Pieke Biermann, who lives in Berlin, is Germany's leading crime writer. *Violetta* was awarded the 1991 German Crime Writers Prize. This is the first translation of Pieke Biermann's work into English.

Other Mask Noir titles

VIOLETTA

Pieke Biermann

**Translated by
Ines Rieder and Jill Hannum**

Library of Congress Catalog Card Number: 95–71060

A catalogue record for this book can be obtained
from the British Library on request

First published in 1990 by Rotbuch Verlag, Berlin

Copyright © 1990 by Pieke Biermann

Translation © 1996 by Serpent's Tail

The right of Pieke Biermann to be identified as author
of this work has been asserted by her in accordance
with the Copyright, Designs and Patents Act 1988

This edition published in 1996 by
Serpent's Tail, 4 Blackstock Mews, London N4
and 180 Varick Street, New York, NY 10014

Phototypeset in ITC Century Book by Intype, London
Printed in Great Britain by
Cox & Wyman Ltd, Reading, Berkshire

This translation is published with the help of Inter Naciones, Bonn

CONTENTS

A human being
isn't much, a couple
of briefcases full
of meat.
*Fritz Haarmann
in 1924 to the court
in Hanover.*

TRANSLATORS' NOTES

1. Until the fall of the Berlin Wall and German reunification one year later, West Berlin was separated from West Germany by territory of the GDR – East Germany. Hence in West Berlin (and not just in East Germany) it was common to refer to West Germany as somewhere else. Legally, indeed, West Berlin was not part of West Germany, but controlled by the three Western Allies.

2. When Berlin was still divided, West Berlin underground trains passed underneath the old city centre, which was in the East, to connect parts of West Berlin, but were not allowed to stop at the eastern stations, which had been shut down.

3. *TAZ* = tageszeitung, a leftwing daily newspaper.

4. Republicans: A far right party which, before and after 1989, briefly enjoyed a degree of success in municipal and regional elections. It has since faded into insignificance, partly as a result of internal dissension.

Prelude
THE LAW OF THE EYE

The thunderstorm was overdue like a period, and the city contorted itself in the grip of a kind of premenstrual syndrome. High tension in the pit of the stomach, torpor outside. Streets and houses and inhabitants yearned for the great cleansing downpour and the cool clarity that would follow. It had gone on for weeks. Last season's joke about doing your bit to punch a hole in the ozone was no longer funny. Most of the people living here seemed to have fallen into the hole, and for the first time in their lives seem to sense that the sun can be a violent planet.

The old woman is well over seventy, and the way she's sitting makes her look broader than she is tall. More precisely she slumps, motionless and apathetic, on the sill that juts out in front of the shop window of a Turkish agency for housing loans, insurance and travel back home. Her right shoulder rests against the window-frame, hands folded in her lap, head drooping. Her eyes are half open. Or half shut. The lids too heavy. Her gaze is glued to the space between her black lace-up shoes, where a brownish dog sprawls on the pavement. Its fat rump stretches the short-haired skin like the casing of a sausage. It's as motionless as the woman, only the big eyes in its pointed face are alive. With nervous attention. Fastened on her fixed stare.

It's about six o'clock on a Saturday evening in July. Haupt Strasse in Schöneberg is ready to choke under a windowless pall of smog – heat, steaming asphalt and other city fumes. Those who can avoid the least movement, lie around at home or in the shade close to some water. The buses that crawl along Haupt Strasse at regular intervals are virtually empty; apart from a few bicycles there's almost no other traffic.

In one of the old tenement buildings on the other side of the street, above the wide-open door of an Italian-owned games arcade, a man's fat arse is wedged into an open window. Inside the room a flicker of coloured light. Once in a while, rumbling male voices rise in a chant, then subside into an even, monotonous, indistinct murmur. And once in a while, the man raises a can of beer and pours the contents down his throat without taking his eyes off the big match.

Not a breath of air. The sun burns down on the side of the street where the old woman is sitting, but the shop window with the ads for housing loans and the handwritten sign "Biletleri Otobüs" is still in the shade. A delivery van is parked at the kerb, blocking the sun. Someone has scribbled, in English, "partners of crime" on the hood, in graffiti-style letters. At school the old woman learned Gothic script.

The sausage dog jumps up as soon as the two young women park their Vespa on the pavement in front of the launderette. Whining and wagging its tail, it races towards them on skinny little legs. They ignore it. They pull their helmets off and unstrap two holdalls from the carrier. The fat little dog is afraid of nothing. Like a wind-up toy it jumps up against the women, licking their feet and legs.

"Stupid turd! You'd better watch it or you'll get a fuckin' heart attack," hisses one of the women, and almost cracks its head with her bag.

Then she notices the old woman, registers her disordered but proper clothes, her sweat-soaked but neatly permed curls and gets the picture. Typical old biddy, probably a block warden fifty years ago, always got something to kvetch about, especially women with coloured streaks in their hair smooching on the stairs.

"If you can't teach your mutt some manners before you

let him loose on humans, then at least take him upstairs and make him lose some fuckin' weight!"

The other young woman looks at her, then at the sign on the first floor. APOLLO FITNESS STUDIO. She grins. "Worse than a guy, a dog like that. Bet it's the spitting image of her old man."

"But she doesn't clean up this one's shit."

They disappear into the launderette without another glance at the old woman. And they don't see how the little fat dog lies down panting at her feet again with a look of resignation.

"Yuck! What a stench!" The woman with the bleached cropped hair and the yellow and green t-shirt wipes sweat from her forehead.

"You mean them?" The other woman, ash-blonde streaks and olive-drab army surplus overalls, points at the two young men sitting at opposite ends of the benches along the shop window front.

"Na," says Yellow Green, "it's the chemical brew in here that's getting up my nose."

"You're not kidding! Fucking patriarchy. Makes you wanna puke."

One of the young men is twenty at most and obviously a student. He's marking a manuscript with a yellow felt-tip. He's slight and very pretty and seems to know it. The casual ease with which his body fits his jeans and tight shirt, the half laced up Reeboks and the soft brown curls with blond streaks above a light brown face all suggest it. His eyes, however, tell a different story. Without the slightest movement of his head, he watches the two women talk. There's suspicion in them. Perhaps even fear, but well-hidden. He checks out situations for possible danger signals. Careful not to attract attention, his eyes now wander from the two women to the other man, back and forward between the three of them, shifting from close-up to full-shot. After that, with a demonstrative movement of the head, he turns to look at one of the nineteen washing machines along the wall to his right. And then, just as demonstratively, the young black man returns to his manuscript. He lowers his head, underlines, turns pages. But his ears remain pricked. Like cat's ears. Only his don't turn.

The two young women ignore him. They drop their bags and throw their helmets down on the dryer by the door. On the wall is a notice-board with want-ads – apartments, jobs, stray pets and missing friends. The weekly information sheet of the Women's Hotline is almost hidden by the handwritten notes. WARNING TO ALL WOMEN! DESCRIPTIONS OF THE MEN ARE BECOMING SUPERFLUOUS, WE ARE GETTING REPORTS OF RAPE AND SEXUAL HARASSMENT IN THE NOLLENDORF PLATZ AND WINTERFELDT PLATZ DISTRICT ALL THE TIME. WOMEN, NO ONE ELSE WILL HELP YOU! HELP EACH OTHER! ORGANISE! DON'T BE INTIMIDATED! BE VIGILANT! Yellow Green reads it as she fumbles in her trousers for her wallet.

"Have you read it? Still the same. And still the cops don't move their asses."

"Why should they? They're the worst. Wankers one and all." Olive Drab hoists her bag on to the dryer.

The other man is about thirty and the prototype of the eternal adolescent. He's visibly straining to look relaxed in the here and now, inside his heavy black biker jacket, as though it were an airy verandah and not a leather wall smelling of detergent and exhaust fumes in the middle of an airless summer. Just sitting there casually does not come easy to him. He can't stop tapping one foot and he keeps shifting his backside around on the bench, as if he had to prove by the adjustment that something was really there. His fly is adorned with a safety pin. Wet, thin, mousey brown curls are plastered above a pasty whiter-than-white face with three-day designer stubble. His eyes are very wide-set and, since the two women arrived in the launderette, have strayed from them only once. A brief glance to check out the other man. Apart from that they've been fixed on the women, waiting for the slightest chance to attract their attention. To make eye contact. To be worth noticing.

The two women have briefly looked him over. "Eyes like a budgie." Olive Drab sums him up.

"The neck too," Yellow Green adds.

"Since when did budgies have necks?"

"'Zactly."

Yellow Green's eyes sparkle aggressively in Whiter-than-White's direction. She then gives the other man a probing glance before turning to the dispenser to get tokens for the washing machines, the spin-dryers and the tumblers. When she wants to turn round again she finds Eternal Adolescent right behind her.

"Hey, what were you two saying just now?" From West Germany, no doubt about it.

At the same moment Olive Drab is already standing beside him. Yellow Green completes her turn sideways so that she's on his other flank. Gleaming with anticipation, Eternal Adolescent's eyes flick back and forward between the two, as if he were watching a top class table tennis match. He clicks his tongue, bites his lower lip, slowly opens his mouth to engineer the pick-up line of the century – But doesn't get a word in.

"You just watch it. With eyes like that, I'd get a sunglasses transplant." Olive Drab slowly looks him over from top to bottom and back again.

"Aw, what's the matter with you two. You were just talking about me. And so I thought I'd take a look . . ."

"There's nothing to look at here!"

"Aw, to hell with his eye-ball wanking. He'll never get it." Olive Drab hands Yellow Green her helmet. They walk round the big laundry-folding table and the tumbler to the washing machines. Eternal Adolescent goes round the other way. The black kid raises his head almost imperceptibly and observes the situation.

The two women exchange glances, simultaneously drop their bags and helmets, and menacingly take a step closer to Eternal Adolescent.

"Are you going to fuck off, or do you want those eyes of yours a shade darker?" Olive Drab's voice is already a shade darker. Eternal Adolescent looks surprised and tries to start an argument, at which he is even worse than trading glances.

"Is that the new thing here in Berlin? Isn't anyone even allowed to look at women any more?"

"You got it mushhole. That's how it is. Now piss off."

"But why not? You like to look at something beautiful too. It's human nature. Isn't it?"

"Because women have had it with being looked over. You only see one thing anyway." Yellow Green is enjoying herself. Olive Drab pushes the sleeves of her overalls a little higher, inspects each bicep with satisfaction, plants her feet a little further apart, provocatively taps her right foot and gets ready to take her turn. "Don't even bother. It's not our job to give baby face from Paderborn an educational holiday."

"From Bielefeld!" Eternal Adolescent offers, confident he's at last found the right subject for a conversation.

"And" – Yellow Green is tugging dirty laundry from the bag – "because the way a man looks at a woman is already an insult!" She stuffs the laundry into a machine, glances at the black student who, three yards away, seems to be studying his text, slams the door shut and puts a token in the slot.

"And because it reduces women to an object. To a sex object. And we've had it up to here. And more." She grabs the second bag. Ready for a fight. Olive Drab is still standing in front of Eternal Adolescent.

"Got it?" Nothing can stop Yellow Green. "And you're just

another small town voyeur. Comes to the big city to look at women. Just what we've been waiting for." She slams the door of the second machine shut and puts in the token.

The student goes on studying.

"Am I going nuts? Is everyone round here turning into a prude or what are you trying to tell me?" It gradually dawns on Eternal Adolescent that his carefully chosen defensive tactic is not making any impression here, and he considers more offensive measures. He puts his hands in his jacket pockets, hunches his shoulders, takes a deep breath and tries to look down on the women. "Or have you just finished a self-defence course with the feminist grannies?"

Before anything else can dawn on him, Olive Drab has jumped him, both hands have gripped the collar of his leather jacket and her right knee is in his groin. "With ass-holes like you attack is the best defence."

Eternal Adolescent howls and doubles up. "But I didn't even... man – "

"Right, and we're not going to hang around till you do!" Before he can escape, Yellow Green puts her arm around his neck from behind and squeezes. Then suddenly she lets go and chops at his kidneys with the side of her hand. He howls again and lashes out blindly. Only a few disjointed words spill from his gaping mouth, before Olive Drab rams her knee under his chin.

"Because you fuckers see nothing in a woman. Nothing. Nothing. Nothing." Yellow Green yanks rhythmically at his hair. Each nothing accompanied by a yank and a hook to the chin.

"All you can do is gawk. And think that's what we're here for. So that you can get off. So that you can jerk off over us. But you don't see nothin'. Nothin'. Nothin'."

They go on beating and kicking him after he has sunk to the floor. He is bleeding from several wounds on the head and in the face. They stand over him and stare down. They don't notice that the student has taken his wet laundry out of the machine and stuffed it into a bag. Nor do they see the blood-red imprints his shoes leave on the terrazzo floor as he soundlessly slips out of the launderette.

They notice the safety pin on Eternal Adolescent's fly.

"Look at that!" shouts Olive Drab triumphantly.

"Another of those macho show-offs. I wonder if he's already on the Hotline blacklist or if he's a new one." Satisfied, Yellow Green wipes her forehead.

"It's just because of his hips," grins Olive Drab.

"Huh?" Yellow Green is distracted. One of the bags is caught under Eternal Adolescent's thighs.

"That he needs a safety pin on his zip."

Then they concentrate on getting the bag from under him without dragging it through the puddles of blood everywhere on the floor, and not leaving any of their wet washing at the scene of their triumph.

Across the street the plump ass is no longer hanging out of the window. The whole man is now standing in the frame, a fresh can of beer in his hand, watching the scene on the other side. A fat old woman is lying motionless on the pavement, a fat little dog dashes frantically round her, yaps, jumps up at a black youth carrying a large, dripping bag and hurrying away up Haupt Strasse. He stops, glances at the woman and then at the launderette behind him, bends down and pats the dog's head as if to reassure it, hastily straightens up and continues running the moment a green and white VW bus, blue light flashing, appears from the direction of Kaiser Wilhelm Platz.

Sweat is running down the forehead, into the eyes and dripping on to the chest of the man at the window. He cracks open another can of beer and grunts something. Then he fetches a pillow and makes himself comfortable for the live show in the street below.

Tyres squealing, the police van brakes in front of the

housing loan agency. A woman and a man in uniform jump out; the dog immediately races towards them wagging its tail. The policewoman walks over to the old woman on the ground. The policeman checks the street and the houses in search of possible eyewitnesses. Five yards in front of him, a Vespa starts up on the sidewalk and rolls away. Through the hot, stinking cloud two women can be seen, the one behind gripping two bags in her lap with one hand and two helmets at her side with the other.

"Stop!" he roars. But the two are already so far away that he can't make out the licence number. "Helmets belong on the head, even in hot weather!"

"She's dead." The policewoman squats on the ground beside the old woman. "And you'll give yourself a heart attack too, if you go on jumping around like that." The fat little dog lies down obediently on the pavement and pants, making itself as flat as possible.

"I'll call the ambulance," says the policeman. "Why don't you talk to the guy up there at the window."

She stands up. "'Scuse me. Did you see what happened down here?"

"What's supposed to have happened? Everything's dead. In this heat. I was watching the match."

"Didn't you see anything else?"

"A black guy just bolted out of the launderette. You should take a look in there. Who called you? Somebody musta seen something."

"The bus driver, by radio. Thanks for the tip. We'll be right up."

"Naw, naw. I'd rather come down." The fat man disappears out of the frame, the policewoman disappears into the launderette.

She reappears just as an ambulance and an emergency doctor's car thunder on to the pavement. The policeman jumps up from the low wall behind the old woman. "Well?"

Five men, two in firemen's uniforms, three in white, leap out of the vehicles.

"Emergency doctor into the launderette," says the police-woman. "There's a guy in there on the floor bleeding like a stuck pig."

CASE 235

At 6.30 a.m. on a Monday in high summer, the detective chief inspector stood in the entrance hall of a building like a Norman fortress at 30 Keith Strasse. Just back from vacation and just out of the shower, but already sticky all over. She tugs at her t-shirt to give her body some air. Runs a hand through her damp, blonde hair. Looks at the sign: D III Division III – Homicide and Organised Crime.

This was her regular work place all right. She fumbled with her shoulder bag. Why not Amrum Island? The thought flashed through her mind as she felt for the pack. She had to grin. The idea that she, Detective Chief Inspector Lietze (first name Karin), could have an easy life on an idyllic North Frisian island was ludicrous. Especially as she had spent the last fourteen days there fending off suitors who had never got past the stage of late adolescence, every one of them in the age group between pot bellies and fatty livers. Twice a day, on average, she had searched for a satisfying answer to the question: Why Amrum? On the Adriatic, she could have had the very same pleasure of not being allowed to swim, or enjoyed nature in small homeopathic doses in any big city.

Nonsense. Who knows what it was good for. She had honed her voyeuristic skills and had resigned herself to pure contemplation: the gratifying observation of the rare examples of presentable masculinity. Anyway, they were either New Men, endlessly involved in modern family happiness, or gay. Or possessed that brand of youthfulness on which she had burned her fingers not too long ago ... In which case she preferred to look at the world through the prism of the imagination.

"Morning, Chief Inspector!" The little round man in uniform with a walkie talkie at his stomach, came out of the glass box at the end of the hallway already dutifully holding out his hand.

"Good morning, Ritter." Lietze shook his hand and pulled him closer. "From now on it's just Lietze, okay?"

She gave him a friendly wink, and Ritter promptly turned red. That's what vacations are good for, Lietze thought, satisfied. Stronger nerves.

She had finally managed to pull the pack of Lucky Lucianos out of the bag. She put one in her mouth and offered him one as well.

"Naw. I'm not allowed to any more. My wife threw out all my cigarillos. Make too much of a smell, she says."

"What – now?" Lietze was surprised. Ritter was close to retirement age.

"No, no. I've got a new one. Got married last week. You weren't here . . ." Ritter said apologetically.

'Well, my congratulations! And so sensitive too!" Hope she smells as sweet, Lietze thought, but kept it to herself. "Take one anyway. Otherwise how can I pay you back for your coffee in future?"

The guard turned red again. "If you say so. I don't have to smoke it just before going home. They don't have to know everything the wo – ah, 'scuse me. The wife – oh Christ."

At that moment, to Ritter's boundless relief, the phone in the glass cage rang. He took one Lucky Luciano and ran. Lietze put the packet back in her bag and watched Ritter pick up the phone. He put one hand over the receiver, and waved the other arm at her. She went over to him.

"No offence, LIETZE!"

She flashed the victory sign, nodded and went to the lift. Pleasantly refreshed and in a rare good mood. These old

walls have their advantages, she thought on the way to the
third floor, taking three deep drags with the no-smoking sign
at her back. They keep out the bright sunlight and the heat.

The office was gloomy, cool and smelled of floor polish.
With luck they'll take their time finishing the new building.
She slipped her feet out of the tennis shoes. Or even better:
maybe they'll run out of money. She pushed the shoes under
the desk and sauntered barefoot to the two windows to
open them wide. Central police headquarters. Who needs it!
Ridiculous. She returned to her desk. They'll need the money
for other things now. She opened the roll-top. Now that the
first holes have been punched in the Iron Curtain in Hungary.
She took her diary and her cigarillos out of her bag, put
them on the table and got up again, because the phone was
ringing in the next room.

"You'll have to wait for coffee," said a voice as soothing
as expensive oil in a hot bath after a long day's work. "About
fifteen minutes."

"Good morning, Mimi. Take your time, we'll be sweating
more than enough today." Lietze looked at the coffee maker
standing innocently on a filing cabinet in the clerk's office.
"Is there anything I can read now, or did nothing happen in
the last two weeks?"

"Yes. In the rubber stamp case – "

It wasn't the heat making Lietze's palms sweat. They had
found his last victim four months ago. Nothing else since
then. Maybe he had moved. Or he was lying low as long as
those avenging angels and their nightly patrols made the
neighbourhood unsafe for people like him. So she had
thought.

"Why am I only being told now? Where was it this time?"
she snapped at Mimi.

"The same area. I typed Fritz's report yesterday. It's in my
drawer with the post-mortem results."

So the vigilante dames, these – hadn't managed to scare

off Mr Rubber Stamp. Lietze took the file and returned to her desk.

She hurriedly lit her next Lucky Luciano. Smoke drifted into her eye and stung. Cursing, she slammed the file on to the table and fell into her chair. "Bye-bye, vacation," she said out loud. And softly, barely audible even to herself: "Just take the last little bit of your good mood and admit that you're jealous of these –, these crack-brained women vigilantes who have the advantage of knowing their patch. Damn it. You don't have a single useful clue! And on top of that, two male stiffs in the morgue."

July 31 was one of those days again. She had felt it earlier as she had run her half mile in Kleist Park, carrying a one kilo dumbbell in each hand. A special day, rare even in summer. And practically unknown during the cold, grey months.

It wasn't just the sun and the warmth. They had been the same every day for weeks. But earlier the air had had this particular smell. And now this tinkling in the atmosphere again, as if the sky were made up of a million thin glass splinters, brushing against each other with the slightest breath of air. It was a fatally happy sweetness, a pulsating fragrance, which pierced and burned between her thighs. And the light.

While still under the shower, she knew that she had to put on her tight violet jeans and that she had to go out looking. The water, the soap, the brush, everything felt different. On her skin.

She stepped in front of the mirror. Yes, today they were beautiful again. She could touch them. In all their fleshy heaviness. On other, normal days, she hated her breasts. They were the proof – and all the exercising in the world wouldn't get rid of it – that "nature" had given her a different body. Fuck nature! Nature is cruel.

Every other ounce of flesh – no, of fat – had been removed thanks to daily discipline and two years of karate, one and half hours, three times a week. Only muscles, tendons, bones and skin, sheer power, were left. Provocative contrast to her long, soft, strawberry blonde curls, the big, soft, bright red mouth, the long fingernails painted the same loud red, and her taste for high-heeled shoes.

She left shirt, track suit bottoms and slip lying on the bathroom floor and stepped naked into the narrow, stiff denim. She could always recognise special days because she felt this desire to move and to feel the hard, sharp seam of tight pants between her legs, the unyielding pressure of the material on her clit and her hips. The excitement as, with each step, each turn of her upper body, the cloth moved a few fractions of an inch across nerve endings which seemed to stick up out of her skin. Even her walk is different. It comes from low down, rising straight up from the imperious drumming of her heels. Steel-tipped. Pointed. Tuk-tuk. Tuk-tuk. And from time to time a scraaatch of metal. Off beat. Louder on stone than on asphalt. The spine straight, tense as a harp string.

She would put the wide-angle lens on the VX 1000. It wasn't a day for telephoto lenses. Special days are days for close contact.

She put on her wristwatch and enjoyed each step through the kitchen, buttering the bread, pouring the coffee. The toast in her mouth and the cup in her hand, she went back to the bathroom. She shook her wet hair and ran her free hand through it, arranging it so it would look wild, each movement a source of pleasure. 7.16 a.m. To look as if she had just been dragged out of bed. That was the trick. She painted her lips red and gave herself a seductive smile. Then she put on the red shoes with the steel-tipped heels and last of all a t-shirt. She had cut round the armholes and the neck to make them larger. It too was red and had a purple slogan: "Every new idea is an aggression – Meret Oppenheim."

Detective Inspector Lothar Fritz had tried his best to make his report as easy on the nerves as possible. The facts alone were a massive attack on heart, brain and stomach. The smooth objectivity of the post-mortem results made too many deep drags necessary.

". . . Injuries as a consequence of strangulation . . . Swellings and abrasions on the mucous membrane of the upper and lower lip inside the mouth . . . extensive haemorrhage of the subcutaneous fatty tissue and of the musculature of the throat and from the upper half of the thoracic cavity to the pericardium . . . extensive injuries to the intestines . . . uneven tearing of the rectum with signs of mucous membrane abrasion above the anus to a depth of about ten to twelve centimetres . . . extensive surrounding haemorrhage in the connective tissue of the sacrum . . . haemorrhage at the root of the mesentery . . ."

The woman who had been treated like this had been found last Sunday around noon, close to an old half-squatted building on Winterfeldt Platz known as the "Ruin." One of the residents had seen her lying in the sand and debris of the roofless quadrangle at the main entrance when he had gone to run round the square. To "wake up."

Death had occurred around five in the morning – not, however, at the Ruin. The corpse had been brought there, probably in a Mercedes, to judge by the faint tyre tracks. The tyres were very new and of a type usually fitted on cars of that make. The condition of the corpse suggested the conclusion that the victim had defended herself. "Desperately," Fritz had written. Lietze threw the report on the desk and leaned back in her chair. The last ten minutes had destroyed most of her two weeks vacation. She drew nervously on the cigarillo. She needed a break before she continued reading. Some more pleasant thought. A contrast. Fritz, for example. Lothar Fritz, forty-two years old, strong, broad shoulders, big hands, someone who is afraid of nothing, not even of treacherously gurgling coffee machines. A family man who, without fear of reproach, lived with three women, one of whom wore the pants (usually jogging pants) – the other two, five and ten years young, would at the latest by the turn of the millennium add to the growing contingent of Amazons in West Berlin.

And yet. There was one thing Fritz was afraid of. Almost unnoticeable, but there nevertheless. Fear that something of all that horror, whose meaningless, brutal depths he had to face again and again, because of his job, could touch his wife or daughters. There was no other explanation for the regular fits of rage which seized such a well-balanced man whenever he came across a case of the violence with which men terrorised women.

A man like that has to write "desperately," Lietze thought. Probably he silently screams and bites with the victim. An inch of ash on her jeans brought her back to her desk. She threw the butt in the ashtray.

Traces of white skin and two different types of hair, one very thin, one thicker, both straight, both blond and both very short, had been found underneath the victim's fingernails. The thicker hair was identical with that found on previous victims. There were two different sized prints of trainers made by a well-known German company. Other than that, the usual facts: no fingerprints, no sperm. Again, the injuries to the woman's abdomen, from which she had bled to death, had been caused by some long, blunt object which could be anything from a bottle neck to a rubber truncheon. Again the woman had been strangled. And again, a single letter about one and a half inches high was stamped on her forehead. The same letter had been stamped diagonally across one of the pages in her passport, which had been found in her handbag along with just over eighty marks, an old five złoty piece, seven condoms and other personal belongings.

The woman had been twenty-eight years old and her name was Krisztina Kędzierska. The passport had been issued in Warsaw. This time the letter was a P. Old-fashioned type, just like the last time.

"So now, first of all, get a cup of coffee down you, Karin!"

Lietze started as Mimi Jacob put a cup in front of her. She hadn't heard anything in the past few minutes. She had been staring at the pictures, trying to remember something that had flashed through her mind while she was looking at the dead face. A beautiful woman.

"You look as if you'd rather have a schnapps. Have you eaten anything?"

"So I can throw it all up right away? I'd really like a vodka . . ."

"A Polish one? The murderer . . ."

". . . won't be found in an alcoholic haze. I know, Mimi. But I do feel sick."

Lietze threw the lighter, then the cigarillo, on to the table. She jumped up, tugged at her t-shirt again, and turned round to look at Mimi. But she had gone.

"We had a T for Turk!" she yelled after her, ran back to her desk and grabbed at the coffee. Mimi came back and stopped in the doorway.

"I know," Mimi watched the coffee spilling over, "and a C for Chilean and an N . . ."

". . . for 'Nigger.' "

"Karin! It's only a matter of time . . ."

The door to the corridor opened behind Mimi. A man of about forty, wearing a discreetly patterned dark shirt and white cotton slacks, tried to say good morning but didn't get a chance.

"Right: before we see a J again, right across a page in a passport or on a forehead."

"Or a G. For gypsy. Don't forget that." Mimi turned abruptly and disappeared into the secretary's office.

The man looked at Lietze, who slammed the cup down on the table, snatched the old cigarillo and cursed because a puddle of milky, sugary coffee was spreading over one of the pictures.

"What's going on? I thought you'd had a vacation, boss!" said a surprised Detective Inspector Detlev Roboldt.

She stepped out of the door and turned left up Goltz Strasse toward Winterfeldt Platz. There's no market on Monday, and she strolled diagonally across the rectangle in front of the church. A few years ago they had put down granite paving stones. The cheap, ugly kind, however, and market people, residents and city planners had tried until the last moment to stop them. As bedrock for lustfully tapping heels and well-oiled roller skates, the stones were quite useful. Not as exclusive as the genuine granite around the National Gallery, but useful. Better than the small cobblestones which had once embellished the square. And much better than the layer of asphalt the German bureaucracy had poured over the cobblestones in its fanatical desire to have every inch of the square disinfected after each market day.

Scraaatch. Tuk-tuk, tuk-tuk. The Exacta VX 1000 dangled against her hip. She shook her head and felt the soft, strawberry blonde curls caress her shoulders. She had been holding a book to her chest with both hands. She took it in her left hand and ran her right hand through her hair. These Mr Cleans! They had miscalculated. As they always do. Because they are predictable. One has to be unpredictable! Deny all conventional views of life. Find another justification for one's existence! When the asphalt was torn up again in the course of the militant struggle against the improvement plan for Winterfeldt Platz, the little Bernburg cobblestones were sticking to it, but so gently, they almost fell into the squatters' hands. Under the asphalt lies – no, not the beach, but "anti-imperialist sling shots". Last words.

The Ruin was perhaps the only reminder of the riots. The houses around the square had been turned into luxury apartment blocks. The usual quota of Italian food shops and fancy bars had moved in from Winterfeldt Platz to Nollendorf Platz, just as they had on the squares off Kudamm. And the usual crowd of not-so-poor, modern young people with high disposable income now populated the neighbourhood.

She glanced at the white and silver tables and chairs chained together in front of Café Sydney at the corner of Maassen and Winterfeldt Strasse. Quarter to eight – too early for modern young people who, from tomorrow evening, would look at her photographs there. Or maybe not.

But it was already hot. No, it was muggy. Muggy as it had been for weeks. Two? Three weeks? Weather like this, she thought, must end in a tremendous thunderstorm. Just like last summer. That day. The first time. It had begun just like this: heat, sun, the hard material. Tuk-tuk, tuk-scraatch. And this strange smell of sun on skin. And this flickering light. Distorting movements. Retarding them. Like slow motion. Burning images on to the retina. And freezing them into a still. Demanding new warmth. After the heat that comes from touching.

"Stop! Let me check! The way you're shaking, there'll be no hair left at the back!" Alfred Henke pulled his head away and raised his arm. "Mirror!"

The pale, slight boy switched off the electric razor. With

unhurried nonchalance he put it on the sink and passed both hands over the head and neck he had just trimmed, as if giving a final touch to his work.

"Jump to it! And stop fumbling around, you know I can't stand it!"

The boy put his thumbs in the extra-large armholes of his string vest and pretended to look round.

"There! On the window-sill! Thorsten, you idiot! Are you trying to make me lose my temper?"

Thorsten gave an obstinate grin. "I'm not going to do that for ten marks again. You'll have to give me double!" He still had his hands stuck in the armholes.

Now Henke raised his massive body from the stool in front of the sink. The towel full of hairs slid from his shoulders. He groped for the mirror and slumped back down, naked except for the skimpy underpants that squeezed his butt into an oversized cellulitic cleavage. He swung the little mirror behind his head and looked at himself in the big one above the sink. Thorsten took his thumbs from his shirt and moved his hands closer to Henke's neck again.

"Get your paws off – what's that? You haven't cut it, you've chopped it!"

"I did it just like the picture!" Thorsten grinned innocently.

"Turn on the light! In these cellar dumps you can't even see properly when the sun's shining!"

"What's next? Do I get double?" Thorsten yawned.

"Shut up! Ohhh, fuck it." This time Henke shot up from the stool. He had sat on the towel with all the shaved off blond bristles which were now sticking into his underpants. He scratched his butt and looked through the narrow window into the courtyard. With some difficulty, a man in a pale green linen suit was lifting a big, blue plastic bag into a garbage can. He turned round and stared straight at Henke. Thorsten had reacted quickly for once and turned on the bathroom light behind him.

The man in the linen suit came towards Henke.

"Herr Henke. I think we have to have a serious talk! That was the last time I'll put up with the noise you were making at some godforsaken hour on Sunday morning. I'm going to complain to the management, I can tell you that now. And the staircase hasn't been cleaned since your wife moved out. That's another reason to get you fired!"

He turned on his heel and quickly disappeared through the front part of the building.

Henke had turned red. "You don't need to check the mail boxes. The mail hasn't come yet. You, you – " he grumbled after him.

Bored, Thorsten flipped through a big book with a navy blue cover. "Olympiad 1936."

"I'd like to know where he's going so early!" Henke grunted.

"Ten past eight isn't so early. At least he's got a regular job, eh?"

"The travel agency where he works opens at ten and not a minute earlier. And you, speak when you're spoken to. What's wrong with you?" Henke snapped, slapping at his ass. "Are you getting fresh? Where do you think you are? Discipline and order, my friend! You get nothing without them. Not work, not nothing. And no paying you double!"

Thorsten stared lazily at Henke, who continued to slap angrily at himself. "I've seen how far you've got with discipline and order," he jeered. "I'll get my money, you wait."

Henke looked at him angrily and shook out the towel into the toilet. "I'd really like to know where he's going so early. His old lady is still on holiday."

He was not yet finished with his butt. He took off his underpants and brushed them with the towel. He looked at himself in the mirror. Good and solid, he thought. In good shape for his mid-forties. Boxing and judo are worth it, after all. He just didn't like the way the hair on the back of his head was trimmed.

Thorsten had closed the book and was looking at him and grinning.

"What are you still hanging around for? Have we got a nigger who's going to serve up breakfast, or has the old bitch moved back in? When I get back with the newspaper, I want some food in front of me. Jump to it!"

"Number 9. Yes. Did you get pictures? Take your time. Schade. I know the streets aren't icy! It's hard to overlook that. But you well know people in Berlin drive like idiots and use any kind of weather as an excuse. Yes. We'll wait."

Lietze hung up and walked back to the conference table through the muggy blue haze.

"Here." She pushed a piece of paper in front of Roboldt and Fritz. "We'll have to go there. She gave it as her visiting address."

Detective Inspector Lothar Fritz read it. "That's up in Wedding. Zadko? Sounds Polish. Are they relatives?"

"If I knew that, nobody'd need to go there." Lietze groped for the Lucky Luciano pack. Three pairs of eyes watched. Irritated she pushed the pack away. It slid off the table. She jumped up and, despite her bare feet, stamped loudly over to the windows and opened them wide again. "Satisfied?" she asked combatively.

Roboldt's reply was a fit of sneezing. Then he gave her an extra-sweet smile. "Yes, boss! Was your vacation that bad, or is there some other reason you're snapping at everybody?"

He picked up the pack, took out a Lucky Luciano and offered them to Fritz and Mimi as well. All three smoked and waited. Lietze looked at the three faces in turn. Then she pulled herself together and returned to the table. "Peace?" she said. "Can I have one too?"

Roboldt sneezed again, offered her the pack and lit her cigarillo. She inhaled deeply. "I'm sorry. It must be this case. I'd secretly hoped you would clear up the two dead males while I was away. Instead Mr Rubber Stamp turns up again, and I can't get a handle on anything."

"Problems are there to be solved," said Fritz and got up, taking the piece of paper with the address.

"Schade will be here in about half an hour. Krisztina Kędzierska was here on a tourist visa. And we'll get a picture too."

"So we have something after all, Lietze," said Fritz. "That's what a change of government can do . . ."

"Yeh. Even the Polish Military Mission is getting co-operative," Lietze grinned.

Mimi thought out loud that the willingness to co-operate might have something to do with Detective Sergeant Sonja Schade's gifts of persuasion, and picked up her shorthand pad again.

He harangued the newsagent in Maassen Strasse about the city's decline, because a left-radical daily had been allowed a place on top of the counter, while other newspapers he would have liked to flick through had not even been published that day. The old lady smiled patiently.

"You're not trying to sell me this commie rag!" Sweat had polished the whole of his pinkish-red face and made patterns on the ribbed white undershirt that hung over his shorts.

The woman handed him a *Berliner Zeitung*. "Herr Henke? When do you think it will be possible for you to look at my tap? It's dripping all the time now."

"Bathroom?"

"No, the one in the kitchen."

Henke put one mark twenty on the counter, picking up *Bildzeitung* as well. He rolled both papers together into a

tube and drummed on the magazines on display as if he had
to think about his busy schedule. In reality he was thinking
about the four flights of stairs he would have to climb in
order to fix a dripping tap in the old lady's apartment in the
rear building.

"Of course. I could call the plumber," she threatened softly
and wiped neck and forehead with a cleansing tissue, "but
I thought you might need a bit of extra cash. And since you
are the caretaker..."

He mumbled something like "later, around two," and left
the shop. As he walked up Nollendorf Strasse again, he
saw the postman coming out of number 15. He started to
run, his feet sliding in his trainers, sweat dripping from his
forehead on to his shirt, but his mood was improving. "Give
it to me. I'll take care of it."

As always, the postman gladly accepted the offer and gave
him a pile of mail. Henke exchanged a few words with him
and disappeared into the front of house number 17. In the
hallway, he checked who had got what. The commie rat
with the green linen suit had got a postcard and his commie
newspaper. From the postcard he learned that the man's
wife was to return early tomorrow afternoon. He rolled up
TAZ with *BZ* and *Bild*. As he entered the courtyard, a red
and yellow tiger striped cat leaped towards him. "There you
are, Blondie, my queen!" Henke teased her. "Shall we see if
the grub's ready? Come, come, come."

Respectfully, he gave the cat precedence. He would get
twenty, thirty marks from the dripping old lady, he calculated. Maybe even more, let's go see. He needed something
in his wallet, when his Mata Hari was back again!

Roboldt had almost finished his report when Fritz returned.

"He's got it in for foreigners, women, especially young
women. All of them under thirty, all of them married or

living with Germans. Well, we don't know about the last one yet."

Lietze looked at Fritz. "And?"

"The registration office only says, Zadko, Marek, born 9.7.52, musician, registered there for five years. Single."

"Go there afterwards, Fritz, and check out whether he was the lover."

"I don't think so," said Roboldt. "She must have had a German. Mr Rubber Stamp always does things according to a pattern, someone like him never varies it, he's an orderliness fanatic – look at all his stamps!"

Lietze picked up the pictures of the dead Krisztina again. "He changed it this time, Roboldt. He was with someone. And . . ." she stared at one of the pictures and shook her head, "this time he may have acted without planning it first."

"What makes you think that?" He almost drowned in sneezes.

"Say the dates of the murders again, please."

Roboldt leafed through the file. "Always at night. The first murder, the black woman, on the night of April 19 to 20, the second on April 30 to May 1, that was the Chilean woman, the third, the Turk, was on May 7 to 8, all quite close together. And now the night before last, July 29 to 30, the Polish woman."

"Exactly," Lietze looked round. "Don't you notice something? I mean, despite your sneezing?"

Roboldt looked at her. Fritz shook his head. Mimi nodded.

"April 20th. Do you mean that, Karin?"

"Yes. I do mean that."

"The 'Führer's birthday'," it dawned on Roboldt. "And May 1, everybody knows that."

"And May 8 . . ." Fritz thought out loud.

". . . is liberation day for some, capitulation which amounts to humiliation for others." Roboldt rubbed his eyes. "Could be something to it. And if he 'celebrates' the Führer's birthday with a murder, then the 8th of May is good enough reason for him too. But why May 1?"

"Why not?" Mimi interjected.

"Either he hates everything to do with the workers' movement, or he is a worker himself, but one of the true German kind." Fritz reflected. He looked at Mimi.

She pretended to be noting something down and mumbled. "You can just say Aryan."

"And what happened on July 29?" Roboldt asked.

"As far as I know," Lietze said, "nothing. It seems like this victim just crossed his path."

"Or someone else did it."

"Someone who has exactly the same letters and ink and who does everything in exactly the same way?" Lietze looked at Roboldt critically and realised that she was rubbing her nose. "Have you infected me, Roboldt? I suggest someone checks out these dates, these Nazi dates."

"That could take forever." Fritz protested. "With this guy you'd have to compile a whole anti-fascist calendar."

"Yeah, but there's no other way. We don't know anything about the killer other than that he obviously has racist motives, and that Internal Security has nothing on such a character either. And if the result of this research is that we can expect a new murder almost every day, then we'll just have to sit down with the immigrant organisations and ask them to co-operate with us. I don't see any other possibilities at the moment." Lietze picked up one of the pictures of the dead body again. "If only I knew where I'd seen her before."

Sonja Schade came in. She looked around and without a word put a small black and white passport photo in front of Lietze. Lietze took it, looked at it for a long time and shook her head again. "Looks totally different. No make-up, like a good girl from the country. Well, good morning, Schade! What have you found out?"

"Single. Came here for the first time about three years

ago. Seems to have commuted. Which means, presumably, that she went back to Poland every so often so as to re-enter as a tourist. Looks like she was working illegally."

"Then we might as well forget looking for employers or workmates," Fritz sighed.

"Unless . . ." Roboldt looked at Lietze.

"You're thinking about the seven condoms, right?" Lietze grinned and suddenly she sounded almost cheerful. She also seemed to be in a hurry. "Fritz and Schade, you go and see Zadko. Roboldt, you check these dates. I . . ."

"And what about our trainee? He'll be here at eleven!" Mimi said.

"Oh no! I'd completely forgotten about him. Call him and tell him to come later. He can wait till I get back. And everyone else too. We'll look at him together. At three? Roboldt, will you make that?"

Actually she had resolved to leave this Herr Herrmann to another homicide section, to continue to wean himself from the uniform branch and train to be a detective. But given what had just passed through her mind, she might need every possible reinforcement. If she was right, then she wasn't going to pass Rubber Stamp on to some other section with less work, in order to concentrate on the second case.

"Have you got anywhere with the two dead males?" Schade interrupted.

"We haven't even talked about them yet," Roboldt said.

"Then I suggest," said Fritz, "that we meet here again at two."

"Before then someone should take a look at *TAZ* – there's something in there about our friends from the JoAnne Little Brigade," Schade added.

As soon as they had all left her room, Lietze picked up the phone and dialled. Nobody answered. Satisfied, she put on her shoes, grabbed her bag, threw cigarillos, lighter and the photos of Krisztina Kędzierska into it and said a quick goodbye to Mimi.

"To be sexless is to be fat." The sentence was underlined in violet ink. She had noticed it again as she was leafing through her book at Nollendorf Platz underground station. *"And I'd rather be anything than that again."* She had written *"me too"* in the margin. It was always good to have something with you to read, above all on those special days. It saved her from looking at all the guys who were of no account anyway. Preferably English and French books. They kept everything at a distance. She snapped the book shut and looked at the cover before squeezing into the subway train with the crowd. An ugly photo. Yellow-brown sunset with the obligatory waving palm trees. Dull as a picture in a tourist brochure. Taco paradise. If it even was Mexico. She stood with her back to the door and glanced around the carriage. Zero. Zero faces. Zero bodies. There was nobody here. No candidate for special days. She got off at the next stop and changed to the magnet train. There were only five other people in the carriage. An older couple with their daughter, and two gays. She scrutinised them, the gay couple, she thought, are taking this silly train because they need a conclusion to an energetic night, the other ones got up extra early to fulfil their tourist obligations before it gets so muggy that they can't stand to be outdoors any more. The girl was waving her arms in all directions and giving little lectures about the city's history. The parents seemed inattentive and slightly uneasy. Probably because the only thing they saw in front of them was the picture shown on tv not long ago. The train had gone through the wall at Kemper Platz Station, and half of it had been left hanging above the street.

She ran her hand through her curls and smiled mockingly.

Since then, she liked to take the magnet train. Whenever she felt like a trip through the capital's catacombs and had to get to Anhalter Bahnhof to catch the S-2 line to Frohnau. In the past she used to walk from Gleisdreieck underground station right across the overgrown railway property and along the abandoned tracks. Except on special days, of course. There weren't enough people at Gleisdreieck. And it wasn't high-heel-friendly either.

She was so lost in thought, she forget to get off at Bernburger Strasse. No problem. She'd just pass over Potsdamer Platz on the magnet tracks before going under it on the S-Bahn. She took her eyes off the family and leaned back. She moved her butt back and forward imperceptibly on the seat. The sharp, hard seams of her jeans pressed the right spots. She leafed through the book again. *"I fear only disgust and boredom."*

That cow had woken him up with her bloody chatter, just to postpone the appointment. Why did he have to deal with dames anyway? He slammed down the receiver. He never got up earlier than he had to. Half an hour. At the most. No traffic now during the vacation anyway. Slip through from Heide Strasse in Wedding and along Strasse des 17. Juni like an ace. No distance to Grosser Stern at all. Full power. Fifty minimum.

And what could he do with the new day now? Rocky looked at the alarm clock. Eight thirty-five. The sun was already on the wall of the house opposite. In this heat, sleep's best anyway. Or – right! Go swimming! Lie in the sun as long as it isn't slamming down so hard that you need an action man asbestos suit.

He got up and showered.

When he was finished with breakfast, he pulled off his boxer shorts and put on his black thong with the slogan "I'm proud." There wasn't space for anything more. He wasn't the biggest. Neither was his thong.

He glanced quickly at the wardrobe mirror. He packed a towel and a mat and looked for the Porsche keys.

He managed the distance to Halensee in a record thirteen and a half minutes. No problem if you live right next to the motorway approach and have flashing headlights and can make a bit of noise. The siren wasn't quite legal, but that was no problem for him! The car was ten years old, but it was A-OK. It suited him much better than that asshole he bought it from last year. A real fairy.

The petrol and relining the brakes twice a year was a bit expensive in the long run though. Time for a change, Rocky! You've got to do it, he thought, as he parked the Porsche diagonally in an entry in Bornimer Strasse. And then . . .

He looked for a corner in which there weren't so many long-hairs and unrolled the mat. His last girlfriend had made a sash for it. It got caught on the hem every time. It loosened. She couldn't even sew properly. Fucking women. Good thing he'd got rid of her. They just get in the way.

He snapped the thong's elastic and decided not to put on oil. His skin could take it. The solarium twice a week all winter after working out. Until you could go swimming again. He threw the bottle of tanning oil on top of his pants and sneakers. Then he sat down on his mat, pushed back his blond crew cut and stared at the scene. Nothing but lesbians. And fucking naked! And Turkish women, all wrapped up, and all those kids! How come they're all lying around in the sun doing nothing!

He decided to continue his inspection later, and stretched out. Two minutes later he had fallen asleep. Over images of a horny weekend. Another good one. And he'd been on top from start to finish. Rocky the King!

*

She put down the newspaper, which she had bought on the way to Anhalter Bahnhof, the book and the lens cap next to her. She held the camera up to her eye as the faint light in the tunnel announced the approach of Potsdamer Platz Station. A gesture, no more. It was much too dark and she hadn't bought any film yet. None of the GDR border guards with their sullen faces were to be seen. Nor any of the East German Reichsbahn men who, now and then, stood on the abandoned platform swinging signal lights at the S-Bahn drivers.

She put the cap back on, slung the VX 1000 over her shoulder and picked up the newspaper. She only took pictures of things which — in some indefinable way — exerted an erotic fascination on her. She leafed through the paper. These border guards, for instance. But there was no way of getting to them. Eddy's name caught her eye. Eddy had written another letter to the papers. Eddy too.

She had met Eddy by accident. Over a year ago. Eddy had been in front of her at the supermarket cash register. From behind Eddy had looked like a lot of old men, a beret on carefully trimmed hair, a bulky, ageless leather jacket. Normally she didn't notice men like him. But then something had attracted her attention. A detail had stuck on her retina. She only understood a few minutes later, as Eddy was already pushing out of the door, loaded down with bags.

It had been the handbag. Eddy had put the wallet back into a handbag. Men didn't carry handbags like that.

She had paid quickly and run after Eddy. She had simply asked if she could photograph her.

She looked up and stared at one of the border guards at the Unter den Linden station. He caught her glance. The train passed through.

Later, she didn't know if it had been Eddy's face which had made her ask the question, or if it had been the question that had cast a spell on the face. A fantastic face, very old, very fleshy and with many very deep furrows. A topography that seemed to reconcile space and time. Full of hairs. And sprinkled with the sunspots which old people often have on their hands. But Eddy wasn't any old lady.

At Friedrich Strasse Station, crowds of pensioners from East Berlin got on. She threw back her head to shake the hair out of her face.

Darting, sharp, pale blue eyes. They had scrutinised her. Had wandered over her body like lecherous thoughts. Along her shoulders, her arms, down to her hands. Had observed her nervous movements and then come to rest on her breasts. She could see them reflected in Eddy's eyes.

How they bounced and shook with every movement. She continued going through the newspaper and imperceptibly pressed her arms against the curves at her sides. A hundred thousand splinters of glass rubbing against each other.

"'Scuse me, is this seat taken?"

She put the book in her lap. She didn't look at the skinny panting man who sank on to the seat next to her, but stared pointedly at her newspaper.

Finally those eyes had quite coolly wandered on, appreciatively, as if they were simply grateful at the sight. And gradually she got the whole picture. *"To be sexless . . ."* And in sharp focus. *"Rather anything than that."* Three exclamation marks.

They had made an appointment for the next afternoon. Sitting in her darkroom that night, she knew not only that it had been right to become a photographer, but she was also sure, for the first time, that she was taking the pictures she wanted to take.

The beat up old Renault made a squealing U-turn in front of the building which once housed the Japanese embassy to Nazi Germany, and drove back down Tiergarten Strasse.

Karin Lietze didn't bother about the honking or about the cursing car drivers, but drove slowly along the kerb, checking the narrow pavement and the bushes behind it. An Enduro motor bike with a helmet hung over the handlebars stood in the shade between two bushes. At least Kim was around somewhere.

She stopped and turned off the engine. Before she had got the cigarillos out of her bag, Helga appeared out of the bushes, her handbag on her wrist as always, an empty can of cat food in her other hand, a cosy and warm-looking black wig on her head and her arms and legs irreproachably covered. Even in the tropics Helga would always be ready for a visit to the nearest cathedral. Or worse.

Her professional eye had spotted the car right away.

"Karin!" she beamed. "Need some more erotic counselling?"

Karin sighed, gathered up the pictures and got out of the car. "Unfortunately, no. Where is everybody?"

Helga put down the can, wiped her hands and took a small black plastic box out of her handbag. She pressed a couple of buttons and the machine blared out: "Kim – eight thirty-three – about forty – block warden type – Daimler – beige – B stroke A-M . . ."

Lietze smiled impatiently. "It's paid off, that electronic notebook, hasn't it?"

"And how. Took some time to get used to. But now I know how to work it."

"And Kitty?"

"She'll be here later today," Helga said and forwarded the tape for Kim's next piece of action. "I've collected all th' tapes. Imagine what the tax office'd say. If they got them – "

"Helga," Lietze interrupted, "do you have a pal called Krisztina? From Poland?"

"Sure, our Shishi," Helga answered a bit crossly. "What do you want from her?"

"What's her surname?"

"No idea. Don't even know if she's really called Krisztina. Shishi's usually secretive. Nobody's supposed to know she's toiling for Solli."

Lietze showed her the passport picture. "Is that her?"

"Yeah. That's her. Now tell me what you want from her. I'm not gettin' mixed up in any shit."

"Are you really sure? The woman in the photo's not wearing make-up . . ."

"So what?" Helga turned stubborn. "When she's working, she wears make-up. Is there a law against it?" She looked defiantly at Lietze.

"She's dead, Helga." Lietze returned Helga's look and saw her face sag.

A cream-coloured Mercedes emerged from the small street next to the Italian embassy. It stopped at the junction with Tiergarten Strasse. A blonde in her twenties with endless, skinny legs in a black leather mini-skirt and a yellow and black striped bustier got out and slammed the door. The car pulled away in the opposite direction. She came towards them, walking like a navvy, and adding a whole new dimension to the precarious gold sandals. "Ooh, a state visit," she yelled happily and whistled through her teeth. "An' why doesn't anybody say 'hello Queen Bee'?"

"Ain't nobody in a mood for jokes. Somebody got Shishi," Helga said.

Kim screamed.

Lietze gave a brief report. "And who's Solli? I thought you didn't have pimps."

Helga raised her head, looked at Lietze and laughed out loud. It sounded rough and suspiciously hoarse. Kim sat down next to her, put her bare muscular arms around her shoulders and pressed her face against Helga's chest. Helga was sobbing.

"Solli is Solidarność," Kim explained.

Lietze looked at her in surprise. Kim shrugged. Helga turned away, blew her nose forcefully and collected herself. "Shishi must've fucked enough men to pay for half the underground printing presses in Warsaw! Well just wait!"

"What do you mean?" Lietze tried very hard to sound gentle.

"What the hell? So now they're the gover'ment. But tell me, have you ever seen a single gover'ment guy, anywhere, wanting to be connected with any of us?" Helga jumped up and planted herself beside Lietze. She was no longer interested in giving in to her grief, but in taking up every challenge that came her way.

"There'd been frictions for a while. She told me that once. They treated her like she was bother. But they always took her money. All those years!"

Kim looked surprised as well. "How come you know all that?" Helga waved the question away.

Lietze wiped the sweat off her neck and thought for a while. The prospect of having to work with her colleagues in the aliens' department made Amrum suddenly light up like a vision of paradise on earth. A car, which had already crawled past the three women twice, stopped at the kerb. Kim looked briefly at the driver, got up reluctantly and went over. Evidently she had no desire to bend over, stick her ass in the air and put her head through the side window. She simply opened the door and got in.

"Eight fifty-eight," said Lietze, "white Golf convertible, licence number . . ."

"Thanks. I know. Regular john."

"Well, Helga – how come you know all that stuff about Krisztina. And what else do you know?"

Helga hesitated. "I know some Polish. I don't make a big fuss about it. The circumstances I learned it in, I don't want to think about it every day. I learned it when I was a kid, and that's all. Sometimes after going round the clubs at night, collecting money to pay for our office, I sit down with Shishi – oh no. God, the poor little thing!"

Helga still hadn't quite taken up the gauntlet, but she was pulling herself together. The first two years in which Krisztina Kędzierska had been making a major contribution to Polish perestroika by working on the German male, seemed to have been almost idyllic. Solidarność was proud of her, protected her from homesickness and the immigration police, gave her a place to stay and lots of news and gossip from home. As soon as Solidarność was legalised, Shishi was supposed to get a good job working as a bookkeeper and secretary, as she had done before, maybe with one of the newspapers for whose illegal survival she had laboured so reliably. But nobody had said anything about that for a while. At the beginning of the year, about the time the opposition was sitting down at the Round Table, it had been made clear to her that there were "more important problems" now. She had made a scene, got nowhere, stopped working for a week and never paid "contributions" again, and she had regularly sat down for a good cry with Helga. "I'm more than sixty now, I told her, and the last little bits and pieces of my idea of how the world works would fall apart, if you could count on the revolutionary gentlemen the minute they get a sniff of power!"

Helga lifted her wig and dabbed her forehead. "You can't tell me any stories and you can't tell me nothing either! Shishi wanted to go to Warsaw yesterday for another talk. I told her, Shishi be careful! You've seen a lot of things they don't like to remember too much now. 'That's why,' she said. That was Saturday evenin', and now ..."

Helga had to use her hanky again. Lietze watched her carefully. Within seconds Helga regained her composure. "Karin," she said all of a sudden, full of energy, "you've got to find this guy!"

"Marek Zadko?"

Annoyed, Helga waved her hand. "Bullshit. Not a Pole. Shishi had this guy, I think he was one of her johns. She mentioned him one time, and I thought it sounded funny. Lots older. Sounded like he was married too. He was laying it on about love."

"What's so bad about that?" Lietze asked.

"No, no, no. If she wants to get married just to stay here, there's plenty of men. It'll maybe cost her a few marks, but love's a lot more expensive," Helga explained firmly and added: "For our kind, you know what I mean!"

Lietze looked at her sadly.

"And how am I supposed to find this john? What's his name?"

That was a question not even Helga could answer. All she knew was where Krisztina had last worked and that Kitty had often given her a lift home after the weekly COW – Collective of Whores – meetings.

"Ask Kitty."

"Okay," Lietze sighed. "And a colleague who uses blue nail polish hasn't turned up by any chance?"

Helga shook her head.

In the narrow store in the old Aschinger building opposite Zoo Station, the foreign newspapers were beginning to curl in the damp fug generated by the heat, the bad ventilation and the crowds of people passing through.

The trip to Frohnau hadn't paid off. The usual finds. A small young woman with bobbed and hennaed hair wearing a flower-print dress, looking determinedly out the window and taking notes in a little book from time to time. As if she were collecting material for an autobiography of her lost childhood. And Ginette was there. Just returned from work on Winterfeldt Strasse. The mascara had run and the layer of make-up was so thin that the stubble underneath was quite obvious. Ginette! Ever a fascinating performance! As in the series of pictures she had taken. Always at her best just before she dropped. Ginette didn't think it was funny, and cursed the night, the johns and daylight.

She had been focusing her VX 1000, and had almost got beaten up. Laughing, she had explained there was no film in the camera. Bobbed hair had forgotten the notebook and the scenery out the window. Ginette didn't trust her and wouldn't believe that from tomorrow three of the photos from the series "Ginette Champs-d'Hiver" would be on show at Sydney's. "I won't believe it until I've got the tricks queueing up tomorrow night."

Coming back had been no better. It wouldn't even have satisfied the curiosity of a very ordinary day. At most, perhaps the man with the stop-watch and the four-colour pen. He shook his head angrily over and over again, so that his grey and white pony-tail knocked against the window, or giggled happily to himself. S-Bahn planner. Or thriller writer. She had thought. Not him either. She felt an unpleasant tiredness slowly creep up. A kind of paralysis mixed up with the fear that it might not work out. But it was only a faint hint. Nothing compared to this other thing. Powerful. Big. Afterwards. She had to be patient. The time before it had lasted from early morning until twilight.

She shifted her weight to her left red high heel, shook her right leg and shifted the tight violet-coloured jeans a fraction over her flanks. It was impossible to summon the right moment. Again she glanced casually over the edge of the glossy photography magazine she had been leafing through. For the past ten minutes at least the man had been working his way along the shelf of Italian magazines. The right candidate turned up when he wanted to. Like her desire. It wasn't obedient. It was suddenly there. He was the only one, besides her, who hadn't grabbed his usual paper and quickly disappeared. Her desire spread and grew. Irresistibly, with a hot shock wave. He was smaller than she was. Late forties. A little old-fashioned despite the fashionable suit. And at some point the buds had to burst open. That's how it was. And it was good like that. He looked scared, as if you were not allowed to read magazines without buying them. She put down the photography magazine and looked straight at him. He immediately started to turn the pages faster, at a rate which made reading impossible. He didn't suspect that this little lie was the first step. She kept on looking at him. Then he gave in. Putting down the magazine, he looked over to her. Drawing his head down even further between his shoulders. Furtive. Expectant. The image burned on to her retina as she seemed casually to shift her gaze on to something an inch to the side of his eyes. It froze into a still. She seemed to give someone behind him a cruel smile. He turned away and fumbled clumsily through the magazines. She repeated the same game twice. Twice her stare forced him to risk a glance and stumble into a seductive smile, which supposedly was not meant for him. He didn't dare look behind him, Picking a magazine, he knocked another to the floor. He bent down. As he rose, she was already on her way to the cash register. He got there before her. With two magazines he wasn't the least bit interested in. Her stare and her tense body at his back. Tugging at his lemon-coloured silk tie, he asked for *Espresso*. Acting as if she belonged there, she rested her arms and breasts on the counter.

"If there isn't an 'Espresso' to read, how about one to drink?" she asked out loud, and registered the waves of pressure vibrating through his body. He followed her out of the store like a disoriented dachshund.

"Herr Zadko?"

The young man standing naked behind the half open door

now opened his sleepy eyes wide. "Tak – ah. Yes, what is it?"

"Police," said Sonja Schade and showed her badge. "May we come in?"

He clicked the door shut, and when he opened it again, he was wearing a bathrobe. He rubbed his eyes, excused himself and led them into the kitchen.

"My name is Schade. This is my colleague Fritz."

"Herr Zadko – Marek isn't it?" Fritz asked, for the sake of routine. "Is it true that Krisztina Kędzierska lives with you?"

Schade had the impression that Zadko got nervous when the name was mentioned. "Yes. Ah – she comes to visit. Only to visit."

Fritz disregarded it. "Is she your . . . girlfriend?"

"Ahh. Yesyes. My girlfriend." Zadko pulled the belt of his bathrobe tighter and seemed to be listening for some sound from another part of the flat. "Are you from the immigration police?" he asked finally.

"No, not at all," Schade responded gently. "How long have you – I mean, how long has Frau Kędzierska been living here?"

"Well, since . . . you know, she doesn't live here. She comes to visit!"

"Since when, Herr Zadko?" Schade wondered if it was really the immigration police who made him evasive. He seemed distracted.

"Ah, February. No, January. No – middle of February. But why . . . ?"

"And you had – let's say, a relationship?" Fritz continued.

Zadko was quick to confirm it, but he didn't seem to be paying attention.

"When did you last see her?"

"Last Tuesday. I've been on tour. We just got back last night. That is, this morning. Around five thirty."

"You are a musician?"

"Yes. I play saxophone. We play free jazz."

"The Marek Zadko Group – is that you? That poster?" Schade nodded approvingly. "Excuse me, it's none of my business, but can you make a living at it?"

It worked, as always. Artists like nothing better than to be asked about their art. Especially the hard parts of being an artist. Marek Zadko relaxed and even seemed to have forgotten that there was something else in his apartment worth listening out for. He proudly announced that the Marek Zadko Group had almost made it. And that Pagart might as well pack it in, because now . . .

"Who?" Fritz asked rudely.

"Pagart," Zadko explained, "the state agency for artists. All they do is take money and snoop, but they never organise any gigs. In seven years, they never got a thing for us, not a single thing."

Sonja Schade listened carefully and tried to remember details without taking any notes. Zadko's angry torrent of words made Pagart seem like a gang of pimps. Not only did they negotiate all the contracts and payments, but they also took a fifteen per cent cut. They'd also send two people along on each trip who, according to Zadko, reported directly to the secret police and in turn took bribes whenever possible. "This is how it works, dear lady. For example, they negotiate with the promoter that we get hotel rooms at, let's say, eighty marks. But they demand cash upfront. Eighty marks a head. Then they put us in some cheap dump and pocket what's left of the money. That's Pagart. And it was always me who got the contracts, not them!"

Schade looked at him sympathetically. "And why do you need an agency anyway, Herr Zadko?"

"Why, why!" he got excited. "My dear lady!"

Schade gave him an amused look.

"Please, if you'll pardon me, you really don't understand. You were born with a passport, if I can put it that way. But in Poland, if you are an artist and you want to go abroad, then you get your passport through Pagart, you see?" He mumbled a few sentences in Polish that neither Fritz nor Schade understood, but which sounded like curses, went over to the sink and splashed cold water on his face. "Excuse me," he said more calmly. "Would you like some coffee?"

He didn't wait for an answer, but poured water into the coffee machine and looked around for filters and coffee.

"Those pigs! But that's all over now! They can't do that to us any more. Not after this tour!"

Fritz watched him, but still wasn't sure what to make of him. "No coffee for me, thanks," he said at last.

Zadko looked at him and then at Schade. "But you, madam, you'll have some?"

Schade smiled and nodded. "So your tour was a big success. Congratulations!"

Zadko beamed, and he immediately interrupted his search to describe in great detail the triumphs of the Marek Zadko Group in West Germany's jazz strongholds. "In Munich they wrote that I'm the next Coltrane!"

Fritz began to get impatient and signalled to Schade. She ignored him. "And," she broke in pleasantly, "you weren't upset because your girlfriend wasn't there to celebrate with you?"

Zadko winced. He realised that he had walked into a trap. He started moving nervously around the kitchen again, trying to figure out how to respond casually. At that moment there was the sound of a door snapping shut and being bolted. A toilet door, for example. Fritz and Schade looked at each other.

"Krisztina wanted to get back to Warsaw," Zadko said extra loudly.

"She didn't want to come on tour?" Schade lured him a little further.

"No, ah, yes. She had to go back."

"When?"

"Sunday," Zadko said wearily.

"And instead she's still here? Or what are you trying to say, Herr Zadko?" It was getting too much for Fritz. Schade glanced irritatedly at him.

In a sudden fit of anger, Marek Zadko threw the packet of coffee filters he had found against the wall. Then he sat down in one of the two chairs, crossed his arms on the kitchen table and buried his head. There were no more sounds from behind the door, but soft Polish curses escaped the sounding board of towelling and formica.

"Krisztina isn't my girlfriend," Zadko admitted finally.

"But she used to be?" Schade continued the dialogue.

Zadko jerked his head back and shook it vigorously. "No, not her! Absolutely not!"

"And who was that just now? Your – boyfriend maybe?" Schade didn't let up.

Zadko looked at her indignantly. "No, damn it! What makes you think that? That was, that was ... Well, that was my girlfriend."

"Does she have a name?"

Zadko gave up. "She does. She has to have one, doesn't she? Anna, I think. I've only known her for a week."

Schade grinned. His opinion of Zadko apparently confirmed, Fritz lashed out. "Some kind of groupie maybe. Herr Zadko, we have to tell you something. Krisztina Kędzierska is dead. You don't need to act the mourner. We would just like to know why you felt you had to tell us these fairy tales."

Lietze's face was shiny with sweat. Her eyes lingered wistfully on Mimi's summer outfit: sandals, bare legs, a feather light skirt and a top she'd obviously crocheted herself. Beads of sweat couldn't even accumulate under the straps. It didn't have any.

Mimi Jacob looked up from her desk and waved her hand. "Don't fall asleep, Karin. It's better if you yell out loud!"

Lietze shrugged and gave a startled smile: "Do you have another of those tropical outfits with you?"

Mimi remembered a white smock someone from the police lab had left behind. Lietze rolled up the bottom of her t-shirt in both hands and wrung it. "Show me."

Mimi took a crumpled white cloth square from one of the cupboards. Lietze sniffed at it. Then sniffed at herself. She unfolded the square, held it up to her and sighed: "Tell the others to come to my office. Oh, and Mimi – what did our trainee have to say?"

"He was pissed off, I think. Because he wasn't allowed to start work at eleven."

"Is that so? What kind of guy is he?"

"Sounded like four and a half feet small."

"Like what?"

"Well, a small guy with a big chip on his shoulder," Mimi explained with the sweetest of sharp tongues. "Sometimes those guys have something mucho macho . . ."

"Mimi! You're not prejudiced?" Lietze rubbed her nose and frowned. Mimi was bent over her paperwork again.

"Experience. By the way, we've hit 235, Karin."

"What? Fahrenheit?" Lietze took the smock and opened the door to the corridor.

"No. Krisztina Kędzierska is the 235th case of so-called sexual assault this year. If things go on like this, we'll have at least a third more cases this year than in 1987."

Lietze let the door swing shut again and dropped into the chair by Mimi's desk. "You've got a funny way of jumping from one thing to the other today . . . But they're not all murders."

"Fortunately, no. In 1987, we had 312 rapes and 120 sexual

assaults. Plus three sex murders. For the whole year. We've already beaten that last number – four in just over six months, and all committed by just one person."

"If we only really knew that!" Lietze's fist hit the table. "And what about 1988?"

"I don't have the figures yet, but I don't think they're essentially different from 1987. And even if they were a bit higher, Karin – we can't get round the fact it's going up with a bang this year."

Lietze asked Mimi to write down the figures for her and then got up.

The camera is a kind of a passport. She groped for the carton and tore it open. Slow motion. A hundred thousand very fine splinters of glass tinkled after the hot wave of pressure. Flickered across her retina. Burned. Cut in. Drilled deep. To face life's horror without squeamishness. Photography is a licence. To go everywhere. To do everything. She shook her head from side to side and up and down. The soft strawberry blonde curls swung and pulled the glass splinters with them. The image froze on her scalp and burned like dry ice.

She picked up the heavy VX 1000 and opened the case. A desiring machine. Whose use is addictive. An endurance test. Without squeamishness. A kind of lust. Insatiable. She stretched. The splinters became millions and sparkled throughout her whole body. And formed heaps. Cutting, stinging heaps. At the tips of her heavy breasts. There above all. Powerful. Big. Too powerful and too big to touch. She loaded the film and snapped the back shut. She set the speed meter. 800 ASA. That's how far this film was ready to be pushed. That, and the sun coming through the window, should be enough. It was on the third floor.

She got up and went to the window. The street lay lifeless

below her. The few people were walking on the opposite side in the shadow cast by the houses with their top-heavy balconied façades, dirty plaster frontages embossed with scroll-work and heraldic devices. Houses like shabby monumental safes. Safes! Crammed with the tarnished valuables and second-hand furniture of a bankrupt middle class.

The breeze from the window drove the jingling splinters right down to the tips of her toes. She wound the film on and pressed the button. Three times. Then she took off the lens cap and retreated. The breeze engulfed her bare back and congealed the film of sweat. The coolness followed each of her movements as she put the camera to her eye and tried different angles. Aggression implicit in each tiny shift. Cool violence. Disembodied. Untouchable. The glass splinters began to fade, and a calm blue light, violet at the edges, spread through her body. A photograph is a secret about a secret. The more it tells you the less you know.

Fritz's eyes almost popped out of his head when Lietze entered the room a little later. Schade rolled her right sleeve up to the shoulder and presented her arm: "Nurse, take my blood pressure, please! I'm sure it's below zero. And Fritz's thyroid . . ."

Lietze ignored her, got her bag and stuck a Lucky Luciano between her lips. Then she sat down at the conference table with Lothar Fritz and Sonja Schade. "Principles are there to be relaxed," she said, "and we're not about to start a debate about skirt or pants . . ."

"If you call that a skirt," Fritz smirked.

Lietze looked down at herself, slipped off her shoes under the table and crossed her legs. They were tanned and almost entirely naked. She tugged and wiggled back and forth. The smock didn't get any longer.

"Look!" She pushed the piece of paper with the numbers

across the table. "What we have to deal with is already the 235th case."

Fritz stopped smirking and glanced at the figures. He thought Lietze's remark cynical. "235 isn't even the whole truth. Those are just the reported cases."

Schade rolled down her sleeve again and seemed to be shivering all of a sudden.

"At least I'm slowly starting to understand the JoAnne Little Brigade, or their motives . . ."

"We'll get to that, Fritz," Lietze cut him off. "What's happened to Roboldt?"

He had probably got stuck in some archive digging up historic dates which might provide the stamper with an occasion for murder.

Schade looked at her watch. "I'll start then. One thing's certain, Zadko isn't her lover." Marek Zadko didn't seem to know very much about Krisztina Kędzierska. If they did happen for once to be in the same city at the same time, they met in the kitchen in the afternoon, blind as moles, searching for coffee to get their eyes open. "She worked at night too, he said, but didn't say where. Maybe he really doesn't know. He only seemed interested in the fact that she paid half the rent and didn't complain about his music and his frequent affairs. But otherwise, quite a nice guy."

Fritz didn't think he was nice at all. "I'd like to know how they arranged their residence permits. As far as I know, the aliens' section is only open in the morning," he complained.

Lietze thought for a while. "How Zadko managed it, I don't know. Solidarność is supposed to have taken care of it for Krisztina Kędzierska. Is it true that she moved in with him at the beginning of the year?"

"Yeah. In February. How did you know?" Schade looked at her.

"Did he say anything about an apartment in Belziger Strasse? Number 29?"

Fritz and Schade shook their heads.

"Then it's my turn. She used to live at 29 Belziger. At the end of last year." Lietze leafed through her notebook and gave a brief summary of the most important points she had got from Helga and Kitty, said nothing about her source, however, and concluded after exactly four minutes with the information: "The last place she worked is on Zieten Strasse. It's called the Olàlà."

"That's a brothel!" Fritz exclaimed.

Schade threw down her pen. "So she was . . . I could kick myself. I meant to ask Zadko!"

"And why didn't you?"

Schade started to sweat again. "It seemed stupid. Polish woman, tourist visa, comes here regularly and returns for short periods – everybody immediately thinks: whore."

"Or cleaning woman." Lietze gave her a challenging look. "And?"

Schade bit her lip. "I think I wanted to come across a bit more sussed," she finally admitted.

Lietze started to lecture her, pointing out that in cases like this, wanting to come across as smarter might be pretty dumb. "So, just for the sake of completeness – Zadko didn't seem like someone who would hate women who are black, Turkish, Chilean or from his own country – or did he?"

Not even Fritz would go that far. "But he could have been her pimp!"

Lietze looked at him pityingly. She suspected Fritz couldn't shake off the idea that some day one of his daughters would turn up with a musician and rogue like that. Fritz wasn't very musical.

Schade defended him. "That would be a classic motive, at least. Maybe she wanted to quit? Or she didn't want to give him a cut any more?"

"My god, Schade!" Lietze sighed a bit too dramatically. "Don't go dropping clichés all over the place; just because you don't want to come across as too smart any more! Being on the game and handing over money are two different things, as far as I know. And so far, nobody has proved that Krisztina Kędzierska was doing the second, or am I wrong?" For some reason, she didn't want to tell Fritz and Schade that there really had been someone collecting the takings and that someone was called Solidarność, and was now in control of the money for a whole country. She herself hadn't quite digested this insight into the real existing entanglement of politics and women's work.

"That's true," Schade said. "She must have been too political, if she was involved in Solidarność, as you said . . ."

"Okay," Lietze stood up abruptly and went to the window, "we'll keep an eye on Zadko. Even though I can't imagine that he would have stamped her for being Polish. That's nonsense."

"It's not impossible," Fritz said.

"I know, Fritz. And pigs might fly!" Lietze groaned. "Nevertheless, I don't see any logical reason for the copycat theory. The first murder was a big thing in the media, with pictures of the corpse and descriptions which were virtually instructions. Anyone could read that and do a re-play. But after that we put a complete news black-out on it. I hope it was maintained while I was away!"

Schade nodded.

"There you are! And you don't seriously think that any of the relatives of the other two victims have talked to anyone, do you? They nearly died of fright themselves!"

At a loss, Fritz said, "There was nothing else in the papers. But still." He evidently didn't want to let go of Zadko and described him as "rather weak looking," with a "cherub's face" and "puffy cheeks" and faded blond hair that was already thinning. "I doubt whether the tears were for real."

"Shoe size?" Lietze asked ironically.

"Normal for his size," Schade said. "7 or 8. He's about five foot nine."

"Where's Roboldt got to?" Lietze returned to the table. "It's twenty-five to three. Tell me what's new with the two dead males, and then . . ."

Mimi put her head round the door. Roboldt had got held up at *TAZ*'s library, but was on his way.

"It's time he read something beside books. But why does it have to be now?" Lietze leafed through her notebook.

Schade whistled softly and grinned. "If I'm not mistaken, a certain Larry works there now."

Lietze tapped her pen on the table impatiently.

"The enchanting American." Fritz smiled too. "Who talks like Robert de Niro!"

"Oh please, no. We really don't have time for Roboldt's love life . . ." She stood up and rummaged loudly in one of the drawers.

"At least he has one!" Fritz sighed.

"Why? Don't you?" Schade asked.

Lietze came back before Fritz could reply. "I'm expecting your report. This, this trainee – what is his name? – is going to show up any minute."

"Herrmann," Schade said. "With two rs and two ns. And that's only his surname!"

"Just tell me his first name, so we can get back to business."

"Roland!" Schade and Fritz burst out together. Mimi closed the door behind her with a malicious smile.

Lietze rolled her eyes weakly. "Terribly funny! And so what's new with the two dead males?"

This chick was really worth a second glance. Rocky clicked his tongue as if rhubarb had got stuck between his teeth. Might be worth the effort. The blonde coming out of the cloudy water of Halensee only five yards in front of him was wearing a shrill green bathing suit consisting first and foremost of strings, and then of a few square inches of material.

He followed her, but at a safe distance. Once learnt never forgotten. She really didn't seem to have seen him. She went over to her mat and gathered up her long hair to wring out the water. The next instant, Rocky was in danger of being discovered, because in a single movement she had untied all her strings and was standing there completely naked. He saved himself by looking at his diver's wristwatch. Twenty-five past two. Just enough time and no more. She put on a little rust-coloured shirt and khaki shorts, gathered up her things and stalked across the grass towards the street.

He made a flying leap to his mat, pulled his pants over his dripping thong, snatched up his stuff and followed her.

Maybe she parked her car around here too, he thought. I just need her number. And then – only a phone call. He clicked his tongue again. Home game! Just you wait.

The blonde weaved gracefully through the traffic on the city freeway exit and strolled casually across the approach road on the other side. She turned into Bornimer Strasse.

He was lucky on the exit side and got to the central reservation. But a green light at Rathenau Platz brought him up short. Traffic thundered past him on three lanes. He saw the blonde heading straight for his Porsche. Then he lost her, because his eyes fixed on something else for a few precious seconds. Who's that asshole? What the fuck's he doing? Take your dirty paws off my Porsche!

A slight, pale boy wearing combat trousers and a string vest had started fumbling around Rocky's car. He bent over the windshield, wiped it and looked inside.

Rocky pawed the ground, as if he was trying to polish the stones of the reservation with his feet. He cursed every single damn driver who had to get from Kudamm on to the city motorway at this moment. Now get the machine gun in both hands. Turn with it. Baddaddaaddam! Step on it, you prick! This is Rocky!

When he looked at his car again, his eyes almost popped out of his head. Two chicks were standing beside the guy, one on either side, and they had – hey man, don't fuck about! You haven't got sunstroke! They were wearing ski masks! And all three were waving their arms about.

He had missed the lights again and he had to risk causing a mass pile-up. This was a kidnapping, man. A clean job. No guns. At least none visible. The little nerd plodded obediently behind the two broads and disappeared into a beat up VW Golf.

Rocky sprinted the last yards to his Porsche and revved up. The Golf was fifty yards ahead. It turned the corner into Kronprinzen Strasse. Rocky accelerated, spun the steering wheel and hit brakes and horn at the same time. Exactly one yard in front of him, in the middle of the street after the curve and in his sights, stood the blonde. She had turned round to look at the Golf, and now, startled by the full blast stereo sound of the River Kwai March, she stared straight into his face. He registered the pleased excitement in her face. So she saw me after all, it flashed through his head. Sorry, honey, but I'm busy now. He clicked his tongue for the third time in fifteen minutes and winked regretfully at her. And now move aside, darlin'. But the blonde had turned round again, still in the middle of the street, hands in her pockets. The scrapyard Golf disappeared from view. Rocky revved his motor, breaking up and distorting the sound of the Colonel Bogey March. He yelled something at her. Slowly she turned round again. "What's your hurry? Got a train to catch?"

She moved aside even more slowly. He accelerated. He didn't see her give him the finger.

*

Both men had been killed in their apartments in broad daylight. In their beds to be precise. The absence of any clues
which might have pointed to the use of force or even a
struggle, but the presence of generous and scattered sperm
traces on sheets and covers, suggested that in each case
death must have occurred suddenly and after enjoyment of
sex. According to the post-mortem, both had been killed by
an expertly placed karate chop to the carotid artery. What
the post-mortem had not revealed was the motive or
whether it had been murder or possibly self-defence. There
was evidence to support both possibilities, and yet, at the
same time no evidence at all.

There was a strong probability that both crimes had been
committed by the same person. They showed the same
forceful hand, so to speak. But whether this hand belonged
to a man or a woman remained undecided. Lietze and
Schade had consistently argued for a woman.

One clue, a tiny flake of shiny blue nail polish, had been
found on the front door of the first victim, forty-five-year-
old Hans-Joachim Seifert. It was a cheap brand, usually sold
during carnival. Seifert had been single, and had had a
couple of girlfriends, but neither were known for unconven-
tional finger nails. Or for their karate skills. In addition,
one of his colleagues at work had said that Seifert had
occasionally ordered "house calls." From where, or if
recently, he didn't know. The phone number of a bar in
Friedenau had been in Seifert's address book, and the local
neighbourhood cop had confirmed that the bar had also
arranged house calls. But it had been shut for two and a
half years. Lietze had visited the trio from Tiergarten Strasse
and they had told her that it was one of the many bars and
clubs where COW had never been able to get a foothold.
And Kim hadn't seen much blue nail polish of late. "But we

don't know every single girl, Karin. There must be – what do you think, Helga? A few hundred?"

Helga increased the figure to "a few thousand, if you allow for shiftworkers and part-timers. Anyway, I've seen a few men who sometimes like to paint their nails blue."

After that, Lietze decided not to lose any more time. "If we call all the ads in the *BZ*, we'll be doing nothing else for days. And why should we bother prostitutes? Did we find a single condom beside the corpses?"

There was no sign of anything missing from Seifert's wallet, briefcase or apartment. Nothing was missing except a reasonable explanation for his death. In the case of forty-six-year-old Werner Neiss, two whole bottles of nail polish were found, both red. They belonged to his former girlfriend, and it couldn't have been her. Not only had she been in jail at the time of the crime – she was a therapist working with prisoners who were drug addicts – she had also left Neiss a week earlier. He hadn't left her.

"He was always being Mr Nice Guy, the good neighbour, every mother-in-law's dream," the ex-girlfriend had declared, and then started weeping after all. "Always obliging and friendly, especially with women. Not a lady-killer, quite the opposite, faithful, reliable and – well, that was it. You know, you can't light a fire with wet paper."

The reports on Seifert had been almost identical. Quiet, polite and gentle, old ladies fell for him on the spot and all his younger girlfriends quickly left. "He never wanted any-thing for himself! Always the same question: Did you have a nice orgasm, darling? At the beginning I thought it was great. But after a few weeks, I thought I was in training for the Olympics. And anyway, I don't believe that from any man!" one of them had exclaimed.

Fritz and Roboldt had found these statements hard to take. "Still waters run deep," Roboldt reflected. "And what if both of them were only playing good, like Dr Jekyll?"

"And went around as Mr Hyde at night, exterminating foreign women and stamping them?" Lietze and Schade had immediately dismissed that idea.

"No, not that. But molesting women. And they were caught doing it by these avenging angels . . ."

". . . and they went after them and killed them," Fritz had finished with gleaming eyes.

"And neatly timed to coincide with the first two stamper murders? On April 23, the first murder, revenge for the black woman. On May 5, the next, revenge for the Chilean, or what? What do you think, Schade?"

Schade had found it all pretty baffling, and since she was the youngest and had the lowest rank, she was even able to admit that, for completely intuitive reasons, she still thought it was a woman.

D III had already got stuck at this point two weeks earlier.

"In other words," Lietze said, and put down her pen, "you've made no progress at all while I was away. And I still don't believe that Neiss and Seifert were killed by the JoAnne Little Brigade. There would have been signs of a struggle."

Fritz raised his eyebrows.

"I don't believe that it was a man either," Lietze continued. "What kind of man? And why? Do we have even the slightest reason for suspecting that? It must have been a woman, and, damn it, I haven't the faintest idea why."

"But that's impossible, Lietze!" Fritz had got cross, because they were going round in circles for the hundredth time. "There is no such thing as a – what should I call it? Female sex killer!"

"Yes Fritz, you're right," Lietze scratched her nose. The door was flung open, and Roboldt charged into the room sneezing. He sat down at the table and stared at her with red swollen eyes. "We can forget this as well, the thing about the dates!"

He threw his notepad and a Red Diary on to the table and devoted the next few minutes to his nose and his handkerchief. Schade started to look through his notes. "There's a whole bunch of dates, so where should I start? July 31, that's today – 1941, Göring orders the final solution of the Jewish question in the German-controlled territories in Europe. August 27, 1914, Battle of Tannenberg. September 15, 1935 – Nürnberg Laws ..."

"Are you trying to give the stamper a history degree, Roboldt?" Lietze, almost bursting with impatience, looked at her watch.

"Bullshit, boss. Guys like that even get to be Chancellor these days. I wouldn't rule out any possibility," Roboldt yelled as loudly as his strained vocal chords allowed. "Why do you tell me to go and do all this work in the first place?" Angrily, he jumped up and went towards the office door.

Schade was just about to mention September 1, 1939, when Roboldt almost collided with Mimi Jacob. A delicate smile on her lips again, she led in a wiry young man who was five foot seven at most. "Herr Herrmann is here," she announced.

Everybody looked at him. Herr Herrmann stood there as if he were on parade. The only thing missing was the salute. He was content to stand at attention, both hands pressed against the seams of his trousers – and exactly midway between the seams was a triangular wet patch. "Herrmann, Roland," he barked. "But colleagues may call me Rocky."

"Oh," said Roboldt, and turned pale.

He couldn't have seen it coming. The dark thing raced towards him from the side at the outer limit of his vision, while he was sunk in contemplation of his tool cabinet, and his thoughts were galloping straight from the forty marks he had collected to her and the new life he would start with her. With her! It had happened to him. With her of all people!

He recoiled and dropped the pipe wrench. It had been at the window, he expected shattered glass. He pulled the cupboard door over for protection and jerked his head round.

Everything remained quiet. It was just Blondie, now sitting on the window ledge on the other side of the drawn curtains and demanding to be let in.

Alfred Henke released the breath he had been holding in and felt new waves of sweat pour down his face, neck and armpits. "Yes yes yes yes yes, my angel," he panted. "It's all right, I'm coming. If you please, your majesty!"

He opened the window a bit and lifted one side of the curtain just enough to let the cat slip through. He glanced suspiciously into the courtyard, closed the window and straightened the curtain. "Why don't you come through the kitchen? That's where your door is. You know very well this window always has to be kept closed."

The cat ignored his sycophantic fussing and stalked towards the kitchen. He hurried to fill her bowl with fresh water. But she was neither interested in his water nor in his lectures about these times in which even water turns mouldy and how, after all, this wasn't Africa. She sat in front of a second, empty bowl and stared lethargically in front of her.

"Of course! Yes yes, you'll get it. You'll get anything you want, my angel!"

Henke fetched a carton and poured some dry food into the bowl. She condescended to eat half of it, turned around, stalked back to the workshop and settled on top of a big, flat wooden box, covered with a kitchen towel. "But make sure everything stays the way it is!" he ordered and moved the box a bit. "That's right. You watch, so nobody gets at it."

He picked up the pipe wrench and finished cleaning it. Then he put it back with the other tools, which lay or hung

in rows in the cabinet. "Order is heaven's first law. Yes yes.
My work area was always the tidiest. But nobody's interested
in that nowadays. Once, my angel. Once, a tidy work area
was a plus. But today? Today they fire you. If you keep
things in order, they get rude. Rude! And they kick me out!
Na. What on earth!"

He wiped the shelves with a cloth, making sure not to
disturb the tools. "But I'm telling you Blondie, you've got
to look after the little things. If a nation doesn't demonstrate
any discipline in the little things . . . Na! Anybody can come
here and . . . you can't do anything about it any more, by
yourself. But at least the old cow's not coming in here again,
not her, I'm telling you!"

He caressed the screwdrivers, lined up like organ pipes
on the inside of the cabinet door. "She shouldn't have done
it. Mess everything up. I found the smallest gimlet on the
floor under the cupboard. Imagine that. Three hours to clear
it all up! The slut's got no respect. What on earth. And that
hooligan's the same. Takes after her and no one else. He
was supposed to be here at one on the dot. And where is
he? All he can do is scream for more money. But not from
me, I'm telling you. He won't get a penny. He'll get a bloody
good thrashing. Just like the old bitch! What on earth. Na."

The cat stopped licking herself and gave him a disapproving look. But it didn't register with Henke. "Yes yes yes, my
queen. I know. You're happy, too, that we've got rid of her.
And that brat, it'll be his turn next, I'm telling you that for
nothing. It's time to sort things out here. Once and for all.
In a big way!"

He locked the cabinet and put the keys in his pocket.
Then he picked up the big broom, which Thorsten should
have been using, and went into the courtyard. He made slow
progress, because every few minutes he had to wipe away
the sweat that was dripping into his eyes.

Blondie sat in state on top of one of the partition walls and looked down on him.

From time to time Henke looked up at her and gave a half bow. My queen, he thought and his mind returned to *her*. To his Mata Hari. Who would have thought! One of them. And on top of that from . . . What on earth! You never can tell with love. He laughed silently. Mata Hari! So different from that, that old besom! That slut! That . . . But her. Slim and young and sexy and on the ball. She's going places. And she'll make something of you too, Alfred! She's a queen and she loves you! She appreciates quality! Solid.

Every time he looked at her, Blondie turned her head to one side and displayed a mocking grin. But Alfred Henke didn't see it that way.

The old bitch has got to go! Vigorously he pushed open the door leading from the courtyard into the street. She'd better keep out of my way! Not screw up me and my happiness. And once Mata Hari is back, that'll be the end of it. The whole thing'll be put in order. He swept the dirt from the courtyard out on to the pavement, and worked his way forward inch by inch behind the broom. I have to put this mess behind me. She has to be there for me. Only for me. My queen. He tore a sticker announcing some rock concert off the wall in the passage leading to the courtyard. Well. Maybe he'd have to bear it for a while yet. He wouldn't get anywhere with piddling amounts like the forty marks from the Thurau woman upstairs with her dripping tap. But when . . .

He swept the pavement outside the front house. He had to wipe the sweat out of his eyes again. His eyes fell on the historic plaque on the left above the entrance. Let them stick their ads over that pervert! Then he looked down again and realised that the broom was leaving a brown trail behind with each sweep. He jerked it up, cursed and saw the pile of dog shit he had swept right through. He turned round and stopped dead in his tracks. A brief flash of joy, which immediately evaporated. He saw the back of a woman walking down Nollendorf Strasse toward Maassen Strasse. That was ... no. Mata's got blonde hair! But if she was wearing a wig ... Had she come out of his building? Maybe she hadn't left, but ... He thought about chasing after her. Impossible. She can't ... That's as far as he got. A cab came down the street behind him, honking loudly. He winced and looked round. A big blonde waved her left arm, which was covered in black and yellow marks, out of the driver's window. "Alfred," she yelled, "I'm returning your slippers. They're too hot right now."

"Aw, stick 'em up your ass," Henke growled. "I've got more important things to do."

The woman stopped the cab right in the middle of the road. Then she took off her sunglasses. The skin around her left eye was discoloured too. "It's not for you to decide what's important. I've thought about it and we have to have another talk. I'm just going to look for a parking place and then I'll be back."

Eyes shut, bare feet on the table, the open newspaper with the headline RECYCLING THE BLACK SKI MASKS on her knees, Detective Chief Inspector Karin Lietze rocked on her chair, trying hard to get things straight in her mind – though she'd settle for a rough overview. She didn't hear Detective Sergeant Sonja Schade come in.

"One of us really should take a closer look at all these self defence courses." The door closed behind Schade.

Lietze jumped. "Schade! For heaven's sake!" She groped for the cigarillos and took out a Lucky Luciano and immediately threw them back on the table. "Do you think these women vigilantes could have a base there?"

"Oh, I see, yeah," said Schade. "Well – no, I was thinking

about the murdered men. It must have been someone who knows their karate chops. And if we don't want to exclude women . . . It might even lead us to the JoAnne Little Brigade as well. Have you read the article yet?"

"No." Lietze folded the newspaper and put it next to her bag. "What a nice word – self defence."

"For the Brigade? Attack is the best form of defence. They're not the only ones to see it like that."

"True, true, and the best way to avoid being scared is to make somebody else scared. I know there are plenty of reasons to be scared. Especially in Schöneberg, around Nollendorf Platz and Winterfeldt Platz. It's really exploded in the last six months."

"Still no reason to take the law into your own hands!" Schade reached for the cigarillo on the table and lit it. "A few strong women knock some men around and denounce them – it just won't work. Or do we want to go back to the law of the jungle."

Lietze stared at her, shook her head and closed her eyes again. Finally she said, "No, Schade, it's unacceptable and we don't want it. But when the police and the courts can't protect women from sexual violence or at least find the perpetrators – that's unacceptable, too. I try to imagine what kind of effect it has. Over and over you're confronted with cases where you don't even have to look for the perpetrator because he's married to the victim, and he's standing right next to her when she's being carried out on a stretcher all covered in blood or with broken ribs. And our model colleagues are standing right there as well. How can you seriously expect women to trust these same policemen to catch guys whose only motive was that the victims were women."

Thoughtfully Schade inhaled a couple of times. "Not to mention the times our model colleagues chose to make fun of the victims."

"Or turned into culprits themselves. Fritz is right, taking the law into your own hands has a certain logic to it."

"Still. It's assault. And how do those ladies know that they've picked the right one?"

"Snap!" said Lietze. "Did you get it?" She fished for the pack. "Suddenly the trap is sprung. Who is the right one? Nobody deserves to become the victim of lynch law. That's what you said just a minute ago, Schade."

"Yeah. True."

"But it's also true that women who are intimidated, raped and maybe even murdered are the victims of lynch law too. What then?"

Schade sighed angrily and went over to the window: "But all that they achieve with campaigns of revenge and punishments is that the guys disappear from one neighbourhood and keep on doing it all the more brutally somewhere else."

"Probably. It looks like this Brigade is labour intensive, and if our little trainee wasn't lying to cover up the embarrassment with his wet pants, it's not just limited to Schöneberg, but has spread at least as far as Halensee. But, of course, you're right."

Schade came back to the desk and threw the cigarillo stub in the ashtray. "It's a nasty way to clean things up. Makes me think allotment gardeners who throw their muck over their neighbour's fence at the back and proudly display their polished garden gnomes in front."

"Me too. Let's see if we can at least get somewhere with this serial stamper case. And if we can clip this would-be Rocky's wings and teach him the basics of detective work." Lietze got up and accompanied Schade to the door. Then she went back to the desk, dropped into her chair and put her feet up. The basics of detective work. Which basics? Detection is hardly the name for what we're doing. More like poking around in a fog. Or throwing chips around, so you get the feeling you're working hard chopping wood.

Especially with the two dead males. Basically all we're doing is waiting for a third, and hoping we'll get one or two useable clues then.

There was a knock at the door. Lietze took her feet off the desk and sat up to look a bit more official. It could only be Herrmann and he was someone who was crying out for authority.

There was a second knock, but the door didn't open. Completely new customs.

"Yes," she barked.

The door opened, and Herrmann was standing at attention again. "I would like to report."

"Wrong! You are reporting, young man. Large as life. Not to be overlooked!"

She had no time for arse-lickers and bootlickers. Oh Mimi! "Have you been shown everything?"

Herrmann nodded obediently and remained at the door. There was something contemptuous about his obedience, Lietze thought.

"You may as well sit down, it doesn't cost extra." She watched him as, quite the athlete, he swung a chair from the conference table, placed it in front of her desk and sat down, legs apart. And waited.

"Okay. If you want to, you can knock off now. We'll meet at eight fifty-five. Did you take down the Olàlà's address? Fine. Be on time, please. And we don't want to take the place apart, just ask a few questions. Is that clear? Anything else?"

"Yes. Ah. Regarding. Ah. About. Ah. Dress, Frau . . ."

"You can save yourself the Frau," she interrupted him. "Rank as well. Lietze is enough. I know that I'm a woman and that I'm the Chief Detective Inspector in charge of this division. We work as a team. Regarding dress, since you asked: wear something comfortable and don't overdress.

Finally," she looked at him sarcastically, "make sure your pants are dry."

Herrmann turned red, but it seemed more with anger than embarrassment. When he was gone, Lietze put everything in her bag and went next door. Mimi Jacob was sitting at the typewriter. "Do you want your jeans and t-shirt back?"

Lietze nodded. "And I want something else, Mimi. Please tell me, there is such a thing as a short man with class!"

Mimi smiled wisely and put the clothes in Lietze's arms. "Oh yes. Sure. Of course," she said at last.

"Well – thank god," Lietze sighed. "Name a few. Maybe that'll calm me down." She hesitated a moment, then put on the jeans and unbuttoned the smock.

"Come on, Mimi," she begged. "Just don't give me Rosa Luxemburg again!" She stood half dressed in the secretary's office of Section D III (Serious Crimes), and hastily pulled on her t-shirt.

"Nope," Mimi grinned. "Golda Meir!"

His eyes were so swollen they were almost closed and the wet Kleenex behind the driver's seat were piling up. Detlev Roboldt had his thirty-seventh attack of sneezing and pulled out the next tissue. As he opened his eyes wide between sneezes and got a clear look at the object of his surveillance, the front door of the building opened and a stocky man stepped into the street. About thirty. Cherub face was a good description, he thought. It had to be him. Roboldt kept the tissue in front of his face and glanced at the clock on the dashboard of his BMW. Seven thirty-three.

A lanky, quite tall man was approaching from the direction Zadko was about to take. Zadko didn't seem pleased to see him. From the way he gesticulated and talked to the other man, Roboldt gathered that Zadko wanted to get rid of him fast. He looked back towards the entrance twice. But the front door remained shut. The light on the first floor was still on. It had been on for at least half an hour, even though it was still daylight outside. Probably lighter than in a north facing apartment on a narrow street in Wedding with nothing but four-storey tenement buildings.

Now Zadko wrote something on a piece of paper and handed it to the other man. He read it, looked sceptically at Zadko, thought for a moment, put it in his shirt pocket and crossed the street. Roboldt's stinging eyes followed Zadko, who disappeared into a corner bar three houses down the road.

The stranger was right beside the BMW when Roboldt found he couldn't hold back his thirty-eighth barrage of sneezes. The man turned his head and stared for a few seconds into a face whose lower half was veiled by white tissue. Roboldt squeezed his eyes shut and blew his nose extra loud. When he looked again, the stranger had disappeared. Roboldt cursed each and every virus in the world. Then he threw open the car door and clumsily went about gathering up the pile of paper handkerchiefs. If the stranger had gone into the café next door, Roboldt would have to see him as he was depositing the wet bundle in the garbage can on the lamp post. At the same time he could keep an eye on Zadko's apartment. The light was still on.

The stranger really was sitting at a table by the window and seemed to be observing the house, too. Roboldt took the initiative and smiled at him. The man looked sullen and didn't react. Why isn't Fritz here yet, Roboldt thought angrily. Even without a cold I don't have three pairs of eyes. At that moment Fritz came walking down Bastian Strasse. Roboldt stepped out of sight of the stranger in the café and signalled Fritz not to come closer. Fritz stopped. Roboldt gave him a brief report. "Grey track suit bottoms, trainers, polo shirt, also grey. Sitting in there. He knows me now."

Fritz looked at Roboldt pityingly. "You should be in bed, Detlev," he decided.

"You may be right. Because he only noticed me because he heard me." Roboldt's nose started twitching threateningly again. "Zadko is in the corner bar."

"Go home, man. You'll screw up the whole surveillance. I'll just get my car." Fritz walked off. "And," he yelled after Roboldt who was slinking back to his BMW, "don't you dare stick to Zadko! Have you got any chicken soup at home?"

As, with deliberate clumsiness, Roboldt was taking his seat in the car again, the light in Zadko's apartment went out. He contrived four ignition failures. Finally he saw a very young, dark-haired woman in a black minidress that fitted like a second skin leave the house and stroll up Bastian Strasse towards the corner bar. He started the car, drove around the corner and stopped two houses down and out of Fritz's field of vision.

A rather unfashionable family car came down Bastian Strasse and stopped as if by chance right in front of Zadko's building. Fritz got out, opened the hood, stuck his head between some radiator hoses and waited. Nothing happened. He had repeated the act of looking for tools and fumbling with the cables and other parts of the engine three times, before the lanky stranger dressed in grey track suit bottoms left the café and went into Zadko's building.

The bellows with the lens slid smoothly up and down. She kept adjusting the focus. Calm after the storm. Hundreds, thousands, of splinters were tinkling gently now. Her damp legs stuck to the chair. The slightest move caused a tickling as the skin detached itself from one part of the wood and stuck fast to another.

She swung the red filter in front of the focus hood and placed the photo paper on the plate. Then she swung the filter away and counted. Rivers poured from her armpits down to her thighs under the red extra large t-shirt with the purple slogan *THINK BIG!* Tickling her nerve ends. *I think I've penetrated the male attitude towards sex.* Was that the phrase? That was it. The missing caption. Look it up. Later. Not now. Now six prints with different exposures, but the same developing time.

When all six were floating in the fixing tray, she switched on the white light, looked at them and chose one. Thirteen seconds, different developing times. She put them in the water, switched off the light again and made three more enlargements. *I prefer sexual contempt.* Later. First the perfect print. It had to be alongside the others in Sydney's — that picture. Although it didn't fit. The edges were different. But they're too dumb anyway. They won't even notice. I always thought of photography as a very naughty thing to do. When I first did it, I felt very perverse. Diane Arbus. To immerse oneself in experiences which cannot be prettified. The encounter with whatever is taboo, perverse and evil. Was that Arbus or Sontag?

It took nearly an hour to get the perfect print. Then the warm, dull picture emerged from the print dryer and she put it with the others on a big table. She looked at the collection. It really did stick out. But nobody will notice. The cards with the captions lay sorted at the right hand edge of the table. The glass splinters had almost stopped tinkling, a cool feeling of happiness began to spread through her body. She opened the window of the darkroom and felt a soft breeze. It was still light outside. She watched her Greek neighbour, who had taken on the caretaker job with her German husband, remove the washing from the line. Was the thunderstorm coming? At last? Tonight?

She went to the kitchen to get a glass of wine. When she came back to the darkroom, a gust of wind had swept the cards from the table and disordered the pictures. Perhaps not such a bad thing, she thought, as she picked them up. Put them in a different order. Photography is essentially an act of non-intervention. Richard Avedon. That was supposed to have been for Ginette. But perhaps it fitted this last one here much better. And that one with the *male attitude towards sex? Sexual contempt*? To present oneself as a work of art. Be the erotic centre of attention. She took a sip. What, if not that, made life worth living?

Then she collected the little bottles of paint and the brushes together and went to look for the quotation.

Cars had been banned from the eastern end of Nollendorf Strasse and from Zieten Strasse which intersected it at a right angle, the car-free zone forming a cross. There were parking bays at either end of Zieten Strasse. Lietze cursed. She had turned into it from Bülow Strasse. Going by the street numbers, Club Olàlà must be at the other end of Zieten Strasse, towards Winterfeldt Strasse.

"It's a short street, let's walk." Sonja Schade extinguished her cigarette. "There's a parking place."

Lietze manoeuvred the Renault into the space. "Who knows what it's good for."

It was eight minutes to nine. They strolled across the intersection. Lietze looked round. Nollendorf Strasse and Zieten Strasse both looked peaceful and clean in the sun's last rays. People were sitting on benches and chatting or making sure that the kids romping around didn't hit each other. The children were the only ones who were unafraid of physical activity. Aside from that, the scene looked as if someone had stopped time.

"It's all this nostalgia kitsch," Schade said scornfully. "They've not only restored the old tenement buildings, they've even put up street signs from the last century."

Lietze pulled a face. "They look like they're polished every day."

Schade grinned. "Wouldn't surprise me. A true caretaker wouldn't shrink from that even in tropical heat."

"Well." Lietze took off her thin jacket and slung it over her shoulders. "That little breeze earlier didn't do it. I hoped it would save us, but . . ." In annoyance she tried to smooth her crumpled jacket.

Schade nodded and watched Lietze's efforts with amusement. "It's no use, Lietze. In weather like this, wrinkles are part of the pattern. It must be over there. A woman just went in."

Lietze looked in the direction Schade was pointing and bumped into a white Porsche. She staggered as she rubbed her shin which had struck the bumper. Sonja Schade took her arm.

"This weather is really no good for the circulation!" Lietze cursed and stared at the car. Some stickers were resplendent on the rear window. A Playboy bunny. Next to it an elongated rectangle: "Five past twelve is better than none after midnight." Underneath, an oval: "Screwdriver seeks screws."

Lietze didn't know whether to laugh or explode.

"How very funny," Schade said. "Bet it's the owner's car."

As they were standing at the door of Club Olàlà, Roland "Rocky" Herrmann came around the corner of Winterfeldt Strasse and walked towards them with a spring in his step. "Legs like a donkey's haunches," Schade mumbled.

"And on time to boot," Lietze added.

"Are you disappointed? You don't want to get rid of him or anything?"

"Me? Never." Lietze grinned. "I've nothing against . . . against . . . dickheads. In the right place!" She tried to remain serious and ignore Schade's look of surprise.

"I'll have to bear that in mind. Here he comes." Schade scratched her head.

"Good evening, Herrmann. Have you begun to make enquiries?"

"Yes," Herrmann beamed. He had already walked round the block and he had even done a bit of thinking. "The thing with the car, umm, that is supposed to have picked up this Polish woman here, it couldn't have been like that," he concluded. "A car can't get to the door here."

Lietze and Schade looked at him with something like pity. "And who said it had?"

"Well. Er. It was in the report. The, er, corpse was only found in the Ruin. And if the woman worked here. Er. I thought . . ."

"Yes, the trouble with thinking," Schade interrupted him, is that . . ."

"I think," Lietze cut them both short, "we'll take a look round first of all."

Fritz had been staring at the two windows on the second floor for at least twenty minutes. But no lights had gone on. Had the man given him the slip after all while he had moved to a less conspicuous spot? He considered whether he should get out and go into the house. Maybe there was another exit, across the courtyard or something. In that case he could safely stop the surveillance and go home and take a shower.

He waited another five minutes. His neck slowly grew stiff, even though there was still hardly the slightest breeze. He sat up again and rubbed his neck. Finally he grabbed the car handle and at the last moment saw the door of the house, which first Zadko and then his "groupie" had left more than three-quarters of an hour before, open. The unknown male came out, looked around quickly, then walked along Bastian Strasse in the opposite direction. He seemed to be in a hurry.

Fritz started the car and followed him at a safe distance.

The stranger turned left into Bad Strasse and disappeared into the U-Bahn entrance at the Pank Strasse intersection.

Fritz drove left down Pank Strasse, made another left turn into Böttger Strasse and looked for Roboldt's BMW. He was sure Roboldt hadn't taken his advice to go straight home to bed, but had stationed himself next to the bar Zadko had gone to, and was waiting for him. But the BMW was nowhere in sight.

The rectangular peephole in the iron door opened and closed quickly. The door was half opened and a slightly hoarse voice barked: "What do you want? We don't need anybody. We didn't run an ad."

Sonja Schade gave a friendly smile as she pulled her I.D. out of her pocket and showed it to the woman standing in the darkness behind the door. "I already have a job," she explained. "It's about something else. Can we come in . . .?"

"We?" the voice barked again. The door opened all the way. The woman stepped out and saw Lietze and Herrmann. "The three of you? Did some government guy's heart seize up in a brothel again – or maybe it was the Catholic Charities boss?" The woman seemed to have no intention of letting them in.

Herrmann shifted impatiently from one foot to the other.

"We just have a few questions," Lietze intervened, as Schade put away her I.D. again.

"No problem, you know. We get some pretty weird requests here. And since I can't refuse yours anyway . . ."

"You can," Lietze assured her. "But maybe you'd like to know what it's about first."

The woman looked the three of them over. "Can I see that thing again?"

"Certainly," Schade said and showed her I.D. again.

"Well, come in."

It took a while for them to get used to the dim red light. On the right against the wall of the small room there was a bar, and to the left were couches, chairs and tiny tables on a rather showy dark patterned carpet. Stylised dark red and green flowers. The upholstery was dark red and black too, but the pattern was different. The walls were papered with photographed scenes of Paris by night, Times Square by night and a tropical sunset, punctuated by cosy old-fashioned wall lamps with floral pattern lamp shades.

"I'm Minou. The others are in the dressing room. I'll get them."

She disappeared down a hallway between the bar and the easy chairs, opened a door and closed it behind her immediately. They could hear a low murmuring.

Lietze and Schade stood at the bar. Herrmann was undecided. He looked as if he wanted to chase after Minou and personally haul all the women out. And have everything lit up. Lietze calmly lit a Lucky Luciano and waited.

Minou was the first to come out. "Martha hasn't arrived yet, but she's always late. Something to drink – just this once?"

Lietze politely refused. "It only makes you sweat even more."

"You were going to say what it's about," Minou began.

Schade suggested they wait until everyone was there. "Is your boss – oh, sorry, are you the boss here?"

Minou broke into a raucous laugh. "Na!" Finally she said. "Nobody would give me that kind of loan!"

The hallway door opened and a thirtyish redhead with long legs encased in thigh-length boots, hotpants and a bra, came over to the bar, followed by an almost childlike little blonde wearing white stockings, red garters and a red and white striped bodice with a little skirt.

"The boss was away for the weekend; he'll be back late tonight to collect some money," Minou explained. She was the oldest, forty at least – the feisty, motherly type. She was the only one wearing a long and almost decent dress, if you didn't count the sequins and the scallop décolleté.

Schade introduced herself and the two others. "Let's see, what's it about – you've got a Polish girl working here . . ."

"I told you that already," Minou interrupted, fiddling with an already open bottle of sparkling wine. "Martha's usually late."

"She can get away with it," the blonde complained. "Gimme a glass too, Minou. Just because Ebb thinks she's taking care of most of the clients anyway!"

With a professional swing of her hips, the redhead sat on one of the bar stools and scrutinised her legs with a bored expression.

"Do you want some too, Natalie?" Minou asked. Natalie tossed back her hair and shook her head. "I don't understand why you start on your own. We have to drink enough with the clients later on. And you can't take a drink anyway, Ramona. You better be careful Ebb doesn't cotton you're working at the bar when you're tanked up."

Ramona pulled a face again and picked up her glass.

"Cheers," Lietze said. "I like your names. Is Ebb your boss?"

Minou nodded. "Eberhard. First name's Richard. But when everyone started calling him Greedy-Dick because he was always after every bit of skirt, he put a stop to that. Now we call him Ebb, like the tide, because he always acts like funds are low, especially in the morning when we ask for our regular pay and our bonuses. They're all the same. At least Ebb provides rubbers. That's progress. Is it about Ebb?"

"No," Lietze laughed. "About Martha, assuming it's her. Describe her again."

"Knew all along there was something not right about her," the sensual Natalie put in. "You can never get close to her."

"Ach, you're nuts. Just because she's from Poland. You're jealous because she goes down better than you do with your tray, tray French trip!" Minou wiped the bar in front of her.

"She snatched clients away from me a couple of times too," Ramona complained, draining the last drop of champagne.

"She didn't snatch anyone away, honey, she just took over those clients who don't dig a Lolita. There are men who don't and you'll have to live with it."

"Ladies," smiled Schade. "You've got the rest of the night to talk about that. What did, um, what does Martha look like?"

Minou looked at her suspiciously. "Detective you said, right? And him, is he a detective too? Or is he from immigration? Martha's papers were in order, I can guarantee that!"

Schade sighed. Herrmann didn't feel he had to do anything which might inspire trust. Lietze waited, then took over the questioning. "Is Martha about thirty? Slim and delicate? Long blonde hair? Blue eyes?"

Minou nodded each time. "A beauty. She speaks pretty good German, and some English as well."

"When did you last see her?"

Natalie looked up from her legs for a change. "Why? Has something happened to her?"

"Let's see, Saturday night. Sundays we're shut. It's not worth it. Saturday's pretty dead too," Minou explained.

"'Cause Daddy has to be at home with the family," Ramona added.

"Tell me a bit more about that night."

"Dead too," Ramona squeaked.

"How do you know, you were plastered," Natalie interrupted.

Finally, Minou came up with a roughly chronological summary of the sequence of events from Saturday night to

Sunday. Nine customers had found their way to Club Olàlà. Two had to go right out again. "Scandinavians. They're always tanked up and are just abusive. Back home they don't get any juice, so they're always drunk when they're abroad. It really pisses me off. I bet Rosso dragged them in, I'll have to have a word with him about it in a minute."

Rosso was some kind of house boy, apparently a youngster who mostly hauled in crates of bottles and beer kegs but, occasionally, customers too. None of the women knew his real name. He got his nickname because for a while he had been going on about the Tupamaros and the Red Brigades and the RAF. Martha had started calling him "Raffke" – money grubber – which had infuriated him. She thought he was a scrounger, and that didn't square with his speeches on "property is theft". Finally, to prevent an escalation of hostilities between him and Martha, the others suggested calling him Rosso. And were careful not to tell him that the name suited his complexion perfectly. "Because he's got the kind of skin that turns as red as a fire engine if he stays out in the sun, and a couple of hours later it all peels off," Ramona explained triumphantly.

Anyway, Martha had taken care of three of the seven remaining guests, the last one around four, just before closing. At the same time, Minou, who usually looked after the bar when the boss was away, and Natalie had work as well, and occupied both cubicles. By that point Ramona had already been semi-comatose behind the bar, if one could believe Natalie, and could not remember Martha's customer at all. She didn't even remember that Martha had passed a note totalling her earnings to Minou in her cubicle. Minou took the piece of paper from a concealed pocket in her dress. "Here, I'm supposed to make sure that the money – oh shit, I completely forgot! Martha won't be in today. She's taken a week off."

Lietze nodded, satisfied.

*

Detlev Roboldt was sweating buckets, but those two didn't have a care in the world. Zadko had left the corner bar again pretty quickly, his arm around the young woman. He would never hold his saxophone that perfunctorily, Roboldt had thought.

Then, arm in arm, but without displaying particular tenderness, still less any sign of being in love, they had strolled up Pank Strasse, crossed Bad Strasse, into Prinzenallee, looked at a shop window now and then, and had finally gone into a tiny African restaurant. During the whole time they had exchanged a dozen words at most. He had watched them through the window. They had eaten and then looked through a magazine. It seemed to be one of the listings magazines, because they had only been interested in a single double page.

God, you're an idiot, Roboldt thought. They're going to have a good time and go to the movies. And all you get is an even higher temperature. Just try to get home safely before the shivers start!

"So you saw her for the last time shortly before four, and then she left the bar with a john?" Lietze summarised. "And you're sure it was a john? Where was this Rosso at the time?"

"How should I know? He was probably roaming the streets. Or putting crates away. Martha told me she was leaving with one of her regulars. And said I should keep an eye on Ramona, because if someone came in, all the money'd be gone. No wonder my client was mad." Minou looked reproachfully at Ramona.

"And you've no idea who this regular client was?"

"I guess Martha has three or four. But they all pay cash, no cheques. And we don't take credit cards. It just causes problems, because the credit card companies take an extra percentage from bars like ours, and we have to make up the difference ourselves. But what's up with Martha? Why do you want to know all this?"

"She's dead," said Sonja Schade, trying to be as gentle as possible. Lietze looked at the three women. Rocky Herrmann was still standing arrogantly in the middle of the room and looking as if he'd like to hose the joint down.

"Murdered. And that last john might be the last one who saw her alive."

"Shit, Ramona, you fucking lush!" Minou started to yell, trying to hide her shock. "You must have seen him! Who was it! Open your mouth, girl!"

Ramona was sobbing. Even Natalie had lost interest in looking seductive, and was slumped over the bar staring at Minou.

A red lamp behind Minou started blinking.

"Mon dieu, clients!" Relieved, Natalie jumped from her stool and ran to the door. "More slime, ah, police," she said, her nose pressed flat beneath the peephole. "Did you order them here?"

Lietze and Schade looked at each other and shook their heads. Herrmann still stood, legs apart, next to the bar and radiated discomfort.

Minou came out from behind the bar and opened the door. "Good evening, gentlemen. Please come in. We're having a party tonight!"

The two young men in uniform stepped a bit uncertainly into the red glow. "Well, ah," one of them began, "there's someone lying next to your door and we wanted to see . . ."

Lietze and Schade leapt from their bar stools to the door.

Right in front of Lietze, a combination of grey track suit pants and grey polo shirt disappeared behind the parked cars. The lanky man in them was wearing sneakers.

Sonja Schade had knelt down just to the left of the

entrance. A very young man was propped against the wall. His head hung down loosely. He didn't seem to be conscious. His pale face was bruised, his head was shaved and had red, inflamed patches, his string vest, the skin beneath it and his arms and hands were smeared with blood. There was no blood on his combat pants, but they were covered in dirt from the street, like the wide black belt with its big buckle embossed with the letters K A O S. There was a circle round the A. The boy wore a tin ring with a death rune. There was a cardboard sign on his knees. THIS IS A WOMAN HATER: TODAY WE GAVE HIM THE PUNISHMENT HE DESERVED. This was followed by a long text in smaller print. At the very end, in big letters again: YOU WILL ALL END UP LIKE THIS, IF YOU CAN'T UNDERSTAND – WHEN A WOMAN SAYS NO SHE MEANS NO! JOANNE LITTLE BRIGADE.

"Rosso!" Minou screamed.

"No, Roboldt! You stay . . . yes Roboldt, I know we have two cases at once – no, I don't know what it's good for either!" Lietze leant barefoot against the desk, and fanned some cool air under her t-shirt with a folder.

"No, Roboldt, we can't do without you, but nobody around here wants to deal with an invasion of your germs. Fritz took care of everything himself last night, didn't he? He discovered the break-in at Zadko's apartment, called the duty guys and checked the place out. The two of you couldn't have done more . . . no, Roboldt! Or did you want to spend half the night waiting for Zadko on the stairs? Well, then."

She listened to the croaking at the other end with only half an ear. Almost eleven thirty. With luck Schade and Fritz would be back in an hour with some information about Rosso. She tried to figure out if she could take time to run over to the Europa Center and buy something that wouldn't stick to her like these airtight jeans.

"Yes, Roboldt, I know we have to find the big lanky guy. Probably he got the Olàlà's address from Zadko. Yes, Roboldt, in that case Zadko was lying. But you stay where you are! Until your temperature is normal. Look at it this way Roboldt, it'll simply get too hot if you start heating our office from the inside as well. We'll keep our Herrmann busy . . . no, I don't like him either. But he hasn't been sent to us to be somebody's sex toy, just to be trained, for heaven's sake. Yes! No! Yes, Roboldt, I know, but for the time being let's assume he's a – a sheep in wolf's clothing!"

The next wave of sweat was on its way. As if this dumb Rambo or Rocky or whatever he was called, this two stroke mixture of bullshitter and baby, who would like to hold mummy's hand and be given the world on a plate – as if he wasn't costing her too much energy already. Now Roboldt was whining for an extra dose of mollycoddling too. She thought about calling his mother. ". . . I was at the back of the queue when they were handing out maternal instincts, Roboldt. Basta. What? Well, I must have been thinking out loud. No, Roboldt, not you. Yes, and you keep on top of things! Like your nose. What? Yes. Good idea. Read all the books you've always wanted to read –. Nice, Roboldt. And I'm not your boss!"

Unnerved, she put down the phone and at the same moment got a whiff of something burning. She raced into the typist's office. Mimi was just unplugging the coffee machine.

"Mimi!" She sounded almost hysterical. "Keep your hands off that monster!"

Mimi calmly investigated the connection.

"I knew it. One day the thing's going to implode! But nobody listens to me round here!" She wanted to take a dive at Mimi and pull her under the nearest table.

Mimi looked up and gave her a smile that should be mandatory for the staff in old people's homes. "Karin – trust me. This isn't a tv. Just an ordinary coffee machine with a cord which, for unknown reasons, has begun to smoulder. Here – do you want to take a look at it?"

Lietze looked with dismay at the yellow-brown discoloured cord which Mimi had pulled from the machine. Then she closed her eyes, told herself to take a deep breath and thought about the beautiful blue North Sea.

"I think it's finished," Mimi said.

"Thank God!" Lietze groaned. One less hassle. "I'll go and buy some instant coffee right now!"

*

"Oh, it was yours!" Sonja Schade would have preferred not to believe her eyes. But it was the very same white Porsche that had been parked in front of the Olàlà last night. And at that moment, Roland "Rocky" Herrmann was getting out of it.

He patted the roof. "It's a goer." Full of pride, he winked at Lothar Fritz and only at him. Fritz glanced inquiringly at Schade. She bristled. Cop, she thought. That's what I couldn't stand about you. From the very first moment. Guys like you either turn into pimps or dealers or cops.

As she walked behind the two men, she noticed how Fritz tried to restrain Rocky's chatter with a flat, "yesyes" and "well, I don't know". Teach this guy something?

He ran ahead and opened the glass swing door for Fritz, letting go of it as soon as Fritz had passed through. Wait, Schade thought, watching him strut into the entrance hall. Will Fritz at least remember I'm still here and that I'm going to have the door in my face?

She was relieved when Fritz pulled the door back at the last moment. "How considerate," she said pertly. "Everybody on his best behaviour."

"There's a full moon tonight," Fritz laughed. "Men always go mad then."

It took at least ten minutes until a nurse in casualty found time to check where the pale, badly beaten youth, who had been brought in the night before in the emergency doctor's car, had been put. She didn't seem to be someone who was particularly obliging with the police. She'd probably been working in emergency wards too long.

Schade felt anger rising in her again. Images of those nights she'd spent in casualty rooms and intensive care units because of Anita. Police bringing in junkies, drunks and prisoners in custody and behaving like bulls in a china shop. Usually several of them in uniform, throwing their weight around. Wanting to poke their noses into every cupboard.

You're one of them too. That's what you're like. Fritz had given up trying to act as if he was taking part in a conversation. He wasn't interested in speed limits. He only drove a car when he had to. Luckily, the nurse came and gave them the floor and room number, before Herrmann could get going on his next heroic tale about big engines and fast cars. There was an uncomfortable silence in the lift. Once on the floor, Schade took charge, running after one of the nurses.

"Oh, that bum! No. Checked himself out," the nurse reported, after Schade had shown her I.D.

Schade broke out in a sweat and a dangerous wave of heat shot through her body. For a moment she didn't know whether to cry or smash everything around her. Including the nurse. "How long ago? Why didn't you call us!"

"Some nerve you've got!" The nurse went on filling feeding bowls and pill cups. "We hardly manage to keep our records up to date, and you're asking – that's too much! We admitted the little guy this morning. There was no guard. Drunks like him come by the dozen and leave by the dozen."

"That wasn't any bum! That was a damned important witness!" Her voice still sounded shrill and angry. She didn't know what made her madder: the face that Rosso had disappeared or that she herself was behaving like a bull in a china shop.

"And how was I supposed to know that? Was it written down somewhere? There are too many like him. And if it was up to me, they could all leave as soon as they're patched up. All they're into is fighting and rioting. I only had to look at his belt!"

Schade was silent. Once she had calmed down she muttered a quick apology. "Did you find any I.D. on him? Did he say anything?"

The nurse softened and even interrupted her work to look Schade in the eye. "He didn't say anything to any of us. And he wouldn't have said anything to you either. We talked about it after the rounds this morning. As if he was shit scared of women. That's how he came across. Ask the doctor. Maybe he did him the honour. Oh, and he didn't have any I.D. But he must be barefoot. We hung his sneakers out the bathroom window. They stank too much."

The doctor kindly made them wait only fifteen minutes. Rosso had tried to make him believe that he was suffering from amnesia. "Didn't even want to say his name. Of course there is a possibility that he did have some lapse. That can happen with concussions. Is there anything else I can do for you?"

Nothing, Schade thought. That's the problem.

"Only to ask the nurse to give us his shoes," Fritz said resignedly.

Throughout the whole conversation Roland Herrmann had jiggled his foot manfully up and down and spared his speech organs.

"Look, Daddy. We both got it in. You got it in, and me too. And wasn't it easy, huh . . .?" Now hurry up, old man! she added to herself, cursing because in the last two hours he had been the only one with the courage to engage in sweat and circulation stimulating activity. Encircling him like the legs of a compass, she held him tight, riding on his potbelly, both her hands stuck between the two of them to stop him from moving freely or seeing what was happening down there. Let there be big cars around me was her next thought. Well upholstered and with space to move your legs. Going by the licence plate, this one came from Cologne, but judging by his behaviour, Daddy had learned his manners out in the farmyard. The first few minutes he had called her things like "pony" and "lamb", but then decided she could be "his daughter". The familiar cocktail of cosy resentment and suffering horniness. That did it. As usual.

As soon as she felt something warm dribble into the thin latex in her hand, she switched from girlish cries of delight to a stricter tone. Nothing against your fantasies, old man. Sure, any time you want to with me. But if you ever dare touch your real daughter! Her words were more carefully chosen of course. Part of her routine too. A Sunday sermon with a double purpose. So first, he didn't notice her get rid of the latex. And second, it reminded him of his respect for no trespassing signs. In Kim's experience, prominently displayed signs were the only thing that kept men at bay. Most of them anyway.

"I could be your father," he beamed in a final happy reminiscence. And I could be mayor, Kim thought. Of course, he was welcome back, she said aloud. Whenever he was in Berlin. "And next time, you bring a little more dough – then we can do something really nice!"

And now fuck off out of here, man.

It was impossible to ignore the babble coming from the cab. The radio news programmes seemed to have been taken over by sports reporters weeks ago. What they broadcast sounded like hysterical commentaries at some soccer match. Every person who climbed over the embassy fence in Prague or Budapest, a penalty, every illegal border crossing, a goooooal!

It was likewise impossible to ignore the heavy-set woman in the prime of life who now switched off the engine and heaved herself out of the cab in the middle of the road. Alfred Henke swung the broom at her threateningly.

"What on earth! I told you yesterday to piss off, Erika! Before there's an accident, before I . . ."

"Before you what?" Erika Henke put her hands on her hips. "Before you hit me again?"

Henke was waiting for every window on Nollendorf

Strasse to open. He knew the power of that voice. He lowered the broom and waited.

"No, no, my dear," her voice was no quieter even though she had come closer, "those days are over. This," she pointed at her left temple, "was the last black eye you'll ever give me!" She planted herself in front him.

Henke changed colour again. He pretended to clean the broom by knocking it against the wall of the house, and wondered how he could get rid of her. "I've packed up your junk," he said as softly as possible, "and you can take all the brat's stuff as well! I don't want to see either of you here any more!" He tore open the door to the courtyard.

"I've told you, it's certainly not up to you. I'm glad to see that you've learned how to sweep the pavement. At least I won't have to take care of that in future."

He stopped in the middle of the gateway and turned round. Sweat was dripping into his vest, which might have been white before it got put in with the wrong load of laundry. Now it was piggy-pink and made the bright red of his neck and shoulders look even more ridiculously theatrical. "You don't need to do a thing around here. Na. Nothing. You don't have any future here!"

Instead of answering him, Erika shoved him in the chest and continued to storm his territory unperturbed. Finally, when Blondie joyfully ran towards her in the courtyard and rubbed against the fat bluish-white calves and big feet, Alfred lost all self control. He threw the broom into a corner and seized Erika by the arm. She howled. He had grabbed one of the green and yellow bruises. Blondie jumped away and disappeared.

"Go. Get out of here! Once and for all!"

Erika didn't even think of it. He realised with astonishment that she no longer seemed to be afraid of his fists. What on earth! What was wrong with her? She always used to knuckle under when he hit out and slapped her around because she was nagging and pestering him. Now she counter-attacked, pushed his arms aside and hit him full on the jaw and the chin with the side of her right hand. "You shit. Beat up your wife, that's all you can do. And spend my money on whores. You creep!"

Henke stood there flabbergasted as Erika seemed to swell to giant size, while he just felt his chin and cautiously moved it from side to side.

"And that's over. ONCE AND FOR ALL!" she jeered. "You can bet your life on that, you – oh, hello, Fräulein von Thurau!"

Henke turned quickly. The woman from the newspaper shop was coming out of the shadowy gateway into the glowing, burning sun. He attempted a super-friendly smile, but it faltered because of the pain. Even his, "So, off to your siesta?" disappeared in a sea of glittering stars.

The newspaper woman glanced at him with pity, but then stared appalled at Erika's black eye. "No surprise that you left, Frau Henke," she mumbled in her ear and hurried across the courtyard to the rear wing.

As soon as the door closed behind her, Erika started again. "You're a washout! For all those years, if I hadn't . . ."

Henke had recovered from his astonishment and had only one thought. He took her good arm and pulled her into the concierge's apartment. Erika didn't shut up. ". . . driven the cab for all these years, you would have been out on the street, you and Thorsten, you fucking . . ."

"I told you, you can take your degenerate of a son with you. I've fed that hooligan long enough. But he never had a chance with a mother like you. It's hereditary."

"You fed him?" Erika slammed the door shut after Henke had dragged her into the hallway. "Nonono, Alfred. You fucked him up. You let him run around with the terrorists instead of putting your foot down. If I hadn't stepped in, he would have ended up a homo as well and brought niggers into the house."

Henke ran into the kitchen and glanced out of the window. There was nobody in the courtyard. Through the glass of the gate he saw an elegant woman get out of a cab and disappear in the direction of the front house entrance with her suitcase. Then he closed the kitchen window and turned up the little black and white tv full volume.

Erika dropped down on to the kitchen bench and stared at the screen. "They're a bunch of wasters as well," she continued. "If they all want to come here with their Trabis and foul everything up and get money shoved up their asses, well poor old Germany! First the Polacks and now . . ."

"Just shut up!" Henke yelled both at the tv reporter and at his wife.

"I'm not surprised you don't want to hear about Polacks!" Erika continued to stare at the screen. "But you just wait! Mummy took care of that! Remember that, you prick! You won't manage. Any fucker can take you to the cleaners. What are you anyway? Unemployed. At forty-four. Even though you learned a proper trade!"

"Is it my fault if they shut down the printing press?" Henke crowed.

"It's always somebody else's fault, just like Thorsten!" Erika's voice filled the kitchen because a politician on tv was mumbling with conspiratorial self-importance. "Did the Public Transport Authority close down too? Did it?"

"I couldn't go on driving buses when my hearing went."

"Tsk, hearing went! You don't need to tell me any fairy tales. I know damn well why you were fired you waster, because . . ."

"Shhh!" Henke jumped up and turned down the tv. "The Fahlenkamp woman's coming. Is she looking for us?"

Erika Henke glanced out the window too. The woman who had got out of the taxi a few minutes ago was running across the courtyard towards the concierge's apartment. She lifted her fists to bang against the kitchen window. Henke opened it. The woman was dreadfully pale and completely confused. "Quick – you must do something – Hartmut – the police – my husband . . ."

She dug her well-manicured red nails into the plaster beneath Henke's window, as if she had to hold on to something. Alfred Henke ran outside. Erika's heroic baritone was finally silenced.

Red high-heeled sandals were dangling out of the open back door of the navy-blue Mercedes. The picture was cut off at the knees.

"My nerves! Another daddy-daughter number again. Puke. I think I'm done for today."

"Well, isn't that nice. Incest – a game all the family can play. Glad I'm too old for it." The rest of Kitty, who had been stretched out across the back seat, sat up. "We really could use our time better. Just remember our office – everything's been left lying since yesterday afternoon!"

"Where's Helga? Feeding cats?" Kim opened the front passenger door, sat down, eased open the zipper of her khaki-coloured hotpants and shook the sticky high heels from her feet.

"In the little girls' room. Man, she's divine. We were talking about Krisztina and how to organise the funeral an'all, and you know what Helga says?"

"There goes our direct connection to the condom manufacturers."

"No kidding! There's nobody to cook borscht any more or whatever it's called."

Kim suppressed her desire to burst out laughing and said quickly: "Pretty soon we'll have a whole crowd making genuine Thuringian potato dumplings!"

Helga had never eaten as well before COW was founded. Food was cooked regularly once a week – Italian, Polish, Turkish, even African and Caribbean food. Depending on whose turn it was. Everybody was talking about multicultural society: COW was living it by cooking!

Now she came teetering through the bushes with all the grace that the heat and her more than sixty years allowed, one hand on her wig, the other holding on to the branches.

"Well, Kitty," Kim looked at her thoughtfully. "Helga just wasn't born with a gold tray to carry around her feelings on. But she'll work her arse off when it matters. For all of us. You know that."

"I feel like a roast chicken! This weather's killing me!" Helga always seemed relieved when she had the two of them in front of her. Especially since yesterday. She ran her hand over her neck and her chest. "Give me my bag, Kim."

"Sit with us. It'll do your legs good." All of a sudden Kim could have burst into tears. She felt a wave of total tenderness for Helga roll over her like one of those big, black clouds everybody was waiting for for weeks. It felt like deliverance. From the awful pressure. Always having to be on top of everything. Having to skilfully pull all the strings so as not to be caught and choked by some guy who has slipped out of one's control. Not to lunge at the empty, greedy faces of moral Neanderthals, but to let them go on believing that they are grown-up men to be taken seriously. Little Red Riding Hood on the outside, Maggie Thatcher on the inside. You could never let them catch even a glimpse of such a thing, such a piercing, glittering desire to curl up very simply and very quietly in Helga's lap and be sheltered by her big, soft old breasts. Not here, not in the middle of Tiergarten Strasse, the last but one surviving autonomous red-light street of West Berlin, City of Women. Not here. Don't cry. Laugh!

"No! You're not going to get me into that oven." Helga

almost tore her bag out of Kim's hand and marched the yard
and a half to her favourite spot on the little wall, in the
shade under the branches. "Who's going to Belziger Strasse
again to see these Solli guys?"

There was still not a trace of a thunder cloud. But Kim
laughed. Tears.

You still had to make your own breeze, but then at least the
thin, loose-fitting desert-brown linen pants and the equally
thin pale-green shirt displayed their true virtues. The faster
one ran however, the sooner the next wave of heat struck.
If one were a computer, she thought, racing down the hall
with five giant jars of instant coffee in her left arm and a
bag with her old clothes and another new batiste shirt on
her right wrist, then one could figure out the precise balance.
Then one wouldn't sweat either! I wonder if Roboldt's
keeping his garbage pail in the refrigerator. Semi-skilled
housewives get ideas like that – "oh, shit!"

Because she had to open the door herself, she almost
buried Mimi under an avalanche of giant coffee jars. Jars
and person were only saved from free fall by a spontaneous
embrace between Chief Detective Inspector Karin Lietze and
her typist Mimi Jacob.

"I'm buying the first round," Lietze panted. "I'd rather have
watery coffee than – Schade! What are you doing!"

Scissors and cord in her hands and a screwdriver in her
mouth, Sonja Schade stood in front of the coffee machine,
pulling a piece of sheathing from the wires. "Fixing this –
what else?"

"Oh man, I'm so glad the thing is broken! Why don't you
write your report about Rosso!"

"First," the screwdriver was still between Schade's perfect
teeth, "I'm not a man. Second, the thing isn't broken, the
cords have been smouldering. I've been fixing things like

this since I was seven. And third, I can't stand instant muck. Wow, nice pants. New?"

Lietze nodded. "Where is everybody?"

"In Fritz's room. He's teaching Herr Herrmann the basics of knotwork." The way Mimi's voice intoned the name of their beloved trainee, it tasted like an irresistibly sweet honey which had been gathered from carnivorous plants by praying mantises.

Lietze grabbed her bags, threw them down on her desk and went to the small, dark room two doors down the hall.

Attract attention. Then force it on to the pictures. Or the other way round? What works better and costs less? To attract them with the photos? Or, because they have set eyes on me and desecrated me, force them to pay by looking at my photos? Grab them anyway. Get them involved. Lure them into the trap. Let it snap shut. The art of it. Exact *timing*, faultless *setting*. What else?

Black! The stretch pants. No t-shirt, no slogan. But? The patent leather bodice. The transparent blouse over it like a jacket. Open. Trompe l'oeil. No jewellery. No violet. Just the shoes. The open-toed high heels that obscenely reveal the cleavage between big toe and the next one. And her fingernails. Each a different shade of purple, and one in red and one in blue.

Black is good. Colour photos lie. Nothing is authentic. Everything is artificial. Black and white photos. That's a lie too. It's all about the grey tones. The palest, those closest to white, get artificial tints. That makes the photos true! Life is a constant movement between shades of grey. Fraying into violet at the edges. She thought of the time when she only wore black, had her hair skinhead short and painted thick black lines of kohl around her eyes. The phone rang and she put down the paintbrush with the purple egg-white varnish on it and got up. And had been more than two stone heavier. Black is a magic colour. It can make outlines razor-shape or blur them completely.

She had given up art school. A futile slog. What for? To slot in. Conform. Every new idea is an aggression. *I think I've penetrated* . . . Oh, you paint pictures? What's in them? Paint, you idiots!

"Yes?" She jammed the receiver between shoulder and ear and wiped the rivers of sweat from her stomach and thighs with her extra-large t-shirt. "I don't really do photojournalism any more . . . I get bored. I always need a push, to . . . What? Well, you can come to Sydney's later. Then you'll see what I'm doing now. If you can pay for that kind of . . . It starts at seven, I think . . . Come a little earlier, then we can talk about it . . ."

A thousand wasn't bad. For three, four days. Plus air-fare and expenses. Budapest is supposed to be beautiful. Prague as well. It was about time somebody took different pictures and not just the usual people jumping fences and queueing for the toilets. All of them in snow jeans. Yetis! But there must be an underground. Fraying at the edges. Violet. Some kind of volcano. Violence. Spies maybe. Closed society. How does one seduce them? Not the gays, the blackmailed. The real ones. The ones who are really committed. They've either got their male bonds and are starved, or they're vain. Or both. Chamois-greys. With brown edges, perhaps. And perhaps in the long run a connection to those blank faces at the abandoned S-Bahn stations . . .

She smoothed her t-shirt, watching her big, tough hands glide over her flat, muscular stomach. They had called her "starlet". You think everything should fall into your lap. Well, what else? If you just spread it wide enough. Not at all. Ignoramuses! You spread your laps long before there's anyone who even wants to get in. Because you don't know that you should never reveal the desired, or it will stop being desired. It's all a matter of seduction. Seduction and nothing but. And never fulfilment. And you're so predictable it's offensive. Starlet – ridiculous! I am Eva-Maria Adam. The work of art in the age of advertising seduction. And for me there is only the blue of noon and the red of fire and the black – black of Eros and? Thanatos. Eros and Thanatos. Exactly. And different shades of violet. With chamois-toned greys which taste of burnt earth. Definitely no green!

Five hand-tinted photos lay finished on her work surface, their captions beside them. The five framed sets of three were arranged in the shape of a star on the floor. Tinted in shades of blue and violet. The single shots, the last of which she was working on, were red-violet. Twenty-one altogether. Good number. Three times seven. Sum of the digits equals three. Magic.

She wondered if she should after all paint her nails in different shades of violet, and forget red and blue. The only blue she had wasn't the blue of the sky at noon, which guides the story of the eye. More like *United Colors of Benetton*. No secrets.

She dipped the delicate paintbrush into the bowl of diluted paint and looked at the photo. ORWO paper is the best. Exactly the right tone of chamois. Greyer than the paper from the West. ORWO film is different too. A very particular tinge. Visible.

That's also what makes this picture different. But they won't see it. They'll see me. And then they'll stare at the frames and be shit-scared of the pictures and be thankful that they've got something to read. *I think I've penetrated the male attitude towards sex.* Oh shit! Where is that book? I could quote it from memory. Nobody will know. And how did it go on, something about how *I prefer sexual contempt*? But I still need the book back. It must be in that café.

*

". . . not particularly exciting. And time-consuming as well," Fritz was just explaining. "That's the first thing you have to understand: first and foremost our work consists of painstaking attention to details. Doesn't look like much. But sometimes leads to something. Statistically, maybe every five years we can pull a Rambo. Some colleagues have worked for thirty-five years without ever having to draw their guns."

It was obvious that such a job description was not to Herr Herrmann's taste. He preferred to dream about the televisual aspects of undercover drug squads. Why else was he paying so much attention to the clean curve of every one of his muscles?

"And," Fritz continued after exchanging glances with Lietze, "compiling as complete a list as possible of all the JoAnne Little Brigade's victims means contacting every precinct one after the other. And when we have it, we'll contact them one after the other. And if that still doesn't lead us to anyone who might be part of the Brigade, then we'll probably make an appeal to the public and look for victims who haven't reported anything to the police to come forward."

"That isn't in the computer?" Rocky Herrmann asked obediently, but with a sour undertone.

Maybe he'll go voluntarily after the first week, Lietze thought. "In what computer, Herrmann?" she asked loudly and sharply. "There are no computers here even for the other way round. Just a Special Section for sexual offences against women and children, and that relies on its card index and a good memory. Fortunately, violence in the other direction hasn't been an issue until now."

"I'm always seeing women knocking their kids around," Rocky protested. "The boys too!"

"You have to admit that there are certain . . ."

". . . differences," Fritz added. "Between women who take

out their aggression on defenceless children, and those who take revenge on men they consider to be rapists."

"I don't know." Rocky remained stubborn. What had he got into? Nothing but women, and the only man in sight was even more into women's lib than the rest of them. The other guy, the queer, didn't count. Good thing he was sick. "One has to, er. Yeah, it's no surprise, er. With all this, er. You know, women's lib – "

"I beg your pardon," Fritz exploded. In discussions like this he knew his ground. Thanks to Beate. "First of all, young man, most children are the victims of their fathers, uncles and brothers. Second, women who are violent with their children are themselves victims of male violence and are hardly in the vanguard of women's liberation. And I don't mean that as an excuse. And third, you've still got a lot to learn. Because the motive mentioned over and over again in the communiqués from the brigade really is one. And one we have to take bloody seriously. As repugnant as what these women are doing is – they are right on two points: violence committed by men is a very serious problem and we are bloody incapable of getting a handle on it!"

He leant back and took a deep breath. Lietze, who was still standing in the doorway, frowned. She didn't have the slightest desire to discuss such matters with Herrmann. And up to now she had never been willing to share Fritz's feminist view of the world. Ever since she had learned to think she had believed that the state's monopoly of violence was cultural progress compared to everyone taking the law into their own hands. Despite all the problems. Even despite the possibility of abuses. Could that principle really be revised? Was there more going on in the world than she wanted to acknowledge? Between men and women, for example? Why did she get so upset about the stamper that she couldn't think clearly any more? Why did she respond so – so, yes: unthinkingly to women who had simply had enough and were fighting back? She tossed her head and did nothing to break the tense silence in the room. If she was honest, she had to admit that she was shit-scared of such questions. Who knew what would be left after such fundamental revisions? Any solid ground at all? Hell, solid ground! A few tent pegs maybe – in order to – in order not to. In all his short life this trainee had been spared these dimensions of police work in general and life in particular, she thought resentfully. Even more resentfully, she registered once again how unproblematically stupidity and insensitivity combine with a hunger for power. Rocky had sensed the subterranean disagreement between the chief inspector and her subordinate. And now he leapt to agree with the senior officer.

"Er. Because er. Excuse me, but these er. Er. These women terrorists! Frau er. Lietze sees it, er . . . a bit differently." And then all in one go and triumphantly: "And that's how I see it as well!"

Fritz was almost throwing a fit. "I don't excuse anything. I'm a detective and as such I have to recognise a motive, even if I believe that what someone with this motive actually does has disastrous consequences. I even accept the fact that you want to join the Serious Crimes Squad."

Herrmann's colour changed alarmingly, but he couldn't think of an effective argument. When he realised that Lietze was by no means going to reassure him that – in contrast to Fritz – she considered him a godsend to D III, he moved on to the next stage. "In my opinion er. Things like that er. Must be stamped out. Root and branch."

During her more than thirty years in the force, Lietze had never got used to such opinions, and the corners of her mouth twitched pityingly. "I see. And how is that going to happen, Herr Herrmann?"

"A big manhunt, huh? He can't escape from Berlin."

"How do you know that?" Fritz asked.

"Well, they took er. His papers? That's what *you* said.

That's what they always do, those bitches. With their ski masks. I told you about it, yesterday on Bornimer – "

Lietze sighed. Even at first hearing, she hadn't taken Rocky's Halensee story seriously.

" – er they looked just like that. In my opinion his papers will show up er. Just like in the case of the other er men. With something stamped on them or whatever."

"Interesting," Lietze yawned. "Did you say stamped?"

Rocky slid back and forward on his chair and started to stutter again. "Or, er. Something scribbled on them. That's also, er, possible. Scissors and er. Penis. Or something." Lietze tried not to laugh. Disconcerted, Fritz rolled his eyes and concentrated on the beads of sweat on his forehead.

"That er guy he looked like him!"

Lietze's ears pricked up. "Who!"

"The one they er kidnapped. Where I was. He looked like the Rosso guy."

"Now you remember that!" Fritz snapped. "What else did you see?"

"What else? Well, nothing exactly. I was too, er, far away. But it could have been er him."

Fritz stared silently at Herrmann. Then he leaned back again. "How do you imagine your big manhunt? The boy had concussion and who knows what else. I'll tell you what he's going to do. He'll crawl home to his mummy. Can you tell me how a big manhunt would tackle that? Will the Riot Police search everybody's bed or what?"

"That's it!" Lietze had had enough. "Herrmann, you make yourself comfortable at this table and call all the stations. Draw a tight net and please write legibly. If there are problems, please let me know. And," she tried to look as much like a teacher as possible, "remember lesson number two. There are no manhunts for witnesses."

She turned round and grasped the doorknob. "Fritz, you come with me. We have to sort out with Schade who's going to check out Krisztina Kędzierska's regular clients. And who's going to 29 Belziger, where she used to live . . . "

And see if there might not be a faster way to get hold of at least a couple of those women from the Brigade. A way she didn't want to discuss in front of the trainee. After all it wouldn't exactly be official channels.

"Look at this one, Marek. Don't you think it's sexy on me?" The very young woman with short brown hair twirled in front of the big second-hand mirror hanging between the two windows in Krisztina's room, pleased at the image of herself in the white lace corsage with matching garters. Zadko was busy looking through bags and drawers, and this was the fourth time in fifteen minutes she had disturbed him with the same question.

"Marek! Why don't you look!" she complained, without really paying much attention to his reaction. "Or don't you fancy me any more?"

He looked up briefly and mumbled "tak, tak". The box labelled "family medicine cabinet" in old-fashioned lettering, which he had just opened, was taking up his attention. It was full of photos, hand-written notes and documents. Postcards addressed c/o Brzeżinska, 29 Belziger. The word COW was on one big envelope full of pictures. As far as he knew that was a farm animal, and the photos had nothing to do with a farm. They showed various women posing for group shots. All laughing and all wearing the same t-shirt with a slogan on it. – en you go – he read and didn't understand anything. Two were black. Krisztina was on the far left of the group. She looked very proud. Another picture showed two women flying a miniature zeppelin from a balcony. Nothing looked like the countryside.

And then there was a big black notebook with red corners. Zadko wanted to pick it up, but then he reconsidered. He looked over at the self-absorbed woman who was busy posing in front of the mirror. "Anieżka, you look great."

She turned round, came over to him wiggling her ass and put her arms around his neck. "It fits as if it was made just for me. Except the top," she cooed flirtatiously and slid the half empty bra across his bare stomach.

He pulled her round a hundred and eighty degrees, because it suddenly occurred to him that she might see the notebook behind him. Then he took her chin in his hand and pressed his mouth to hers. He closed his eyes only after he had made sure that her lids were closed too.

Now he only had to find the guy who had broken into his apartment last night and searched Krisztina's room. He had to know if he had found anything. Apart from money. But then, he might not have been looking for money.

The slow-moving cab pulled over to the kerb and parked in front of Kitty's Mercedes.

". . . anybody'd recognise us as 'a trade', Herr Paplowski, I tell him," said Kitty, "and we just want to be registered as one."

Kim had noticed the woman in the cab, who was paying the driver, and turned to look at Kitty again. Helga, however, kept an eye on the cab.

"Then he jumps up, runs off and comes back and sticks this piece of paper into my hand. The Law Regarding the Regulation of Trades. Appendix A. It lists all the trades allowed to register: 125 so-called occupations requiring apprenticeship and exams to qualify as a master or engineer."

"As if we don't provide training?!" Helga commented, not taking her eyes off the cab.

"And God knows I'm not the only mistress of the hand

job!" Kim was getting more excited than was appropriate in view of the weather. "And I've got letters to prove it!"

Helga's laugh sounded like a rattle. She smiled at the woman who had got out of the cab and was coming towards them.

"Just imagine, Kim! Our apprentices'd have to take some commission's exam! As officially recognised nurse for gentlemen with sexual hang-ups. With stamps and a signature from some official, who could maybe come by after hours and make his inspection. And pay for it! Hi, Minou!"

Kitty began to laugh uproariously. She squeezed her knees together and spun round, balancing on her hair-raising high-heeled sandals, and snorted till she could hardly breathe any more. "You're im-possible!"

"Who, me? Do I look funny?" Minou stopped, put out. Kitty had to insist several times before she accepted that nobody had been laughing at her, and then she flopped down on the wall next to Helga. "You're all in a good mood. Just thinkin' about your organisation, but no respect for Martha!"

"Just leave be." Helga patted Minou's arm. "Your Martha and our Shishi, she's dead, and nobody's gonna bring her back. But if we were an association or something official, we could deal differently with the Solidarity guys. They don't even want to let Shishi have a decent funeral!"

Minou looked first at her, then in disbelief at Kitty and Kim. "Is that true?"

Everyone nodded. "So," Kim said firmly, "we gotta go to them. And make sure they don't sneak her out of the mortuary an' take her to Poland. They wouldn't want to let us even put flowers on Shishi's grave."

"But I thought you were already an association! Your letterhead reads COW – a registered charity," Minou said.

Kitty smiled. "It's not official yet."

Helga's attention had shifted back to the traffic. Nothing apart from a green and white VW van slowly cruising down

Tiergarten Strasse was of any significance. And it didn't really matter either. Except to Minou. "Oh shit! Here they come. I knew it!"

Helga gestured dismissively. "Those are our boys. They're just taking a look. Sometimes they want to have a chat. They won't do anything."

"Well, I don't know." Minou quickly took a big pair of dark sunglasses from the pocket of her respectable beige trouser suit, put them on and tried to disappear behind Helga. But the only thing that disappeared was the inconspicuous façade. "Anyway, last night three cops came to the shop. The two girls were okay, but I couldn't stand the guy. And Ramona told me she'd seen him before at another place. During a raid. Everybody had to fill out questionnaires, then he wanted to see their health certificates!"

"He's not allowed to! Hope she didn't show 'im anything!" Kim shoved her hands as far as possible into her tight shorts and stuck out her right hip.

"She hasn't got one. She wasn't eighteen yet, and he took her name and everything. Last night we gave them all our names and addresses, because one of them, Mieze or something like that, said she wanted to check out Martha's regulars."

Today, the police car stopped. An older uniformed officer with an ingenuous face forced himself out. "Ciao, ladies! Got a new recruit?" He looked down at Minou with unconcealed curiosity.

"Oh, not at all, Herr Police President," Helga joked. "That's my niece from Spandau. She's an expert on trade issues an' she's just advising us about all the rules and regulations."

He didn't seem convinced. "I don't think that you'll succeed with your trade association. And if you do," he scratched his head and continued to stare at Minou, "then I wouldn't have the pleasure of dealing with you!"

"Course you would," warbled Kim, "we'd train you as a client."

"Sure, sure! Maybe you really should try it as a professional association!" He winked at Kitty, who was standing in front of him in a perfect hooker's pose. "You look a real pro."

After the van had gone, Minou sank on to Helga's shoulder, exhausted. Helga shook her head. "You really are dumb! Why are you wearing those glasses! With those guys it's best to show them yer face. I been talkin' with him about our association ever since we got the idea. That gives him the feeling he knows everything, an' we get left in peace."

"Well, I don't know," Minou said for the second time. "I'd like to have your self-confidence. But you don't have kids . . ."

"I do so!" Kitty gave her a friendly look. "So what? 'Specially in that case. Or do I have to apologise to someone, because I'm on the game to earn money for them? I couldn't give a flying fuck. The cops are just ordinary guys too. So what do you want? We've learned how to deal with men, haven't we?"

"I thought you had a police contact, some guy," Minou finally came out with what had brought her here.

"A wo– " Kitty began, but Helga interrupted. "Yeah. Why?"

"Well, I don't want to end up in their files and get visitors all the time from the Schöneberg Public Health Department. Lots of women have lost their apartments because of that."

"What was that one yesterday called? You said Mieze?" Kim asked with interest.

"Something like that. But she was okay. The guy got on my nerves. A young one, short legs, figure like a warning triangle and behaved like the offspring of the pimps I slaved for in Hamburg for a while."

The three exchanged glances. "We'll ask our contact, Minou," Kim appeased her. "An' the deal is, you come with me when I visit the Solidarity guys. Is that fair?"

Minou nodded, a bit offended.

"So, okay, who's gonna come to Krisztina's apartment with me?" Kitty demanded.

"I would," Helga said. "But I don't think I'd be a big help."

"Na." Kitty laughed. "You hold the fort here instead."

"Look like they belong to a giant." Lietze put the two shapeless trainers on the table. Rosso had professed his devotion to KAOS on them as well. But the A didn't have the anarchist circle around it. Instead it was indicated by a stylised death rune. "Maybe he should be given a chance as an artist . . ."

"Orange boxes," was Fritz's comment.

"Everyone has something they can show off," Schade joked, "with some it's their feet."

Lietze pulled the plastic bag back over the shoes and went to wash her hands. "Don't forget to have them checked. Who knows, it might turn out useful."

She sat down at her desk and stuck a Lucky Luciano in her mouth. "If Herrmann hasn't put together a useable list by the end of the day, one of us will have to work on it tomorrow morning as well. This JoAnne Little Brigade is no longer secondary. They've really got in the way."

Fritz nodded and sighed. Schade got up and went into Mimi's office to see if the coffee machine was still working. "I don't know how we're going to manage it all," she said, returning with a full pot and three cups. "Why don't we ask Elkau to check her files for us?"

Maren Elkau was the head of the sexual offences department, the special unit where all cases of molesting, sexual assault and rape were registered. "What's she going to find there, Schade? Any number of women and children who have been victims of male violence, and any number of offenders who have never been charged. But we're not looking for them."

"No, but maybe among the victims there are some indi-
cations of – "

" – a desire for revenge? I'm sure. Any amount. So?"

Fritz filled the cups. "Besides, they don't have any time
either. If I think about the figures you mentioned yesterday
– they're probably so buried under reports, they don't know
if they're coming or going."

"I don't think so," Schade insisted. "I don't think many
women report any more. Doesn't pay off. Take a walk
through Schöneberg – there's the same slogan on every fifth
house: Women, form your own gangs! Even the Women's
Hotline advises women to get together and to rely on themselves."

"We could regard that as incitement to violence, if we
wanted to." Fritz emptied half his cup. "Do we want to?
Should we get heavy with the Women's Hotline?"

"Nonsense. I've been there. They don't know any more
than what's been written in those communiqués. And if they
do, you can bet they won't tell us. I left my card and told
them to let the women from the Brigade know that we
would like to talk to them. Doesn't matter how. That was
two months ago. Result: nix."

"No, Fritz," Lietze joined in, "to give you a definite answer:
at this particular moment we really don't want to accuse
the Women's Hotline, of all things, of anything criminal. And
certainly not on the basis of that kind of law about incitement to violence. We don't need to pretend that we're doing
something. We can leave that to others."

Satisfied, Fritz smiled. "It wouldn't be my idea either. In
that case we'd have to go to every foreigners' organisation
too, and to all the antiracist groups . . ."

"What have they got to do with it?" Lietze finally lit her
Lucky Luciano.

"You didn't read yesterday's *TAZ*, right? There was a very
informative article."

"About the Brigade, yeah, I know. Supposedly, they're a couple of women who are frustrated because Kreuzberg has been pacified since the red-green coalition came to power and are also pissed off about the macho men in the Autonomists, and so they've expanded 'time for action' across the whole city and shifted to the struggle between the sexes." Lietze inhaled deeply and looked at Fritz and Schade. "Maybe there's something to it. But a few frustrated black ski mask fetish girls from Kreuzberg just aren't enough to cover so much ground and strike so effectively. So what's the conclusion? That we have to look into every radical feminist corner, but surely not the antiracist groups!"

"You should have read on," Fritz said. Lietze looked at him.

"Do you know where they got their name?" Schade asked.

"JoAnne Little? Going by the logic of these direct action groups, it must have been some woman who was raped."

"Right. She's still alive by the way. But the rapist isn't. She killed him with the ice-pick he threatened her with. In a jail in North Carolina. He was her guard and – "

" – white. And she's black!"

Lietze finally understood Fritz's triumphant voice. The stamper's first victim was black. "But so far we don't have any indication that the Brigade is made up of black women. Okay, you can hide faces. But not hands. And nobody said anything about foreign accents."

Still, if the neighbourhood militia named itself after a black woman who had killed her rapist, then the hypothesis that the murders of the two men had been acts of revenge became more probable again. But they weren't exactly rapist types. If there was such a thing. If not, then every man really was a potential rapist, and that was a kind of logic that Lietze didn't care for at all. What if it had been a mistake to think the JoAnne Little Brigade capable of all kinds of assaults, but not murder? What did her nose tell her. Nothing useful either. What nonsense anyway, to pin one's hopes on an average nose just because she sometimes had a reliable hunch, and her nose had happened to give her some kind of signal at the same time. Probably just an allergy! "Are you trying to tell me that the young man last night was supposed to be Number Three?"

At a loss, Fritz shrugged his shoulders and remained silent. Not Schade. "Bullshit! Rosso and Seifert and Neiss are two different stories. There was no statement with those two murders. Nothing, no reason, no motive, no connection made with anything the victims had done or not done. With Rosso and the others it was described in detail."

Lietze stood up and got the cardboard sign that had been lying on Rosso's knees. "So does that mean it's the JLB only when it actually says JLB?"

Clumsy chapped hands were pushing and shoving at Elvira Fahlenkamp. As clumsy as Erika's clodhoppers and everything else about her, thought Henke. Watched by Fräulein von Thurau's keen eyes they had taken Elvira Fahlenkamp into the concierge's apartment and tried to calm her down. But Frau Fahlenkamp did not want a schnapps nor did she want to lie down on the brown and yellow flowered plush couch, so badly scratched by Blondie. Frau Fahlenkamp didn't want to stay at all, but neither did she want to leave. And so, after a couple of minutes of being pulled one way and the other, she had simply given up trying to decide and collapsed. Now Erika lifted the small feet in the dainty high heels and tried to put them on the arm rest of the couch.

Henke looked away. No comparison with Mata! He left the living room.

"You're not going upstairs!" Her voice followed him.

"Why don't you shut your mouth!" he yelled back. "I'll go where I want!"

"Alfred!" Erika dropped Elvira Fahlenkamp's legs to chase after him. Elvira Fahlenkamp started to slide and was about to fall off the couch again.

Alfred Henke turned round briefly. "Watch what you're doing, you clown!"

Erika Henke had her hands full, and he left the apartment, slamming the door. She had to go! Once and for all! Just those big mitts ... And she had touched him with them! Pushed him! Pushed *him* away! What on earth! We can't have that! That's – that's – anarchy! Oh, Mata, please come back soon, my Mata Hari. Once one of the women she worked with had passed out, and he had watched as she put her on a couch and taken care of her. In the club. The other woman had probably had too much to drink. With her warm, tender fingers. And she had stroked her. And carefully unbuttoned the armour. A corset or something.

Those hands! Delicate and. Capable. Yes. Capable. Why not? No comparison! He looked up at the fourth floor. Fräulein von Thurau had all her windows open, though the dark curtains were drawn everywhere, except for the kitchen window. The second he stepped into the courtyard she looked down. "What's the matter with Frau Fahlenkamp?"

"Out cold. The police are just coming."

He felt her hands all over his body as he walked through the courtyard doorway to wait for the police. It was exciting. Pleasurable, but dangerous too. Because between him and those hands there was Erika. And if she doesn't – and if he – her – and but. . . . And suddenly the idea took shape and took possession of him. Why hadn't he thought of it at once? Right after Erika had turned his workshop upside down! His workshop! Yes, of course. This would even – that would be two birds with. . . . Once and for all! Na!

He didn't see Thorsten until the boy stepped out of the dark corner behind the entrance gate. Blood all over his clothes, his face covered with bruises, his hair shaved off and not even shoes on his feet. "I – they're after me!" he managed with some difficulty.

"I've had it!" Henke yelled at him. At that moment, he heard the "laleelaleelalee", ran to the rear door to see if Fräulein von Thurau was still at the window, ran back to Thorsten, grabbed him and shoved him into the courtyard. "Don't go into the house, wait in the cellar."

Once more, Lietze carefully read the small print that came between the statement THIS IS A WOMAN HATER and the warning SOON YOU WILL ALL END UP LIKE THIS. As usual, there were details of everything of which Rosso, according to the Brigade, was "guilty". During the women's march against sexism, held on Walpurgis Night every year, he had stood in front of a sex shop and heckled the marchers. A couple of them had recognised him. In the past he had been hanging around the "scene" and been suspected of being a "narc". In the mean time he had become a "skin", and his punishment was also a warning to all neo-Nazis. "He has stamped himself as a fascist pig," she read aloud, "as a macho-viper, who only gets pleasure out of throttling women's power."

Schade sighed. "I'm glad that Roboldt doesn't have to listen to this. He'd puke."

"Come on Sonja," said Fritz, "they've no interest in being poets or philosophers."

"No . . . judges and executioners! Imagine if they were in control here . . ."

A "confession" signed by Rosso, was also glued to the cardboard. He had denounced himself as a "fascist asshole" and had been forced to swear "never again". The signature had evidently been attempted several times and turned out quite different each time. "It looks as if they weren't satisfied with the first version . . . That could mean that at least they really did have his I.D.," Lietze concluded.

"As Herrmann claims," Fritz reflected. "Wait a minute, read it out again."

Lietze repeated the last sentence of the small print.

Fritz got all excited. "Stamped – throttled – and a fascist on top of it! The choice of words puts it damn close to the stamper case!"

Lietze looked at him. "Really Fritz! If you're serious and not just saying that because you're standing in for the office poet, then you're saying Rosso is the stamper. At least in the opinion of the JoAnne Little Brigade."

Fritz hadn't actually got that far. But Schade took a sudden liking to the avenger hypothesis. "Or – his accomplice. For Krisztina Kędzierska we have two sets of footprints!"

Lietze jumped up, ran to her desk and leafed through the file. "Size 7 and size 8. Fritz, what size are those trainers?"

Fritz turned over the plastic bag with Rosso's shoes. "Can't read it any more." He held one of the shoes against his own. "Could be size 8."

Lietze picked up the phone and pushed a button. "Mimi? We've got something which has to go to the police lab urgently. Shoes and a cardboard sign. Can you take care of that? Thanks." She went back to the conference table and threw the butt in the ashtray. "And how is the JoAnne Little Brigade supposed to know about the stamper's last murder? And if they do know about it, how come they don't spell it out clearly?"

"Someone has to go back to the Ruin place and pump the guy who found Krisztina Kędzierska. Maybe he didn't keep his mouth shut," Fritz said.

"That too. And I had an idea – good God! Maybe our trainee will get his big manhunt after all!"

"How nice," Schade said poisonously. "I'm sure he'll be there first – in his pimpmobile! Okay, who? When? Where to?"

"So what was your idea?" Fritz asked.

Lietze winked at him and then looked straight at Schade. "One that might lead us to the Brigade without going through official channels."

"Oh, really!" Schade returned her gaze just as directly.

"The two of us, you and I, do all the women's bars . . ."

Fritz grinned. Schade thought out loud, "You mean all the lesbian places? Hoping that some of the Brigadistas will fall into our laps?"

Lietze also grinned. "That too, if necessary. If they really are part of that milieu . . ."

". . . and they also belong to the radical man-hating faction – right? They used to hang out in the lesbian bars."

"We don't have to wear a sign saying we're slime."

"Nice word!" Fritz's grin grew even broader. He was happy to have biology on his side and be spared such night shifts.

"Or are you too well known there, Schade?" Lietze ignored Fritz's innuendo.

"I haven't done those places in ages. Since Anita can't any more . . . I'd have to ask around to find out who goes where these days. And who owns the bars. Maybe nobody knows me any more."

"Tonight?"

Schade thought about it. Lietze got up and went to the desk to answer the phone. Mimi came to get the evidence which had to go to the police lab.

"Yes . . . When? . . . Yes, I'm writing it down . . . Yes? . . . No, absolutely no one, please. Wait until we arrive . . . Thanks."

She took the piece of paper back to the conference table.

"Number three?"

"Looks very like it, Fritz."

"Then nothing's going to happen tonight," Schade said, relieved.

"Looks very like it, too." Lietze picked up her bag and her

cigarillos and went to Mimi's office to leave some sugges-
tions for Herrmann's occupational therapy.

For him the door bell rang at just the right moment. He
wasn't in the mood to deal even superficially with Anna's
over-emphatically expressed libidinous urge. And since the
mood was lacking, he didn't have anything else that might
have satisfied her deeper desires. For at least ten minutes
he had been lying half underneath her on the red-white
striped cover of Krisztina's bed and the only thing he could
think about was how to get the notebook and make it disappear without his little muse noticing. She was just about
ready to masturbate again. "You go open the door, Anieżka!
But put something on first!"

Anna didn't even consider interrupting her flight of
pleasure, and only after the soft landing was she even willing
to open her eyes. "I don't need anyone," she purred innocently. "I've got you."

Zadko sat up and pushed her aside. "Anna open the door.
It could be police. I don't want trouble!"

In a huff, Anna got up, took Krisztina's robe from its hook
and strolled toward the front door. The bell rang a fourth
time. Marek Zadko jumped up, took his clothes and the
notebook and slunk into the bathroom. There he put the
notebook behind the heater. Then he listened at the door,
but he couldn't understand a word. He could distinguish two
women's voices. One was Anna's. He quickly put on his
clothes.

When he came out of the bathroom, he saw a woman
with long red hair and dangerously high heels striding
straight towards Krisztina's room. Anna didn't have the
slightest chance of stopping her, and was trailing helplessly
behind.

"Who are you?" he asked loudly.

Anna turned round. "She isn't a cop."

"Hello. I'm a good friend of Shishi's." Kitty turned back, came towards him and held out her hand. "You're Marek, right? Shishi sometimes told me about your concerts. I've been here before." She spoke with a broad Berlin accent.

"What do you want?" Zadko ignored her hand and crossed his arms.

"Are you part of Sollidarnosh too?" Kitty asked, still with her friendliest face.

Anna started to giggle. "Not him! Marek is a musician, not a politician!" She forced herself between Kitty and Zadko, who was far too close for her liking, and tried to throw her arms around his waist. He shoved her aside roughly. "You be quiet! What do you want?"

Kitty looked at him attentively, but with an imperturbably friendly smile. "You should be nicer to your girl. I'm not from vice." She felt how hot she was getting. "Like I said, I'm a friend of Shishi's, or was a friend." She could forget about the little tart. If necessary she'd deal with her. "That is, we're a whole group of women who worked together . . ."

"Curva!" Zadko knew why this woman looked familiar. She was in the pictures he'd found in Krisztina's "family medicine cabinet".

"What's that?" Kitty looked him straight in the eye.

"You're whores!" It didn't sound like a neutral statement and it wasn't meant to be.

"Yes, that's right." Kitty didn't appear to have heard the contempt in his voice. "So it's called Kurva in Polish. I'll remember that. Could we maybe . . . It's not very cosy here in the hallway." Now or never, she thought. She took a deep breath, stuck out her chest and shoulders, swung around hazardously, turned her back on him and stalked straight towards Krisztina's room again. She'd know right away if it was a mistake. Rule number one occurred to her: always keep an eye on the guy.

For a moment Zadko was taken aback and stood rooted to the spot beside Anna. Then he shot forward and grabbed Kitty's arm. "What do you want – from Solidarność?"

Kitty was trembling inside at each step, but she kept going and relied on her more than twenty years in showbiz. "Nothing at all. I just know Shishi had some trouble with the Solli people. So I just wanted to know if you were maybe a member too."

"Could you tell me what you want?" Zadko was getting nervous. He couldn't stop the woman. She was already in the middle of the room and looking round. He didn't notice that, as she was looking, she kept an eye on him. He saw her stare at the rumpled bed on which Anna had spread out all the lingerie she'd tried on earlier; an oddly confident smile appeared on the woman's face and a glance he couldn't quite fathom. He realised he had run out of threatening gestures. He turned towards Anna and nodded to her to come closer. Anna sauntered into the room and sank down on the chair diagonally opposite the junk shop mirror.

Kitty realised that not only Krisztina's bed, but other things as well had been thrown about. As if someone had been looking for something. "First thing is," she said, apparently staring only at the box labelled "family medicine cabinet", "we want to give Shishi a decent funeral. But we don't know of any relatives or anything. And second," – Zadko was still standing motionless – "we think her private stuff ought to be protected from getting into the wrong hands. You understand, Marek?"

"Are you a real whore?" Anna interrupted.

"Yes," Kitty smiled and looked at her. Maybe she wasn't as stuck on him as she had feared? She opened the box. Maybe . . . "What were you looking for, Marek?"

She didn't understand what Zadko was mumbling. But then, Kitty didn't speak Polish. "Money?"

He gestured angrily and his mumbling got louder and less friendly.

"You won't find money here," Kitty continued unimpressed. "Shishi put it where nobody can get at it." She went through the contents of the box, took the pictures out of the envelope, looked at them and picked out one to show Anna. "Here," she said, "that's us. A whole buncha whores."

"Someone broke in here yesterday," Anna said, as she came to take the picture. Kitty looked at Zadko. He nodded. But he didn't know who it had been. Or what he had been looking for.

"Maybe money, what else?"

Kitty thought he was starting to sound friendlier.

"What's the problem with Solidarność?" He lit a cigarette and gave her an almost trusting look. Though not trusting enough to fool Kitty.

"Wish I knew," she said quickly. "Shishi never said exactly." And if she hadn't told him, she must have had her reasons. She rummaged a bit more in the box, found a few sentimental souvenirs, postage stamps, the letters M and H, which must have come from an old fashioned type case for headlines, and other knicknacks. "No letters from relatives?" she asked Zadko. "Or a diary?"

Zadko shook his head and continued to puff on his cigarette.

"She had a black notebook," Anna announced.

"Really?" Zadko asked.

To Kitty's ears he sounded a bit too surprised.

"Didn't you see it Marek? It was in there."

Kitty considered. She wasn't going to get at the notebook on her own. Only the box. She put on her sweetest voice. "Marek, I'd very much like to take the box with me."

*

Once again it was a dead body of the male sex, whose pleasure had become eternal, innocuously exposed. Clean. Except for the anticipated pale spots on the synthetic silk sheet. No question – Hartmut Fahlenkamp was number three.

He held one cognac-brown and rust-red striped synthetic silk corner in his left hand, which was clenched into a tight fist on his stomach. His right hand hung off the edge of the bed, long-fingered and spider-like. His hands were disproportionately large, just like his box-shaped head with its thin, grey hair. The whole scene looked posed. Like a parody of the oh so beautiful sleeper in the full page ad for Davidoff perfume. Going by the wrinkles, this one could have been the sleeper's father. Otherwise he was neither the most beautiful nor the biggest. Nil nisi, Lietze thought, trying to picture the incident, which, according to the forensic doctor, had happened at least twelve, at most thirty-six hours ago. The corpse was completely stiff.

Probably they'd only discover good things about this man, too. And all too many of them. And someone in this city seemed to loathe this nice guy type so much that he, or maybe she, had decided to get rid of him wherever he or she could lay hands on him.

"Nice sweet guys like this don't fit into the picture for the dear ladies of the JLB either," Schade pointed out. "In the long run, he really upsets their ideal world view of the big bad wolf and the dear little lambs."

"Except that none of them would make the sacrifice of going to bed with him before sending him off to the great beyond with a karate chop." Lietze lifted up a pair of pale green linen pants and found two lemon-coloured silk socks. The matching tie was draped over an antique chair by the bed, and a pale green linen jacket hung neatly over its back. Shirt and underwear were white and rolled up in the striped sheet beside Fahlenkamp's legs.

"You bet," Schade said. "Although with a bit of imagination, this looks like the signature under a confession."

She pointed at the copy of *TAZ* which, spread open at the headline RECYCLING THE BLACK SKI MASKS, lay beside the edge of the bed, over which dangled Fahlenkamp's Nosferatu-like hand.

"Nonsense. So far they haven't distinguished themselves with between-the-lines messages. It looks more like a red herring."

"When you're right, you're right." Schade leafed through a book which she had pulled out from under *TAZ*. "He read English. Here, preface by Kate Millet. Another true feminist."

"Careful, Schade. This one had a wife. And she doesn't have to be illiterate . . ."

"As I said, when you're right . . ." Schade sighed. "What time does *TAZ* actually appear?"

"I assume late evening. Don't they sell it on the streets? Maybe Roboldt can ask his Larry. He'll be pleased to know that we haven't forgotten him," Lietze groaned.

"Good idea. Shall we question the wife?"

At D III, apart from Sonja Schade, it was normally Miriam Jacob who was most capable at dealing with machines. Miriam was particularly good at handling the phones and wrong connections without being cut off. Karin Lietze broke into someone else's conversations with unfortunate regularity. And now it had happened to Mimi.

". . . see each other later anyway. But now I need something official," she heard as she picked up the phone and routinely pressed a button. It was Roland Herrmann.

And normally Mimi was also more a model of discretion than investigative zeal. She really couldn't have said why she didn't put down the phone right away. There didn't seem to be any reason. Herrmann was doing what he had been told to do. He had called one of the precincts to inquire about reports on the JoAnne Little Brigade. Maybe it was just the tone in which Herrmann and some "Charlie" on the other end were bragging that no women would "beat the shit out of them", without any need to mention why. The certainty about their own safety. The lack of imagination with which they assumed their own invulnerability.

Mimi felt a little hot wave of hatred and envy.

". . . yes, I've written it down. Two with gas pistols . . . Wait, not so fast . . ."

For a fraction of a second she wished him a full charge of CS gas in the face.

". . . probably blind . . . for the rest of his life . . ."

But then she came to her senses, and they reminded her that no problem in this world could be solved with hatred. And that more than twenty years ago, she herself had refused to do the military service which she had so longed for. And had left the country where neither she nor her parents had been born, for the land of her mothers and fathers. To go back somehow, even though she hadn't come from here at all. And somehow forward. And some time in between she had arrived. For the first time in her life. And in Berlin of all places, a place that was always in transit too. A continuity of departures. Always going somewhere. Never being anywhere.

". . . complain about our Riot Squad boys, and then go and shoot off CS gas themselves . . ." "Charlie" was saying.

Mimi had got back her smile again. It was an advantage to have been born nowhere. In a plane for instance. In mid-air. Somewhere above the ocean. At thirty thousand feet. It made certain earthly things less important. She had stopped paying attention to what Herrmann was noting down about letters to employers, training schemes, universities, about notices in tenement hallways and wanted posters at bus stops and underground stations, about the kicks, upper cuts,

kidney chops and stab wounds men had been subjected to.
She thought that by disliking this Rambo wannabe she was
probably doing him an injustice. At least he was working,
and his tone of voice was only her business when he used
it with her. Gently she put down the phone, before the quiet
feeling of shame could turn into a feeling of guilt, something
that she was still quite capable of, on the most surprising
occasions. But that was *her* problem. She decided to take
him a cup of coffee. She didn't need to tell him why.

Roland "Rocky" Herrmann was sitting with his back to
the door, completely self-absorbed. More exactly, preoccu-
pied with a mixture of logorrhea, thigh slapping and bursts
of laughter. "... she doesn't suspect a thing, the head
cunt ... hahaha ... last year, right? Three men? Well, I'll
remember that ... No, wait! ... it's much worse, I can tell
you ... you might as well forget the two guys ...
hahahaha ... one of them's a poof ... Yes! True! Really is.
In the police! ... No, the other one is worse than a women's
libber ... a real idiot! Hahahaha ... You won't believe it ...
She isn't exactly A-OK either ... Her first name's Miriam ..."

The trembling started very deep inside. It felt like camping
out in Antarctica in an evening dress. Mimi saw that the cup
in her left hand had started to shake, and suspected that
the right had already frozen to the door handle. She tried
with all her strength to keep a clear head. But the desire for
the cup to turn into a hand-grenade increased. She started to
pull the pin with her teeth, and bit into a void.

"... hahaha ... right! If they knew ... Hahaha ..."

There was no pin. Only the pain of clenched teeth. Eventually she managed to close the door without making a
sound. At least she hoped so.

"Get out of here, both of you!" Alfred Henke's voice was
close to breaking. Fräulein von Thurau had herself never

heard him like that, even though various neighbours had often told her about the quarrelling that went on in the caretaker's apartment.

"Once and for all! What on earth!"

Then she could hear some commotion, a door slammed and was flung open again, and above it all a second voice could be heard.

"Once and for all: NO!"

"Erika, I'm warning you . . ."

"You can't warn anybody here."

More commotion. A piece of furniture in the hallway seemed to have lost its balance. Heavy steps and another voice, close to tears. "Why can't you stop this shit!"

"GET OUT OF HERE!" Henke sounded like he was ready to fight. "They could be here any moment. I've got to make a statement!"

"That's just what you'd like!" Judging by her voice, Erika Henke wasn't in as tight a spot as Henke. "I've got my suitcases in the car. And I'm bringing them back in. As sure as I'm Erika Henke, maiden name Vogel!"

"Man, I've gotta go! They're after me!"

Thorsten's steps came dangerously close to the front door. In her fright Fräulein von Thurau didn't even feel the heat any more. A heavy, ice-cold hand gripped her heart. "Stop!" Henke yelled. "First I'll have to check if it's all clear." Footsteps faded away. Erika and Thorsten continued to talk. Then Henke's footsteps returned to the hallway. It was no longer possible to understand what the three of them were talking about. And Fräulein von Thurau was no longer interested anyway. She was busy calculating. What was safer – to run away? She thought of her brittle bones and her fear of falling. Or to seek refuge in an attack?

As soon as the action seemed to have shifted to about two feet from the front door, she resolutely rang the bell under the home-made sign with the lovely old letters: Henke-Vogel.

There was a muffled scream, then Henke: "Who's that now! What on earth!" He tore the door open and came towards her like a steam roller. Fräulein von Thurau retreated a yard and then she mustered all her talent. Every woman is an actress, the least gifted end up in the theatre.

"Oh, er, Herr Henke?" she said very sweetly. "I have to get back to my shop you know ..."

For a moment Henke was tempted to roll right over the old lady. "Well go then, na!"

"... and I was wondering if you would be so kind as to tell the police where to find me because I'm sure that they'll want to question me too and then I want to say could you tell me what's happening here and if there is something wrong with Frau Fahlenkamp maybe I could help ..." Fräulein von Thurau babbled on. There was no room in her head to think about commas and full stops. There was only room for the hope that enough words occurred to her so that she had time to memorise precisely and clearly the scene before her. Alfred Henke didn't seem to beat up just his wife. His stepson looked in very bad shape too. Most of all, however, she hoped that the police would show up right now, before he could attack her as well.

Even on Lietze's words of condolence, it became clear that the new widow no longer wished to pretend that the marriage between her and Hartmut Fahlenkamp had been one of the statistically rare successful experiments in relations between the sexes.

"Just don't try telling me that he was the unique and wonderful husband all my women friends must have envied me for."

Schade's jaw almost dropped in astonishment. Lietze

glanced at Fritz, who had been trying for the past twenty minutes to console the widow, and who appeared a little uncertain.

"There's no point in telling you stories," Frau Fahlenkamp continued unwaveringly. "Your officer told me that he doesn't even believe in the fairy tales he reads his daughters every evening. To be quite frank about it: I wanted a divorce; in the last few months I've wished more than once that Hartmut would simply drop dead. I was with my mother for a week, because I couldn't stand it here any more. I don't know who killed him, I only know it wasn't me. Can I offer you anything?"

She went over to a little antique cabinet that exuded old colonial splendour and pulled open a little door.

"Frau Fahlenkamp," said Lietze, "you surprise me . . ."

"Forget the Fahlenkamp, please! Thank God I won't be burdened with that name any more! If you had known Hartmut Fahlenkamp the way I knew him, then a name like Schmidt would make you happy! Tell me, what would you like to drink?" She looked round. Nobody reacted. "Your problem. I need a drink for my stomach." She giggled. "A criminal water!" As if it were an immense pleasure to be frivolous at this moment. "For once it's appropriate! Hartmut, of course, would be indignant. He is, well, he was, always so pious!"

She gulped down a good blackish-brown mouthful straight from the bottle, shuddered and ran out of the room. Lietze, Schade and Fritz exchanged half-concerned, half-amused glances. "Somehow, merry widows are pleas . . ." Schade began, when a cheerful voice rang out from the kitchen: "At least, don't you want to try a criminal water, too?"

Lietze gave up and called, "Well, okay. And then . . ." The rest was drowned out by clinking glasses and banging cupboard doors. She pulled a cigarillo out of her pack, lit it and looked round the room. Here too, like the bedroom, everything was tasteful. Nothing was placed by chance or simply left over from earlier, less affluent days. Everything was carefully chosen. And everything clashed. The Chinese lacquer tables didn't go with the African sculptures, and the wicker chair, which looked as if it had spent a good part of the nineteenth century on a plantation porch in Central America, didn't go with the polar bear rug, and none of it belonged in a nearly one hundred-year-old Central European apartment.

"This room is all Hartmut, heehee!" Elvira who-would-rather-be-Schmidt placed the Indonesian rattan tray on the ornamental Arabian wood table. The cigarillo pack fell on to the floor. Quickly she bent down, picked it up, glanced at it and then fell back into the plantation chair and giggled uncontrollably. Lietze thought about calling a doctor. Frau Fahlenkamp wouldn't be the first person whose suppressed shock turned into hysteria.

"That's even better than criminal water – heehee! Lucky Luciano! You're okay," Elvira chortled, still balanced between tears of joy and a bout of weeping. "Why don't you take a seat!"

Fritz and Schade sat down on a spartan bench, like the ones in standard saunas, but – as the widow immediately explained cheerfully – it came from Japan. Lietze remained standing by the window. "What did you mean just now – all Hartmut?"

"Oh, all this hotchpotch here. It was Hartmut who dragged it all in. From every corner of the globe. Take a look at the bookcase. He knew everything about every place on earth. But never went there!"

"Why should he?" Lietze asked.

"The number two man at a travel agency? That was his tragedy. Fear of flying! All he knew from personal experience was the little bit between the North Sea and the Alps. But nobody realised that except his boss. He could talk about every destination as if he had grown up there – heeheehee."

"And he didn't get fired?" Schade asked.

Fritz, who had already heard the story once, drank his mineral water, got up, went over to Lietze briefly and then returned to the bedroom, the scene of the crime.

"That might have happened at the beginning, when he was first found out," the widow said. "But you had to know Hartmut. He was set on putting his mark on the history of travel. He simply made sure he was indispensable. As maid of all work. He made coffee, especially for the women in the office. He charmed the boss by imitating his mania for loud ties and socks. Well, you know, the boss could get away with it! With Hartmut it was just arse-licking. He acted like the boss's latchkey kid. Because he was always travelling. Someone had to check out all the package deals. So Hartmut gradually worked his way up. He actually became the good atmosphere in the company. All the women were at his feet. The boss was the only man he had any dealings with. Other than that, he avoided men. Heeheehee, like the devil avoids holy water!" She got out of the wicker chair to pour herself more water.

Lietze was no longer thinking about calling a doctor, but about a question. Schade was quicker. "Was he possibly a closet homosexual? I mean, was he afraid . . ."

"If he was, then he didn't even know it himself! Anything is possible. They're the worst, aren't they? But I really don't care. All the affairs he had with women were enough for me!"

"Ah!" This time Lietze was faster. "He did have affairs?"

"You bet! Didn't look like it, did he?" She jumped up and rummaged through a box on to which Indian patterns and characters had been stuck, and returned with a pile of photographs. Hartmut Fahlenkamp surrounded by his female colleagues. Always slightly stooped, with drooping shoulders and thin lips, always surrounded by radiant female faces and always at the centre. "You wouldn't believe how thankful women are if a guy doesn't come across like a pig, but like a bit of a feminist. Heehee. Out of sheer gratitude they go to bed with him. Happens like clockwork!"

Lietze couldn't suppress a grin. "Doesn't look like there's much jealousy there. Was there a new one recently?"

"Not as far as I know. Do you think a woman did it?"

"Can you think of someone?"

"Me?" Elvira sat down again and appeared to give it some serious consideration. "I hadn't even thought about that. But it must've been someone!"

"One of his male colleagues maybe? Because he pinched his woman?"

"There were no male colleagues. Except the boss, and he got sick of the constant Fahli-here, Fahli-there." As had Elvira, who had long ago stopped participating in any social activities where Fahlenkamp's female colleagues could gush: "What would we do without Fahli," or "Fahli would have done a much better job!" She had left the marriage bed, because Fahli, every woman's best friend, thought he always had to be floating in a sea of gratitude there too. She had moved into a tiny third room, in which there was not a single piece of exotic antique furniture or a single travel book. And had eventually taken advantage of every chance to travel which her job in an advertising agency gave her.

"Oh, so what," she continued giggling, "there's no point in trying to kid you. Of course I wasn't staying with my mother as I said, but . . ."

". . . with a lover," Lietze and Schade added simultaneously. "And? Somebody really masculine?" Schade asked.

"Oh no. I take them even less seriously. Tell me, and I hope I'm not stepping on any toes. But the other officer, is he married?"

"Yes – why?" Lietze asked surprised.

"Well, just keep an eye on him. It's not easy for a woman with a man like that!" Elvira Schmidt, the widow of Mr Fahlenkamp, looked suspiciously dreamy.

"As you've moved out of the bedroom, I assume this isn't your book?" Schade asked, interrupting her dream.

"Maryse Holder? Never heard of her."

"Did your husband read English?"

"English, French, Italian, Spanish, Portuguese. What kind of book is it?" Elvira thumbed through it.

"No idea," Schade said. "But I'm sure it isn't travel literature. Since the preface was written by Kate Millet . . ."

"Seems to be something about Mexico. But anyway – the writing in the margin isn't Hartmut's!"

"Then we'll take it with us," Lietze said. "And we'll take Fritz with us as well. Where's he got to?"

"Here I am." Fritz was standing in the door. He waved a small cardboard box. "I have one more question. Did your husband take pictures?"

"Yes, of course. Every single thing that's in the apartment. And only slides! Too bad he couldn't organise any slide shows, but who wants to look at furniture? And unfortunately, he couldn't take pictures on trips."

The west side of Zieten Strasse was in the shade. A few kids were playing there. The treeless east side, on which houses were mercilessly exposed to the burning sun, baked in the heat. The curtains were drawn in all the windows. The temperature inside the few cars in the parking bay must have been close to boiling, and it wouldn't drop much for the next four or five hours. The two cars parked closest to Winterfeldt Strasse would have to endure the light and heat for as long as it took the sun to complete the whole of its westward journey.

Most of the windows on the shady side were wide open.

A sign that the people living there didn't go out to work all day. Proper families, still ruled by housewives who could respond flexibly to such influential phenomena as the weather.

The door, the two opaque windows which prevented anyone looking in, and the display case with faded pictures of striptease dancers in feathers and sequins, didn't put this shop in the category of what might be called "proper". But that was a relatively recent development. In earlier days, to be more precise, in the first third of the twentieth century, places nominally like it had defined not only Zieten Strasse, but the whole area around Nollendorf Platz and Winterfeldt Platz. Not even the horrors of the First World War had interrupted the tradition. On the contrary. That war created the volcano around whose crater the whole city danced after the eruption, addicted to pleasure in the final, unpredictable, beautiful hundred or ten or five minutes before the end. Pandora's box was wide open. A spiritual meridian ran right down the middle of Motz Strasse. And the gulf stream flowed through the whole area, warming the Dorian Grays and Kleists, the dollar-girls and butches. And those who belonged lit the candle at both ends, and burned up all the most expensive coke with the briefest, most intoxicating effect.

Club Olàlà was part of that tradition and, quite properly, even its name had a history. But the present inhabitants didn't know anything about that. And least of all the rather tall, lanky man in the grey track suit trousers, the polo shirt and trainers or the petite woman with long blonde hair pinned back, who was having a hard time keeping up with his long strides.

They probably wouldn't have been interested anyway. Nothing seemed to interest them except the debate they were carrying on as they walked. They came down Zieten Strasse from Bülow Strasse, and when they crossed the pedestrianised intersection at Nollendorf Strasse, the man nodded towards the Club Olàlà. The woman looked over and started to protest vigorously again: "Why don't you take care of it yourself?"

"Because then it'll cost money. As a woman you'll manage it much more easily. Just say that you're a friend and you'd like to know where . . ."

"No, no, no. I think it's mean. I'm not going to do such a thing!"

"Don't be so selfish! You know what's at stake!"

The woman stood at the entrance and looked at the yellowed pictures. The man pulled her away. He didn't want to attract any attention. But nobody was interested in the two of them anyway. The kids who were playing nearby didn't even look up. A quarrelling couple was nothing special in this neighbourhood. Not just because hardly anyone could understand what the fight was about; it was carried on in Polish. Although – not even that could be taken as certain. Polish had become West Berlin's third most common mother tongue. And anyway, fights in several languages were as familiar here as polyglot love-talk and polymorphous diverse kitchen smells.

"No man! I don't wanna go to some dump in Schleswig-Holstein! Drive me to Neukölln, then leave me alone!" Paler than usual and wrapped up from head to toe, Thorsten Vogel sat in the back of the beige Mercedes, trying to keep a grip on a sports bag. His black satin bomber jacket was zipped all the way up to his neck. His legs and feet were sweating in heavy combat boots and camouflage pants intended for jungle warfare, his shaved head was hidden under a navy-blue baseball cap with the insignia of a U.S. unit which had attacked Da Nang, and his eyes and the scratched and bloody skin around them were hidden behind mirrored sunglasses, like the ones the pilots in Ray-Ban commercials wear.

"But you'll be safe with Onkel Hermann and Tante Karin," Erika Henke insisted. "Nobody will ask about you, you can cure your head, and you can even make yourself useful."

"Just shut your trap. I've got a headache. I wanna be with my mates, not in the West. Can't even go there."

"Thorsten," Erika cajoled, but kept an eye on him in the rear view mirror as she was driving. "Look, I'll drive you there tonight. You go to sleep on the back seat . . ."

"Shut up, will you. I told you I can't!"

"You just can't be running around here as long as your head isn't okay. I'm worried about you, son!"

"Man! Can't you shut up! Since when have you been worried about me? Go tell the old guy about it. I'm telling you for the last time, I can't. And now drive to Neukölln!" My head is going to burst in a second, he thought. Or I'm going to throw up on this plastic seat.

"Don't be a smartass! I hope you realise that, from now on, you depend on me as much as I depend on you! Why can't you?" Her voice was drowned out by squealing tyres, because Erika Henke had suddenly swerved the taxi to the kerb. She turned round and stared sternly into Thorsten's mirror shades, as far as that was possible with a left eye which was now a brownish-green.

"'Cause I got no I.D.!"

"And why don't you have any I.D.?"

"'Cause those fucking cunts took it," Thorsten managed to say, before he tore open the car door and puked into the middle of the road.

"I'm actually a professional typesetter, na! That's really my profession." Alfred Henke had decided that suspicion wasn't the caretaker's first duty in dealing with the two ladies and the gentleman from the serious crimes squad, and he proudly showed them his treasures. "Na! A place for everything and everything in its place, that's important. Take a look here, that's what a proper tool cupboard looks like!" He opened the cupboard and presented the screwdrivers all ranked by size.

Sonja Schade was impressed and let him know it. She didn't say, however, that what impressed her most was the orange striped cat sitting enthroned on top of a square box as if rooted there and, seemingly tired and uninvolved, slowly closing its heavy lids.

Lietze glanced impatiently at Fritz. "Herr Henke, this is all very nice. But let's stick to yesterday morning."

Henke turned round. "Yes, of course. Well, I was in the bathroom. Come with me." He went on ahead.

Startled, the cat dashed across the workbench and disappeared out the window. Schade watched it, as a second later it jumped on top of a wall and paced back and forward, paying no attention to a young woman in cut-off jeans and a t-shirt and wearing big tiger-striped sunglasses, who was coming across the courtyard.

Henke led Lietze and Fritz to the small bathroom window. "Well, I was here, and he came through the entrance. You can go straight into the courtyard from the front house."

"And you said that he threw a plastic bag into the garbage container. What time was that?" Lietze tried to figure out if it was really worth wasting more time here or easier just to find the right rubbish dump.

"Well, I'd say it was just after eight, na! I noticed the time. Because normally Herr Fahlenkamp isn't an early riser – umm, wasn't, I suppose one has to say."

A noise at the front door interrupted Lietze's train of thought. It sounded as if something had been pushed through the letter box. Henke ran to the door, Fritz after him. Through the window Lietze saw a young woman cross the courtyard toward Nollendorf Strasse. She was trying hard to look relaxed. At that moment, Fritz called: "Lietze, come here."

Schade came out of the workshop too. Fritz was holding a temporary, but nevertheless machine-washable Berlin I.D. in his hand. A thick black Mars symbol had been drawn on the front. A circle with an arrow pointing up to the right. But the arrow was broken. On the back was written RAPIST!

"God, then I must have just seen one of our friends." Without further explanation, Schade shot past the other three, tore open the door and chased through the courtyard to Nollendorf Strasse.

Lietze looked first at Fritz and then at Henke and pushed the door shut. Henke was transformed. His face had turned blue and red. Panting, he mopped his wet neck. Fritz thought that he was trembling, while Lietze looked at the face on the I.D. which had been bisected by the Mars circle and read out, "Thorsten Vogel, born August 13, 1971 ... Who's that, Herr Henke?"

"My stepson," Henke forced out. "A really black day."

"Why, what else happened today?" Fritz asked.

"I mean August 13. The anniversary of the day the Wall went up."

Lietze handed Fritz the I.D. "Now that we've destroyed all possible finger prints, could we sit down somewhere where there's more light?"

"Of course, inspector ..."

"Lietze will do. Where?"

"Well, maybe in the kitchen."

The extra light gave Fritz the same idea Lietze had had. She signalled him to wait. "Herr Henke, if you are the stepfather, where is the mother?"

"Yeah, I don't know. Didn't you see her? She had to leave to go to work."

"I see. And Thorsten? Did he go to work too?"

Henke twitched and said quickly: "Yes, yes, if you don't work, you . . ."

"Where does he work?"

Henke didn't really have an answer to that. But his clumsy delaying tactics spoke volumes. He reached out to pick up a napkin at the far end of the table and patted his face and neck as violently as if he were training to take part in a procession of flagellants.

"Could it be that Rosso . . ."

"Who?" Henke almost seemed relieved.

Fritz looked at Lietze. "Rosso. That name doesn't ring a bell?"

"No!" O Mata, Mata, help. What had the asshole done now?

"But you do know that he helps out at Club Olàlà?" Lietze added in a friendly tone. "You know that Herr Henke, don't you?"

Henke sank lower on the bench and sighed deeply.

"Where is he now?"

"Oh, I don't have the slightest idea," Henke growled. "I kicked him out."

"When?"

"Yesterday." All of a sudden, Henke seemed to remember something. Words bubbled out. "What on earth! Doesn't show up to sweep the yard. That lad has to do as he's told as long as he stays in my house! That's all!"

Lietze put the I.D. in her bag and looked at her watch. Fritz started to worry about Schade too. "Shall I go after her?"

"No. We'll wait. Herr Henke, before we find out a little more about your stepson – have you got anything else to say about Hartmut Fahlenkamp?"

Alfred Henke straightened up and cleared his throat. "Well, I'm not the one to talk, but there was something wrong with the marriage. I mean, whoever heard of a wife who goes travelling all the time. Whether they're really okay otherwise – I don't know. They subscribed to left wing papers, na."

To the right, on the short section up to Eisenacher Strasse, there was nobody with cut-offs and a t-shirt. Just two dogs, each leading an old lady across the street to the shady side. Nor was there anything moving between the cars parked at right angles to the new buildings at the far end on the other side of the street. Nothing that looked like a young woman with cropped white blonde hair.

Schade looked left, down Nollendorf Strasse to Maassen Strasse, and tried to sort out with the naked eye the blur of bodies moving about in the glaring light. The street was empty until the third building down. Then a bunch of heads which, because of the distance, seemed to be close together. And there – a white dot, dancing between the others. She released the handle of the heavy courtyard door and started running. Zigzagging among people who seemed to walk or stand further apart the closer she came.

The woman with the bleached cropped hair was running faster too. She hadn't turned round. Somehow she seemed to know she was being followed. Maybe it was in the air. I'm probably pushing shock waves fifty yards in front of me, Schade thought. The woman was about three buildings ahead of her. Then she shot diagonally across the street right in front of a car. Schade changed sides as well. Because it was shady, there were more people. But on the sunny side there were shops with people going in and out. Schade was catching up. Only one building between them. Even though she didn't have such good shoes. And her feet were wet and were slipping inside the soles. The woman was wearing trainers. She still hadn't turned round. She looked straight ahead, shot across the street again to where two other women, who going by their hair and clothes were from the same milieu, were standing beside a motorcycle, shouted something at them and ran on. Schade followed her and lost precious seconds because she got involved in a misunderstanding with a driver about who had the right of way. When she got back to the sunny side, she saw the two motorcycle women strolling towards her. Challenging her and keeping just enough distance between them so that she would be unable to pass through without jostling at least one. She couldn't slip by to the side without body contact either. Eight yards left. She sized them up. They were going to make sure she lost several more seconds. At least. Perhaps even turn rough. Well, if you want it. Show me. Behind the two, a woman was pushing a buggy hung with shopping bags, occupied by a radiant baby. Schade calculated the curves and angles needed to slip between the two women and past the young mother. She fixed her eyes on the two of them, looked first at one, then the other, then back to the first and accelerated.

They really had intended to crash into her. Schade managed to get through with the classic feint, staring at the wall to the left of one of the women until the last moment. And when the woman moved close to the wall, swept between them and past the buggy. The white head was just disappearing into an entrance on the left.

Another one and a half buildings. Fifteen, twenty yards. A big dog, happy finally to have found someone to scrap with. She snapped at it in a voice she had never heard before, and had no idea where she got the breath from. Then she was at the entrance, ran in and found herself in a huge, labyrinthine courtyard. Nobody in sight. Schade gasped and felt the blood pound explosively through head and neck. She panted loudly and rhythmically and jogged on the spot. The courtyard seemed to be the heart of the whole complex bounded by Nollendorf, Massen and Motz

Strasse. It had several proper exits and plenty of walls which would pose no problem for a fit young woman who knew the neighbourhood and whose feet were given wings by a pair of Nikes.

"Are you nuts or something! Coming here in the middle of the day dressed like that!" The wiry young man with a bit of pale fuzz on his face pulled him into the hallway, checked out the staircase, then closed the apartment door.

"I need a place to crash," Thorsten said dully, "just a couple of days." He dropped the bag and tried to hold on to the wardrobe. "They're after me."

"Who? The cops? So you come here? Ya want them to find us?"

A door burst open at the end of the passageway, and a beefy type in a black shirt, with a short blond crewcut that was twice as high as his forehead, appeared. 'D'ya come in the taxi that just drove off? You oughta know . . ."

Thorsten slid down the wardrobe on to the floor. "Yeah, yeah. My old lady . . ."

"Hey, what's goin' on? You conking out?" The wiry one shook him. The beefy one came closer. "Get him outta the hall."

They dragged Thorsten into the room at the end of the hallway and left him lying on a yellow and brown flowered carpet among empty beer cans and three pairs of combat boots. Fragments of conversation and a thousand razor blades were spinning round Thorsten's head. The nausea was rising again. Painfully he sat up and spat a few brown lumps and some sour-tasting white mucus over two or three boots. The bawling around him increased. He felt a kick against his right thigh. Then his head fell back, pulling his body with it. The baseball cap slid off. For a second there was silence. Then he saw a few faces bent over his face and heard, "fight?" and "nothing planned" and "solo effort?" and "doctor maybe?" and the snap of a beer can being opened. The flag with the red cross and black eagle on a white background which hung above the brown corduroy couch merged with the larger than life black and white face of a woman holding a gun aimed directly at the viewer, and into red-rimmed ski caps and muffled screams which grew softer and weaker, and heaps of sand and crumbled walls and black combat boots and and and, and then there was another shove. He pulled himself up, holding his head on the side without bruises and gasped, "Th-th-brigade—"

He saw that two of the guys were trying to clean their boots with wads of toilet paper. "What brigade? Antifascists? C'mon, man, talk!"

"No-the-brig-those-what're they called-who, who beat up guys—"

"What? Tarts?" The beefy one yelled at him. "Ya mean them?"

It was as if someone had stopped time and space. For seconds, not a movement. Then the bawling broke over him like a hailstorm, whose fist-sized stones pummelled his ear drums. In between, rattled fragments of sentences: ". . . cunts beating you up . . ." and "kick him out . . ." and "not fit" and "no use for . . ."

He forced his eyes open again and looked into five faces which seemed to be bursting with laughter and contempt. But for – for thingummy, he thought. For him. You had some use for him. And then the storm of images broke over him again.

To judge by the sounds, the first rear house at 29 Belziger Strasse could have been in Europe's deep South. If one listened more carefully, then it belonged in the Mediterranean crescent between Greece and Egypt. What was pouring from the north-facing windows opening on to the courtyard, when Kim and Minou had pushed open the heavy wooden door, was an ethno-symphony for transistor solos and large stereo orchestra, speaking parts and song, drums, guitars and diverse instruments from other homelands, voices in the most various accents, Greek, Turkish, Arabic, Bavarian and Swabian, with a background of the clinking of dishes, hammering, drilling, electric razors, screaming babies and washing machines on spin dry.

"Good thing it's an old house," Kim grinned. "Social housing would have collapsed a long time ago!"

Minou didn't know much about music. "It smells like being on holiday here!"

"Where d'you go?"

"Turkey. Down on the coast. Ah," she patted her stomach with a wicked, flirtatious look, "I ate far too well."

The brown door on the right on the first floor sported a lion's head which was easy enough to pull, and the bell echoed on at least three of the five floors. But nobody opened up.

"What now?" Minou sounded relieved. She felt altogether uneasy about the visit.

Kim unzipped her short black leather jacket and dropped down on to the steps. She wiped the sweat from her forehead and fanned her neck with her hand. "Wait."

Minou shook her head. "Why did you have to put on such heavy clothes?"

"It's an advantage, believe me. The right outfit is half the battle. Ya wouldn't turn any tricks wrapped up in a chador either."

"Why – we don't want to turn any tricks with these guys."

"You got it."

"I don't get it." Wide-eyed, Minou watched as Kim tugged in annoyance at the leather drainpipes sticking to her legs and beat the sleeves of her leather jacket in the air.

"Look, girl! It's very simple. Kitty an' Helga was here th' first time, an' they got kicked out after five minutes."

Minou looked worried.

"You know as well as I do that most guys will only start negotiating when they can't get anywhere with fists. Or threats. And if you come up against three guys like the ones Kitty an' Helga did yesterday, then you can throw away your poplin and high heels. Unless you've practised kidney punches wearin' four inch heels. Kitty never did."

"You sure there's only three, if we . . ."

"Nope. That's why I'm wearing this stuff and these shit kickers. Even if it's crazy as wanting to go to a sauna in the jungle. But it don't matter. It'll work for the first five minutes, and after that I'd sure like t' see if one of them's still got the idea he can hurt me."

Minou dabbed nervously at her face and neck with a tissue, and continued on mechanically across the front of her P.A.'s outfit.

"Want one?" Kim pulled a pouch of tobacco out of her jacket. Minou stopped dabbing and offered her a cigarette from a pack. Kim wiped the tobacco crumbs from her moist fingers and put the papers back in the pouch. "Thanks."

"Listen," said Minou, after she had wiped a bit of the steps with the soaking tissue and sat down beside Kim. "I didn't understand all that about the trading licence."

"It isn't possible to understand it, it's just the law. They say the kind of work we do isn't a trade, just a travesty of a trade. So if we, like, make an application for, say, a trading licence to the local council office, then they're going to officially reject it."

"So there's no point in wasting your time on it."

"Wrong! Because they've got to have proper grounds for the rejection. In every case. So, now imagine if everybody we know fills out an application. We could bring the council office to a standstill."

Minou looked at Kim. "That's great. Like that time with the census?"

Kim inhaled. "Similar. But there's something else too. Because if you get rejected you also – oh man, what's it called – have means of legal redress or something. Anyhow, we can appeal, then it goes to a higher level, and so on till it gets to the Senator for Economic Affairs. And that way, I think, something could come of it."

"Why? Was he on the game once?"

Kim had to laugh, and swallowed the nicotine cloud which should have gone into her lungs. "Nope," she coughed. "Just the opposite. But we've got this Pampers Senate here now with more women than men."

"It's true," Minou burst out laughing. "There's even one in there who's only responsible for women's stuff, maybe she can . . ."

"'Zactly. Though . . . yeah, well. We'll have to try it out. But second . . ."

One floor down, the main entrance to the building creaked open. Kim looked through the banisters. A woman with shopping bags and a man with a crate of beer. Minou became restless again.

". . . second: who do we know in the Economics Department?" Kim stood up, ground out the cigarette and took up position, her legs wide apart. Minou got up as well. She stood there wide-eyed, and it was impossible to tell if she wanted to see exactly how the knockout blow would come at her, or if she was trying really hard to figure out if the word "self-consciousness" was a little weak to describe what COW stood for.

As soon as he saw the two of them, the man with the crate overtook the woman on the stairs. He stared at them. The woman took all four shopping bags in her left hand, pulled a set of keys out of her pocket with her right hand and walked up to the door with the lion's head.

"Are you looking for someone?" the man asked.

Kim looked at him with an ambiguous smile in her eyes and was silent for a moment. "Yeah – you," she finally said tersely.

The woman turned round now, too, and said something in Polish which sounded more like a sigh than something hostile. She looked at the man. He merely gave a sharp reply and shook his head angrily. Kim moved a tiny bit closer to him and raised her shoulders even further. He wouldn't be able to stay in that position for long holding the crate of beer.

"What do you want?" he snapped.

"To clear up a few things," Kim said without dropping her gaze. "Right here on the stairs, if you want, we've got nothing to hide . . ." She felt Minou's trembling body move closer to her.

"I don't know about anything I need to clear up with you."

The woman started to talk to him in Polish again, but unlocked the door at the same time, went into the hallway and put down the bags. Then she came back out on to the stairs, still talking and now gesticulating as well. Kim didn't understand a word, but from the tone of her voice and the man's face, she concluded that she must somehow be arguing in favour of the two women.

"Really?" she said slowly and risked a bluff. "You ought to listen to your wife."

It seemed to work. The man appeared surprised and he shifted the crate of beer to a slightly different position to gain time. Kim continued to stare at him and squared her shoulders for emphasis, slowly putting her hand into the inner pocket of her leather jacket, noticed that the man noticed and finally pulled out the bag of tobacco. Gravity seemed to be working against man and beer again, at least the fact that he didn't have a hand free seemed to be getting on his nerves. All of a sudden, he turned sharply, strode to the door and bumped into the woman who had been looking

back and forward between him and the two women at the
bottom of the flight of stairs. He mumbled something in
Polish and disappeared into the apartment. The women lowered her arms. "Well, come in!"

"And you didn't by any chance have him on your payroll as
an informer?" Lietze pushed the notepad aside and reached
for the lighter half hidden under the files on her desk. The
best the colleague from Internal Security had had to offer
on Thorsten Vogel was meagre compared to the information
the JoAnne Little Brigade had already put on a cardboard
sign. He didn't have the nickname Rosso in his computer
either. Only details of every riot in Kreuzberg at which Thorsten was presumed to have been present, and in which
Anarchist contingent he had been sighted on demonstrations
in other districts, and which bars and squats he had fre-
quented. He had slipped out of view since last winter, and
he had not been spotted during the last May Day riots in
Kreuzberg.

"I beg your pardon?" His indignation was as heartfelt as
a government denial in Bonn.

"It's okay," Lietze said quickly, before he could start lectur-
ing her that the police Internal Security section had nothing
to do with the Federal Office for Defence of the Constitution
and even it . . .

"Do you have anything on any women he had contact
with?"

"Women or men, it makes no difference to us, there are
several people here who . . ."

"I'm interested in women, particularly ones who might
have withdrawn from the Autonomous scene recently."

That was asking too much for the computer. Obviously
nobody had led it to expect that some day it might have to
provide such answers. It only dutifully collected data which

this one small scene produced. Whoever didn't show up there regularly any more disappeared from its fixed gaze, though not from the computer.

"Does the name Henke mean anything to you?"

"Aren't you listening to me? Thorsten Vogel is registered as resident with . . ."

"Thanks, I knew about that. But you've got nothing else on Henke except his address. Okay. Last question: who's responsible for the far right there now? Aha. Still Lang. Thanks!"

A ray of light at last. Detective Superintendent Lang wasn't someone who had had his perspective distorted by decades of working too close to the government. Neither did he have an exaggerated opinion of himself because it was his job to protect the state and its constitution and not just ordinary citizens. Unlike her, Lang had preferred to go back to school once again years ago, so as to rise up the bureaucratic ladder. Then he got his promotion to superintendent and needed an appropriate post and the only one available was with Internal Security. It was, however, partly because of her that he had stormed off so enthusiastically to attend police academy in West Germany. If she had seriously been able to imagine that an affair with a colleague would not inevitably become competitive and if she had really wanted to grant a relationship significant space in her life, and if he had taken his desires and privileges a little, just a little, less for granted – well, so what! It was okay. It was better than having one's energies consumed by useless and anachronistic debates. And perhaps having to spend years struggling with questions like, should she have children or not after all, or how could a woman even have a career and in a man's world, but she would sometimes have had a shoulder to lean on and . . . enough of that. It was better this way. Even though she didn't have a shoulder to lean on or sometimes a lap to curl up in! This was better. Period. The man who could love a woman not despite, but because of, her independence had still to be invented.

"Oh hello, this is a surprise. Shall we be formal, inspector, or will it be first names?" He seemed genuinely pleased.

"What would you prefer?" Lietze energetically stubbed out her Lucky Luciano to make the prickling at the back of her neck disappear, and quickly started talking business. Fortunately, Lang not only had a particularly pleasant voice – still! – he was also very co-operative. They did have a Thorsten Vogel on file, because he had been picked up twice at punch-ups after football matches. Both times he had been with people under observation for neo-Nazi and racist activities. Not an organised group though, as far as they knew.

"Do you know that he used to be involved with the Kreuzberg black ski mask lot?"

"Sure, Karin. They thought he was an agent provocateur and chased him out."

"And. Was he?"

"Oh no. From time to time our colleagues claim that the Autonomous scene in Kreuzberg is the best infiltrated, but we're much better."

"At infiltrating?" Sceptically Lietze raised her eyebrows and pulled over her notepad again. "You're not trying to tell me that the gentlemen from the uniformed sections who vote for the neo-fascists en masse, and attend their meetings, are in reality your fifth column."

The hearty laugh at the other end of the line was slightly condescending. Maybe Lang too had now come to regard everyone else as a bit dim?

"Do you also have a Henke on file, on Nollendorf?"

"Alfred? Sure. Vogel's stepfather. Just a minute – yes, here. Seems to have retired after marrying Erika Vogel. Although it surprises me a little."

"Why, what did he do before that?"

"Oh, he was involved in everything happening on the far

right. He was under suspicion in connection with two bomb attacks. But there was no proof. A few times he turned up as the contact address on leaflets. For a while he was drinking with that gang who were slipped the famous two thousand marks by our lord and master to make the socialists' campaign posters disappear. Do you remember? That tripped him up for a change . . ."

Lietze relaxed. This part of Lang hadn't changed much. He was laughing again.

"A strange bird. You never know: is he dangerous or just a laughing stock you should feel sorry for?"

Lietze remembered the story about the West Berlin Senator for Internal Affairs and the woman the East Berlin Secret Service got into his bed, and was immediately back to thinking about Krisztina Kędzierska. Had she spied for Solidarność? Or put people into a position where they could be blackmailed? It took her a while to realise that Lang was still making fun of Henke.

". . . and then finally they gave him a job with the Public Transport, and he's allowed to drive buses . . ."

"Drive buses – what?"

"Karin – you do have to pay attention. This is pure Henke. He gets into a fight with a student because something's wrong with her monthly pass. The monthly stamp was missing. Well, she said something like it wasn't her fault, that it must've been the guy at the ticket office counter. And that did it. Henke must have shouted – did you ever hear him talk? Order is the most important thing in life, and a German official doesn't forget anything and so on in the same vein. He accuses her of doctoring the pass, pretty soon everybody on the bus is listening, and she's not at a loss for words, wants her pass back and to get off, he says that's out of the question, it's going to be confiscated . . ."

Lietze saw Alfred Henke in front of her, the incarnation of order, and was only listening with half an ear. Of course, he was no match for the student. And she could very well imagine his face, when, because he wouldn't return the pass, the student grabbed his date-stamp, jumped off the bus, telling him he was a fetishist who needed therapy and that she was going to liberate him from his dangerous fetish, and then disappeared. Lietze remembered officials, who with that tiny dash of pleasure which went far beyond what one might expect from ordinary official duty, slammed the little wooden cudgel down on some form or other. Only then was a piece of paper certified, a postage stamp cancelled, an address made official. She thought about the ridiculously large visa stamps East Germany banged into the passports of travellers in transit. A demonstration against one's own insignificance. Marking territory. Stamping it out. No freedom without stamps. Stamps. Only now did the word itself intrude and evoke another image. A forehead with a letter, precisely placed, above an appallingly abused body. And another one. And another one. And a fourth. Lietze shuddered. The seductive voice at the other end of the line was now cheerfully relating anecdotes from the trial.

"... the student said to the woman judge: Ask him if this is his stamp. I guarantee he knows the number by heart and no doubt he put his own special mark on it as well. Then Henke comes in, the judge asks him to identify the stamp, and he does exactly what the student said he would do ..."

He should tell me something that would help catch the JoAnne Little Brigade. And then we'll see. But that thought wasn't any more comforting. And Henke's quirks no longer seemed funny. What a country, that produces such people. She forced herself not to think about the sealed cattle trucks heading east, their transport lists stamped as carefully as could be. She also suppressed the pictures of crowds of people in Hungarian and Czechoslovakian embassies. People who were no longer willing to wait for their own state to grant them an exit stamp, who crossed the border illegally, and immediately threw away their East German passports, greedily accepting the new West German one. With its forms and stamps and seals and its official acts and . . .

"Karin? Are you still there?"

"Yeah, yeah. Sorry. It must be the weather," she lied and realised that she was shivering. "Where could Thorsten Vogel have got to?"

She should have been annoyed when Lang explained that he couldn't give out the addresses of the three or four people with whom Thorsten seemed to have associated. "I don't want to offend you . . . We want to keep them under surveillance a bit longer, and you could muck it all up." Instead she felt relieved. She tried to sound a bit reproachful, mentioned the words interdepartmental co-operation and noted with satisfaction that he sounded hurt, and he suggested sending one of his people to look for Thorsten.

"Well, okay, I'll make an exception." She wouldn't have known, anyway, who in D III would have been available to do it. "What about the mother?"

"I'd like to know that too. She's been suspiciously quiet."

Erika Henke, born Vogel, had been an activist in the Lower Saxony NPD before moving to Berlin with Alfred Henke. She had run a village inn near Lüneburg, which also served as a party meeting place and belonged to the party or to its boss even after the NPD had become insignificant.

"She wouldn't even have had her toilet cleaned by someone who wasn't German. The name of the inn was 'The German Oak'. She was taken to court a few times because she kept putting up 'Germans Only' signs on the door. A fanatic, not just some little fellow traveller."

She had got to know Henke in the village, because the inn's owner thought he needed a bodyguard. Henke was unemployed, strong, well trained and recommended by Berlin acquaintances. And she had an illegitimate son and needed a husband to stop all the gossip about the presumed father.

"How come you know all that?"

Lang laughed. "I told you, we're better than the boys with two left eyes. Nobody wants to use our information. We'll see, maybe that will change now."

"Because of the Republicans voted on to the council? Has the far right been joining the Republicans yet?"

"Not yet, as far as we know, at least they aren't in any official positions."

"So, small fry. Why are you so interested in them?"

The condescending tone returned to Lang's voice, robbing it of any erotic quality. "Because one can never be sure that these small fry will not one day turn into big fry."

"Did you come by car?" Marek Zadko had an idea how to get the woman out of the apartment at last. Kitty nodded.

"Which way are you heading?"

She thought about going home, which was virtually around the corner, but decided at least to let Helga know about her find.

"Grosser Stern, that direction." Or was he planning a trick to get the box with Shishi's keepsakes off her again. She decided to continue stalling him with watchful friendliness. "You need a lift?"

"Where do you want to go?" Anna broke in.

"I want to be at the club at six. Soundcheck. But I could look in at Pagart before that. Instead of tomorrow morning. It's on U-Bahn line 9. Turm Strasse."

Kitty looked at him. Anna complained that she didn't want to stay in the apartment and then follow him to the club later. He didn't seem to want to have her around, which alarmed Kitty. But Anna simply decreed: "I'm coming with you!"

Zadko disappeared into the bathroom. Kitty sat down and held the box tightly on her lap. The first thing was to lock it in the boot. She watched as Anna took off Krisztina's robe. She was quite naked as she looked for her underwear among the covers on Krisztina's bed. Or had they been Shishi's too? She continued grumbling about musicians in general and about Polish jazz musicians in particular. "First time you meet them, they're gentlemen, the kind you don't find here any more. By the second time, they're patriarchs. Complete Neanderthals!"

Then she disappeared from the room. Kitty heard her banging on a door and complaining, because Zadko was spending too long in the bathroom. She looked slowly round the room. Shishi's room. It seemed strange without Shishi. Dead somehow. She thought about the last time she had sat here. Months ago. She had given her a lift home after a COW meeting. Shishi had clearly not wanted to be alone. So she came upstairs with her. And Shishi had told her that she was going to put four thousand marks into the office COW planned to open, and that she was willing to support it with at least five hundred every month.

"I'm not going to need it," she had said, when Kitty had advised her to spend the money on herself. Officially Kitty didn't know anything about Solidarność. "But office will need it. And COW needs office. Basta!"

Yeah, sure. And how. If only the girls from around here, and who will probably stay here, could see that! But they only moan about every penny they're asked to contribute. And tell you a long story, that because they're whores they have to pay a fortune for health insurance, but when you organise something for them, so that they only need to hand over a couple of notes a month, a little bit devious, but safe – then suddenly they become mean.

She was still thinking about that long after she had put the "family medicine cabinet" into the boot and was sitting at the wheel. Her head didn't catch up with her till Perleberger Strasse, when Marek Zadko asked her to stop so he could buy cigarettes.

"Can you bring me a pack too? And chewing gum," Anna yelled after him. "But not the kind that pulls out your fillings!"

She stretched and gave a satisfied sigh. Then she sprawled out over the back seat. "I've never seen a real whore. I mean, one who says so. Berlin is strange."

Kitty turned round and looked at her. "And what do you do?"

Anna worked as a typist and girl Friday for all kinds of companies. Listings magazines, concert agencies, occasionally a film distributor. That way she usually got in free to events and backstage as well. And had been on more than one tour. Or even home to listen to her current favourite. "I've already been to the south of France," she said proudly, "and soon we'll be able to go east. Budapest and so on."

Kitty was the first to notice that Zadko was taking a very long time to buy cigarettes and chewing gum at the shop around the corner.

"Oh shit! That asshole!" Anna shot up and drummed on the back of the seat. "He's done this twice already! But in Munich, and I know my way around there. The fucking asshole!"

Kitty was astonished. "Nobody'd try that trick more than once with me. Why does he do it?"

"How should I know. Maybe I'm not supposed to see his stupid Pagart people. Maybe he's doing some deal with them. Or they take advantage of him, and he doesn't want to look dumb in front of me. What do I care. He can lick my arse!"

Kitty thought for a moment. "You got a key?"

"Sure. They put in a lock this morning. I took one right away."

"So how about we go back and look for that notebook you talked about?"

Anna stared at her. "Sure, yeah, Great. I couldn't figure why he acted as if he hadn't seen it. He must have hidden it somewhere. Let's go. That'll teach him!"

Fillmore HP5 was the most widely used brand of black and white film. She turned over the little carton Fritz had found next to the Fahlenkamp marriage bed. Might as well forget about fingerprints.

"You can upgrade it up to 800 ASA without any problem, then admittedly the film . . ."

Lietze didn't have a clue about photography. She didn't understand why someone would need an especially light-sensitive film, in order – that was the assumption – to take pictures in the middle of the day in a south-facing room high above tree level. And there weren't even any trees in front of 17 Nollendorf Strasse.

". . . mostly sold to amateurs. Professionals, and we have many professional photographers among our customers," the young man from Fish Eye Photo continued, "hardly buy it. Because they use light quite differently . . ."

Before he could say any more about the subtleties of light and shade and how to produce them artificially, Lietze thanked him a little impatiently and hung up. Hartmut Fahlenkamp had only taken slides, and his merry widow Elvira would presumably deposit the entire end product at the nearest toxic waste dump at the first opportunity. If this carton had any connection with Fahlenkamp's murder – there were enough professional photographers in West Berlin, but if you made all the amateurs the target of an investigation as well, that would make finding a needle in the proverbial haystack look easy.

She threw the carton on the desk and looked at Herrmann. "What would your conclusion be?"

Herrmann lifted the notes from his crossed thighs and

straightened up. "A pervert? There are these porn films. Snuff..."

The phone rang. Lietze picked it up. "Thanks, Mimi... Lietze! What have you got?... By yourself?... Have you gone nuts?"

It was Kitty, and what she had to say didn't improve Lietze's mood. She glanced as casually as possible at Herrmann who was staring at her with curiosity, and was annoyed because she couldn't tell Kitty what she thought of her right away. "What kind of stuff is it?... Yes. Well, I still don't like it... But we'll talk about it later... Tomorrow morning's fine... Yes, I'll drop by."

She slammed down the receiver. Maybe the things would lead somewhere. Not the souvenirs. But maybe the notebook. She picked up the phone again. "Mimi – do we have a Polish interpreter?... Tomorrow... afternoon."

She got up and turned to Herrmann again. "To come back to your suspicion. Snuff porn is, as far as I know, extremely violent. And there was not a trace of violence with this third murder either. What do you make of that?"

Herrmann had also got up and he waved his notes around awkwardly. "Even more perverted!"

"Shall we go?" Lietze glanced at the notes. "Oh yes, how many did you say you've got? Six people? Good. And all of them made statements? You tell me about it while we're driving."

While Herrmann got his jacket, she went to Mimi Jacob's office. She looked at the clock. "Mimi, don't you want to call it a day?"

Mimi shook her head and continued looking at her typewriter.

"Mimi – it's after five! We can use Roboldt as our switchboard. Fritz is going over there anyway when he's done at the Ruin, and all you have to do is call Schade and tell her."

Mimi's voice was strange too. Not a nasty sweet poison,

still less a bath oil. Leaden rather. Something that would immediately clog up every pore if it was poured into your bath. She only seemed interested in whether Lietze and Herrmann were going to take Lietze's car and how long they planned to take at Krisztina Kędzierska's last but one address.

Szczłacz! He turned over the rolled-up newspaper. The black fly was squashed flat in the middle of a brown and red spot. He screwed up his eyes. The outline of the fly dissolved into an image of a pale young woman, dressed from head to foot in black leather, and staring at him challengingly. He opened his eyes wide again, smacked the newspaper against the wall once more and dropped it. Then he reached out to the toilet roll and tore sheets off. He was fed up to the back teeth with this city. And then some. It was cold, not even the muggy heat could change that.

He stood up, pulled up his pants and pushed the button. Hostile. Heartless, all of them. Still. Long blonde hair, like an angel – and? A face of stone. Nothing could move her. That's not a woman! He wanted to leave. Go back. Leave this country where a whore could threaten him. Him. A decent man. A man who had busted his ass for the last nine years. Who had risked life and limb for a great cause. For a free Poland!

And she just stood there in front of him, without any respect at all, and threatened him. Brettzinski! She couldn't even pronounce his name properly. Brettzinski. Hard. Cold. German. He climbed up the half flight of stairs and cursed the stuffy air in the stairwell making him sweat from every pore. He had been against it right from the start. A woman can smuggle messages, deliver illegal material, be the contact person for clandestine meetings, that's okay. Illegality demands unusual measures. But obtaining money is a man's

job. Much too dangerous. Much too important. Not something for women. And especially not for whores.

He pulled the yellow brass lion's head violently three
times. He had always said that there'd be trouble. Who else
knew about it? The two sluts who had just been, and the
two who'd been here yesterday. A whole troop of whores.

The door opened, but the petite woman with the pinned
up blonde hair didn't say a word to him and went straight
back into the kitchen. They had fucked up that idea too!
Ewa couldn't go to that whorehouse now. They'd seen her.
But it didn't matter any more. Who could guess what connections they had. But not with the police. That's obvious.
Women like that don't talk to the police. But maybe to the
newspapers. Another one of those whore professions! At
least here. In the golden West. You scratch my dirty back
and I'll scratch yours. If you let me have a scoop, then –
nice work! Especially now, with the papers pouncing on the
Polish flea market like starved vultures . . .

And who could tell what they really had! If they really
had been close friends of Krisztina, and if Krisztina really had
something, then she must have hidden it with them. No
wonder he hadn't found anything at the musician's place!

Or what else could that blonde bitch have meant? What
was that supposed to mean: We can be unpleasant, Brettzinski, if you stop us from organising a decent funeral for
Shishi . . .

Perhaps they want to steal the corpse from the pathology
lab? He had to talk to the others quickly. It didn't look good.

The three ladies sitting at pale grey desks in front of beige
computers had suspected something immediately. Sonja
Schade had only to ask discreetly for the boss, and then, to
the distrustful response, what was it all about, mention the
words Serious Crimes Squad even more discreetly. The

oldest of the three, a plump brunette in an immaculate short-sleeved suit, had shrieked, "Is it about Fahli?" and had forgotten the customer in front of her desk.

The boss was "out at the moment", the young woman with the blue-green headband and the sweater tied around her hips had explained.

"He went to have a snack, because he'll be here at least until nine this evening. He has to deal with this month's accounts alone, because Fahli didn't turn up yesterday or today."

"And he didn't answer the phone either!" The third had come out from behind her desk, a young woman with shoulder-length red curls, wearing jeans, ballet shoes and wool socks. "We've been calling him all day. What's happened to him?"

"Fahli is usually so reliable," the one with the headband had added.

Schade had sat down on one of the little easy chairs, flipped through a travel catalogue and enjoyed the cool breeze which the huge fan on the ceiling wafted through her short brown hair and across her skin. The oldest of the women had turned back to her customer and red blotches still showed on her face and neck.

Elvira Fahlenkamp's relationship with her husband's colleagues really was far from intimate. She didn't seem to have informed them about his demise yet. Schade had made up for that, once the customer had left the Ikarus Travel Agency. At that the blotches of the brunette in the immaculate suit had spread all over, so that the few remaining pale spots appeared like blemishes on a dark red complexion and she had run into a back room and returned with a bottle of tequila.

"Nothing matters any more!"

"Oh boy, if the boss sees this!"

They agreed that it was always the wrong one who got it,

and all of them knew a whole crowd of people who deserved "such a fate", men above all.

"Fahli would have brought glasses too, not just the bottle," said the redhead with the wool socks.

Schade refused the tequila and gradually began to understand why the three were so warmly dressed. Now she was standing by the desks again and not directly under the fan, where the breeze is weakest. She felt goose pimples. She ticked off the routine questions. All three of them "loved to take pictures" – so they could give slide shows. Probably with sparkling wine and pretzel sticks, Schade thought. She began to understand Elvira Fahlenkamp better and better. "Any karate?" All three of them stared at her as if she had made an indecent proposal.

"Well, it doesn't have to be karate. Maybe a self-defence course? That's even taught at adult education classes nowadays." Schade rubbed her arms warm and looked each in turn firmly in the eye. The young woman with the headband blushed and admitted to having taken such a course.

"Last year. At that women's gym, 'Breathless', in Schöneberg," she stuttered. "But only for a while. The women there weren't my type. They're all supposed to be lesbians."

Schade suppressed a grin and merely raised the corners of her mouth a little pityingly. The young woman hadn't got very far in the course, not even as far as to be able to defend her own neck. She didn't have a clue about attack and didn't even know where a carotid artery was.

"Presumably you were all here yesterday, weren't you?" Schade concluded ill-humouredly. She was beginning to be afraid of catching a chill in her kidneys and felt the travel agency was a waste of time altogether. These three didn't know anything that was a help, and didn't miss the slightest opportunity to join in lamenting, and singing the praises of the deceased. She was looking at her watch just as the phone rang.

"It's for you," the oldest said to Schade and then to the others, "like on *Colombo*, isn't it?"

The door opened as Schade was listening to Mimi Jacob telling her what she had to know. A well-tanned man in his mid-forties entered. The two younger women immediately shot back behind their desks. The immaculately dressed one went over and talked to him. The bottle of tequila stood resplendent on the middle desk. The man wore a silk suit in the same pale grey as the furniture, a grey and blue striped silk shirt and electric blue tie and silk socks. "All that's missing is the blue nail polish," Schade thought and hung up.

She introduced herself. He looked at her disdainfully, told her that he had no time to spare, since due to, ah yes, Fahlenkamp's death, of which he had just been informed, he was up to his ears in accounts, and with a disapproving glance at the bottle, he swept into the back room. Schade picked up her bag from the small table with the catalogues and got the distinct impression that there was something in the by-now polar air. As she was about to follow the boss, she looked at the three women once more. Finally, the woman with the headband pulled herself together and, after checking with the others, whispered, "He was gone for a long time yesterday afternoon. He said he was going to be back here at two, but he didn't actually come back until a quarter to three. He claimed somebody drove into him."

The image of the black ski masks stretching down to cover necks as well and ending at naked shoulders, faded very, very gradually and with painful slowness. Hangman's masks. Masks of hate. Huge pricks with a red-rimmed slit for the eyes. And through the pane of milky glass behind which they disappeared, a big, white square with black and red patterns became visible. It moved. Now the right upper edge drooped. It billowed. The middle sagged. The square lost its shape. Then it was gone.

Thorsten forced his eyes open another fraction. A white-black-red pattern still trembled on the faded wallpaper. The flag lay on the edge of the brown corduroy couch. He saw two big hands pull it aside and he tried to follow them with his eyes. Immediately sand from somewhere crunched beneath his feet, and he started once again at a bare, crumbling wall with an enormous gaping black hole. Through the sand he heard voices. ". . . put it away . . . the tapes too . . . don't know if they're gonna come . . . everything's got to be clean . . ."

Two different voices. He had heard them somewhere before. He forced his heavy eyelids open once again, moved the pupils very slowly to the left, to where the big hands had disappeared in the sand.

". . . with him there, eh? . . . he's gotta go too . . ."

He couldn't tell if they were talking about him. They didn't look at him while they were folding up the big flag, and he had no idea if there was anyone else in the room besides them and him. He was afraid to move his head. The knives would start jabbing away again. The ski masks would hit him again. The car wouldn't budge again, the wheels were spinning round in the sand without gripping. In all the sand. But the voices became more distinct. He began to work out who was talking. The wiry smaller one talked more than the other one, built like a safe and wearing a black shirt.

"Sure, yeah, but we don't know if the cops are after him . . . he said something about fucking tarts . . ."

"Better safe than sorry!"

"We'll have to pump him again, before we put him out of the way . . . How much time've we got?"

The black safe tucked the rolled up flag and a box of video cassettes under his arm and went right out of the frame. "We've got to be there just before seven."

The other turned round and looked at the floor. At him. So they were talking about him! Thorsten felt a hot blade slice him right from his head down to his stomach.

"A good hour an' a half."

He heard the other voice from a distance, but only when it came closer, did he understand: ". . . we'll have him softened up by then."

Then something big and dark towered over him and he immediately closed his eyes. A kick in his side tore them open again. He lay on his side. Four hands were pulling at him, two faces floated right in front of him and sour waves of beer, smoke and sweat filled his nostrils. He felt sick again. They had leant his head and his back against something hard. His intestines were being squeezed. It was as if they were trying as hard as they could to escape through his mouth.

"Hey, man, open your eyes!"

He tried to obey. He looked straight into a pasty face with fuzz on it.

"Pull yourself together man! What kind of cops are after you?" Another face, darker, but with almost no neck or forehead entered the frame from above. Cops? Why cops? "Open yer gob, or else!"

He tried to talk, but couldn't even get his lips apart. Nausea rose again. Everything was so tight. As if someone were holding his stomach between two fingers and squeezing it out like toothpaste. His lips still wouldn't open. He was seized by panic. A choir boomed in his head, alternately chanting "Mama" and "Schleswig-Holstein."

"What kinda cunts were they! Go on, open your trap!" The face without neck or forehead came in close and filled the whole frame. The other voice came from farther away. ". . . what's that car doing! . . . all afternoon . . . now he's eating a curry sausage!"

The face disappeared from Thorsten's view and he heard

an indistinct mumbling again. He could only understand one word. It came from very close by. Mama. From his own mouth.

"Who the hell's going to see that! At least put a big sign at the bottom of the stairs!"

She blew a puff of air up over her face and tossed back her strawberry blonde curls. The owner of Sydney's stopped drying glasses and leaned across the bar. "There's a poster on the door . . ."

". . . and it's always open, so nobody sees that either!"

". . . there were announcements in the press, and word's going round the neighbourhood. But I've got no desire to have my place smashed up because of your pictures! Come on, have a glass of champagne!"

She gave her mane of hair an angry shake, then looked at him contemptuously. Asshole! Because of his cowardice, she had had to hang the photos in the gallery upstairs. Only at weekends, when all the tables downstairs were occupied by breakfasting tourists from West Germany, did anyone stray up there. And then only if it was too cold to sit outside. Or if it was raining. Why doesn't this fucking thunderstorm break! At seven exactly! she thought and realised she was wiggling around on the stool again.

"What a load of crap! If you're talking about the silly cows in the JoAnne Little Brigade – they've got it in for randy old fucks, not shops!"

"Wait and see. Yesterday afternoon they were at the *TAZ* office and demanded a full page. For a 'rebuttal' of what was written about them yesterday."

"So?" she asked absent-mindedly. What did all this tinkling mean? Why was the damned skin on her hips trembling, just where the violet jeans were tightest? And why was she wearing them anyway? She looked at the owner and her mouth twitched in disgust. Not him!

"They threatened that if it's not in today's paper, there'll be trouble. And it wasn't."

"Then what's your problem? They'll have their hands full tonight. Besides," she said, bored, "what have I got to do with those silly feminist aunties?"

"There are black ski masks in a couple of pictures." The owner put a glass of champagne in front of her.

She jumped up, and one bare foot stood on the steel tip of the violet high heel she'd kicked off next to the stool. She screamed. The few customers, who preferred to have their after-work drink inside rather than outside Sydney's, looked over with curiosity. "I wouldn't even put in a film for them. You know that damn well."

She ran barefoot through the bar, trying at the same time to adjust the skin-tight jeans and take something out of the pocket.

"Question is, do they know that too!" the owner exclaimed.

She put three coins in the slot and dialled. It took a while for Eddy to answer. Over short distances with lots of corners, wheelchairs take longer than healthy legs, and for three months Eddy had mostly been using a wheelchair to move around her tiny apartment high above the roofs of Schöneberg. She commented on the few things in this world which still seemed significant to her in grouchy good humour and with a slightly distant realism, happy not to have to come down to earth any more.

"It's not impossible they'll show up," Eddy answered laconically. "Revolutions need the right place, the right moment and the right opponent. And if you can't get the right opponent, you take out your revolutionary rage on the next best thing. Preferably on someone from whom you don't expect much resistance . . ."

"You're not trying to tell me they're revolutionaries! Eddy, really!"

"No. Not in my opinion. But they're convinced that they are."

"They're worse than the cops. They behave like the Mafia!" The jingling didn't stop. It pushed up from the tips of her toes and stiffened her spine.

"The Mafia started as a revolutionary movement too." There were sly, almost obscene undertones in Eddy's voice. "Look at it this way – if the JoAnne Little Brigade attacks your show, then it'll make a splash. The media won't miss a chance to report on women picking on other women. I'll keep my fingers crossed!"

There were at least hundreds or thousands again. She fanned some air under her t-shirt. The glass splinters started to oscillate more violently. Rubbed and rattled against each other. Increased in number. More concentrated. Sharper. It wasn't possible! Not so quickly. Or was it the storm giving notice after all?

She made the most of each step back to the bar. Thunderstorm. A cloudburst. Then Sydney's will be packed and people will go to the gallery. And after that an attack by the furies and it's on tv. And then I can ask three or four thousand for Budapest and Prague! She forced her feet into the violet high heels and reached for her bag. The owner watched her and went on wiping glasses. "You sure you don't want anything to drink?"

She ignored him, passed her free hand through her curls and looked up the stairs once more. "I'm going home now. If someone asks for me – I'll be back at six thirty."

Well, we'll see, he tried to keep his courage up. The name Brzeżinski was on the list of names inside the entrance of number 29. So there was a man too, and not just a woman as he had expected, because the envelopes he had found in Krisztina's "family medicine cabinet" were always addressed to Brzeżinska. A married couple maybe. But then why were they addressed to the woman? The letters were from Poland. Ah, there. The mail boxes. It said Brzeżinski there, too. Like to know how the postman handled that, he thought, hoping to distract himself from the bass lines improvising in his innards. I've seen these Germans go nuts because they don't understand that we can distinguish men from women by their surnames – and that they're still the one family! We! We! He made an angry gesture. Anyway I don't belong there any more. They can do what they like. I'm leaving! For America! At last I'll make a decent living from my music! And they'll get me the money. For the plane fare and the first few months. At least! America isn't cheap. Oh, no! They'll have to understand that. I'm not going to be fobbed off with a few złoty. The thing must be worth something. Otherwise she wouldn't have hidden it. Otherwise they wouldn't have turned her room upside down. It must be worth a lot. And now I've got it.

Maybe there really is just a Brzeżinska, and for some reason she's put Brzeżinski up everywhere! Determined, he pushed open the heavy door to the courtyard. Garden house 1, Right Staircase, the list at the entrance announced. He looked across the courtyard. Not a trace of a garden. Only paving, bikes, garbage containers, dirt and a cacophonous concert from every possible window. The house in the back also had a gateway. Maybe there were two rear houses, and what those dumb Germans called a garden house was just the second house to the back. Because there was a bush in a corner or something!

He climbed the stairs. The stairwell reeked of food and rotting garbage. Half way up he passed a door with a key-hole, but no handle. It smelled like a toilet too. On the first floor there was neither a Brzeżinski or a Brzeżinska on any of the four doors. So the other house after all. He went downstairs again. What did that guy look like? Dark blond, big, at least two or three inches taller than me. Lanky. Athletic. Right, the track suit.

He went through the second gateway again. And what do I say, when they ask why I'm looking for him? The bass lines started jolting his stomach nerves again. I can't tell her what it's about. I could pretend that I've got problems with the police and customs or something. Poor persecuted Pole. They picked me up at the Polish market and took everything off me. And now I need legal help to get my things back. I don't speak a word of German. I met the guy – where then? Feeling jumpy, he pulled open the door to the first courtyard and at the same moment saw a tall, lanky man with dark blond hair pull open the door to the street. Something icy cut through the jolting bass lines. He stepped back into the passageway. That's him! He lives here! Brzeżinski! He stood in the gateway for a moment. Once the front door had closed behind the other man, he followed.

"He saw a cab, Detlev, do you understand? It could have been that Mercedes!" Lothar Fritz had talked himself into more of a state than was advisable considering the heat, which even at half past five was still weighing on Roboldt's east-facing balcony. "It took me three-quarters of an hour to drag it out of those stoned little innocents!"

In his bathrobe, a shawl and wool socks, Detlev Roboldt sat on a folding chair and forced himself to drink hot, steaming tea. He showed barely any resemblance to the elegant, good-looking man in the prime of life who, under normal circumstances, did his duty – as it were – as second in command of D III. His black hair stuck to his wet skin shining greasily, his face was red as a lobster, his nose peeling and sore, his eyes cloudy and almost swollen shut.

His whole body was covered by a film of sweat, and every five minutes Roboldt surreptitiously put his nose beneath the collar of his bathrobe and sniffed. "Do you think it means anything?"

"Who knows," Fritz grumbled. "The idiot who found the body and was told to keep his mouth shut, didn't keep it shut of course. He blabbed to his mates at the Ruin. Thank God, he did, because on Saturday night, or rather Sunday morning at five or five thirty one of them comes out of the pub and, dead drunk or doped up or whatever, sits down on the nearest bench, and sees a taxi backing out of the entry."

"Yes – and? Licence plate? People? What did he see?"

"Nothing. He closed his eyes again and fell asleep. It was too bright, he said. His eyes were stinging. You know what, there's a jinx on this whole thing! Where are you going? Detlev!"

Roboldt had jumped up and disappeared into the apartment. Fritz found him in the bathroom, just as he had thrown off his bathrobe and was shoving his hands into the waistband of his boxer shorts. "There's nothing wrong with me!"

The palm tree in the white pot by the wall opposite the shower shook wildly as Fritz lunged at Roboldt to grab him by the collar, and because at the last moment he realised that Roboldt was naked apart from his underpants and wool socks, he picked the bathrobe up off the floor. "Put this on again so I've got something to hold on to! You've got a temperature, you're sick, and the one thing you mustn't do is work!"

He waved the bathrobe in front of him. Roboldt finally took his hands off his boxer shorts and took it. If he was honest, it felt good to put it back on, because ice cold shivers were running down his wet back. He caught sight of himself in the mirror and what it reflected made him sit down listlessly on the toilet seat. With a face like that he would at most scare his mother, but not a murderer – male or female.

"I beed workid' adyway," he said defiantly, after he had crawled back under the covers with a thermometer in his mouth. Fritz had sat down on a chair next to the bed. Roboldt avoided looking him in the eye and stared obstinately at the opposite wall. The poster of the wrapped Reichstag no longer reminded him of a bed of pleasure. It looked more like a sweaty, rumpled sickbed. "Did 'i dow dat a 'ear ago tree udder men were kilt? Inda same way!"

"What?" Fritz stopped leafing through his notepad. In reply there was an electronic bleep from Roboldt's mouth.

Roboldt removed the thermometer. "Barely over a hundred. That's not a temperature!"

"You stay put!" Fritz decreed. "What's this about the three other men who were murdered?"

At some point between bouts of fever and reading, Roboldt had recalled that the previous summer a scare had gone round the gay scene. In quick succession two men had been found dead in bed, after sex, and they had been killed by a karate chop. They were both bisexual and only marginal figures on the gay scene. "But of course those dud colleagues of ours only investigated the hustlers! And the possibility that those two murders could have had anything to do with one a few weeks before never even crossed their minds. Because that victim wasn't bi!"

"And why doesn't anybody tell us? Why do we have all these meetings?"

"I'd like to know that too. I had to make endless phone calls to get all that information together. Anyway, it looks now as if we're dealing not with number three, but with number six." Roboldt put an especially triumphant emphasis on the little word "we".

"And if it goes on like this," Fritz growled, "we're just

waiting for number seven!" Then he went back to his notes and gave Roboldt a full report on Fahlenkamp.

The phone rang. Roboldt grabbed the receiver. It was Sonja calling from the travel agency, wanting to know where they would hold their next briefing.

"Just come over here first, and then we'll wait for Lietze together. And bring some cake!" Roboldt put down the phone. "I'm supposed to ask you about a book."

"Yes, yes, all in good time," Fritz said, wiping his forehead with the back of his hand. "I think I've told you everything. What do you make of it?"

"A scum bag!"

"Who – Henke?"

"No, Fahlenkamp."

"Very enlightening, thank you." Fritz got up and went into the hallway.

"Did you know that he expired in a famous building?" Roboldt shouted after him. "Christopher Isherwood lived there!"

Fritz returned with a book with a brown and yellow cover. "Who?"

"Did you see the movie *Cabaret*?"

Fritz gave him an irritated look. "Detlev, really. I don't have time for your . . ."

"Do you remember Fräulein von Schröder? The landlady? Check whether she's still around."

"Tell me, have the bacteria got into your brain? A minute ago you wanted to get up and now you're talking enough crap to get you put in a straitjacket. Take a look at this book."

Roboldt took the book, but didn't give it a glance. "Seriously, Lothar. You'll find old ladies like that in apartment blocks like that. Even today. And if you find one, then you could have an eye-witness."

Annoyed, Fritz stared at the beaming face of Roboldt,

who ostentatiously looked through the book. "According to Henke everyone is out of the house all day. Except for a young woman who's a translator and works at home. But she's on holiday. And a woman who runs a newspaper shop on Maassen Strasse."

"Just around the corner. Then I'd have a word with her."

"But she isn't home during the day either!"

"Wrong. The shop is closed at lunch time. And she is a sweet old lady, my dear." Roboldt had stopped beaming. "Lothar," he said finally, "it was a woman who marked up this book. Look – she underlined whole paragraphs. And notes in the margins. A man wouldn't write this, and a man would hardly use a violet felt-tip."

"What about a transsexual," Fritz countered, without believing it himself. "If he identifies completely with women and hates the sex he was born with . . ."

"Nonsense," Roboldt cut him off. "I know the book. That is, not the book. But the film. It's a mad film . . ."

Fritz only half listened. What did an obviously unfulfilled, masochistic woman from New York, who went to Mexico, picked up macho types and got herself killed by one of them, have to do with the job he had to get on with! The situation here was something completely different. These guys weren't machos at all, but more likely the real masochists. Just like him! It was sheer masochism to let Beate and the girls go on holiday! Just at a moment when he desperately needed every word of comfort because everything was a muddle at work. The steaming heat alone made it impossible to get a grip on anything!

". . . you understand Lothar, she was an aesthete. Turn my life into a masterpiece, she says near the end, I just didn't know yet, what with. Or something like it."

Fritz sighed. "We're light years away from that. Masterpiece!"

"And what if our murderess is someone who is following precisely the opposite course with equal vigour? That is, not the masochistic, but the sadistic one?"

"Detlev, you are delirious!" Fritz snapped. "Or is this gay fantasy? There are no such women!"

"That's what people said about Maryse Holder. Women especially," Roboldt grinned. "Promiscuity is unfeminine, and so on, and so on."

"It's not true—" Fritz didn't have the slightest desire to go on discussing something which only reminded him of his own current misery.

"Exactly!"

"But to pick up total strangers and kill them afterwards, that's *not* something that women have on the agenda as far as I know, not even the most man-eating femmes fatales, Detlev!"

"Not so far," grinned Roboldt, even more doggedly.

He hadn't noticed the man following him at a distance of ten or twenty yards since he left the house. He was so lost in half outraged, half worried thoughts, that, as he descended the steps to the platforms at Eisenacher Strasse underground station, he ran into someone, and only realised it a moment later. It must have been a woman, because suddenly a female voice yelled at him. "Hey! Watch where you're goin', asshole!"

Then several women were yelling. He caught bits and pieces. "Typical man . . . stare at 'cha like idiots or don't look at all . . . jist like they drive, like th' street belongs to 'em . . . assholes . . . blind bastards . . ."

He looked behind him to the right, where the voices were coming from. Three young women looking a bit like punks stared at him aggressively. Suddenly he felt scared and weak at the knees and was happy to have the solid platform under his feet rather than the stairs. One of them was wearing black leather trousers and the other two weren't dressed in a way he considered appropriate for a woman either. And they were slovenly. Short straggly hair, greasy clothes.

"... that type, don't let them get away with it ... no messing ... he looks like ..."

Was it them? Was this what those dirty whores meant by getting unpleasant? It wasn't pimps they had been talking about? But these women here? I'll show them. He turned round abruptly, looked at each one of them and gave them a mouthful of abuse and threats. In Polish. He turned away, straightened up and walked off. They'll understand that perfectly! But he didn't even get as far as thinking about the next threat. Before he could swing round, two of them had grabbed his arms and pulled him around, then he was lying on the platform, rolled up like a hedgehog to avoid being kicked in his private parts. And then he didn't see anything any more, but only heard voices, yelling and hissing at him. Thoughts raced through his brain. She had sent them. The bitch. Who are they? Pay attention to names. Remember. Remember everything.

Soon the voices stopped. From somewhere else, which must be close by on the platform, he heard other voices now. Men's voices. "... typical ... I've told you ... they should go back where they come from ... Polish market ... you only need to see ..." And older women's voices.

He didn't dare open his eyes. He hoped the train would come quickly. Then they would all be gone. Did he look like that boy in front of the whorehouse last night? He tried to stay calm. But he felt as if he had suddenly been changed into one of those SEAT engines he used to assemble, and was dangling from an overhead belt speeding through the plant at 120 miles an hour. When he heard someone say something in Polish, he knew there must really be such a thing as hallucinations.

*

"Yes yes yes yes yes, my queen. Just a second, then you can get back up. Yes yes yes." Purring loudly and giving a perfect imitation of a dog's trusting gaze, Blondie weaved around his arms, and again and again nudged his right wrist with her long-whiskered cheeks. "But you can't do that, my angel! Na! You can't jump up on it like that! Look. They're all messed up. Blondie, Blondie, Blondie. Yes yes yes. Sit down properly."

Alfred Henke clicked the box shut again. "So, everything sorted nicely again. And complete." Except for the two – na! She's got them. He pushed the box carefully into the corner between the wall and the tool cupboard. Mata. And if it was her yesterday after all? How on earth. Mata wouldn't do such a thing. She's honest. Quite different from Erika. Honest and upright. And that brat. What had he done to get the police on his heels. No no! They were here because of Fahlenkamp. Like to know what she's doing now. I bet she's got someone else. What on earth. Always away. That's no marriage!

"That's nice, Blondie. Lie down nicely. Yes yes yes!" He stroked the soft, orange striped fur between her ears. Mata as well. She always has to be away. But she doesn't have anyone . . . I know why she has to go there! She wants me. She said so.

He looked at Blondie once again and the box, then left the workshop. "Stay nice and quiet." In the hallway he stumbled over a pair of trainers. There was a crunching underfoot. Cursing, his face blue and red, he fetched a brush and dust pan and swept up grains of sand. The whole left side of his chin was throbbing by the time he got to the toilet and dropped down on to the seat. He shot up immediately. In the mirror opposite the lavatory bowl he noticed that his chin was starting to turn greenish. "And there's going to be a stop to that as well! It's downright – unnatural! To piss sitting. Where on earth? Just because it's beneath her to clean the toilet properly. But she'll have to go. She's not coming back in here again!"

He stood close up to the mirror and pissed into the wash basin. His chin seemed to have developed an odd slant as well. Just wait! He grabbed the hand mirror and looked at the back of his head. That damn brat! Why had he been shitting his pants? They're after me, he said. What on earth had he got up to? It'll be at least a week before it grows out again! Angry, he slammed the mirror back on the window-sill. Good thing that Mata's away until then. What if she hasn't really left? If that really was her yesterday afternoon? With a blonde wig. Visiting somebody. In his house? Of all places? What on earth. Who could it be? He looked straight into his own eyes. He had to go there. He would go there! This evening. You owe it to yourself Alfred! "Na!"

"How long did you say she lived here?" Lietze looked attentively at the petite woman with the loosely pinned-up hair who sat on the couch.

"Two years," Ewa Brzeżinska said. "A bit more."

"And yet you know so little about her? About what she did, about her friends, her girlfriends?"

"Krisztina was very – how can I say this: secretive. I don't think she had a real girlfriend. Besides me."

She really didn't seem to know. Krisztina Kędżierska must have carried on her COW activities very conspiratorially. Lietze thought a bit. Then she glanced at Herrmann who sat there on an easy chair, legs apart and a condescending look on his face. She decided not to mention COW.

"No, no boyfriends either," Ewa Brzezinska continued. "Just our people. But since January, you know . . ."

"Yes, I know. Why did she – fall out with everyone?" Lietze pulled the pack of Lucky Lucianos out of her bag and gave Ewa Brzeżinska a questioning look.

"Tak tak, you can smoke. Oh, cigars! No, no, not for me. Thank you very much. Krisztina was politically, how can I say this, enthusiastic. She didn't just want to distribute leaflets and raise money. She wanted to what do you call it, participate in the decisions." There was pain in her eyes as she looked at Lietze. "You know, our men don't like that."

Lietze inhaled deeply. "Neither do ours. But then there must have been a row about the – money. I'm trying to imagine what it's like, if a woman uses the money she earns as a prostitute . . ."

"What do you want," Ewa Brzeżinska interrupted with unexpected liveliness, "would you prefer the money went to Mossad? Or KGB? or Stasi? Or BND? Or CIA? Or – how do you say – every Harry, every Dick?" She leaned back with a sigh and dabbed her forehead. "Your women's movement has also taken contributions from prostitutes."

"Try telling them about it," Lietze smiled and regretted for the umpteenth time that she hadn't come to Belziger Strasse alone. "Our women's movement, it doesn't like to hear that."

"Nobody forced Krisztina, because nobody could force Krisztina. Nobody."

"I believe it. But I had something else in mind when I asked the question. I wanted to know if your men weren't really annoyed because all of a sudden there was no more money coming in."

Ewa Brzeżinska's eyes were melancholy as she considered that question. Or perhaps resigned? "Andrzej was opposed from the beginning. And others as well. But they needed the money, before. They were afraid someone would find out. And then – bad reputation. Rumours."

"Is that the reason someone broke into Krisztina's new apartment and searched her room?" Lietze watched the petite woman as closely as the fading light in the small, narrow back house apartment would allow.

Ewa Brzeżinska didn't seem surprised by the question.

She shrugged, lowered her eyes and after a pause looked first at Herrmann and then back to Lietze. "Who can understand all this," she said finally. "Some others showed up here before and they wanted something. Just like that. Because they think it's their right."

Lietze was stopped short. Who did she mean? Had COW interfered in her work here too, not just with Zadko? "Women?" she asked sharply.

Ewa Brzeżinska nodded wearily. "Yes yes. One was from Krisztina's club. The other – I don't know. Still quite young." Minou! And Kim! That means trouble for you tomorrow morning, girls. That wasn't part of the deal. As much as I love you! She shot an angry glance at Herrmann, whose eyes were wandering around the room, as if he was trying to commit everything to memory, and as he realised that she was looking at him, put on an innocent ever-alert look. She got up. She would come back tomorrow on her own. She rummaged in her bag and pulled out a purse. "May I make a call?"

Ewa Brzeżinska laughed. "Dobrze, dobrze. No money! It's in the hall."

A good quarter of an hour later, Roland Herrmann was sprinting across the parking lot behind the building at 30 Keith Strasse. He panted rhythmically. Toughens you up, he thought. In this heat. Better than the underground anyway. Changing lines and everything. He'd had to sit around long enough at that Polack's place.

He looked at his watch as he headed for the white Porsche, one of the few cars left there. Five past six. Hot wheels. He patted the Porsche's roof approvingly and unlocked the door. Looks great next to all these family cars. He didn't waste time looking at them. Nor did he notice that someone was sitting in one of those cars and watching him.

He fell into the upholstery. Home first. Shower. Change his clothes. They won't start before a quarter to seven anyway. The old lady could easily have given him a ride back here. That's what they'd agreed. But with the car she's driving! Well, he had something he could hang on her. Full blast! He clicked his tongue and grabbed the notepad from the glove compartment. And the whole gang of them as well. His buddies would be pleased. He scribbled quickly. What a crew. Brzeżinski. Have to see if one of our people knows them. Doesn't seem to be small fry, from what she said. Maybe we've got some dirty stuff there. Financing themselves with whores' money. Paragraph 181a! Pimping – isn't it? Well, it'll be a big hit. If only the old lady hadn't changed the subject every time it got interesting.

He threw the notepad on to the passenger seat, started the engine and granted himself an admiring glance in the rear view mirror. His face was still shiny, but it was no longer tomato-red, just tanned. He was full of pride. King Rocky rode out of the courtyard. Full speed in reverse and then a racing start. As he sped north, all that was missing was the sunset. But the sun was still blinding. And King Rocky didn't see a green Golf leave the police parking lot just behind him.

Ah, nice. The lukewarm stream from Roboldt's shower drummed on Lietze's head and splashed down her face and body, flushing the heat and stress from her pores. She let the water run and merely swung her head and arms slowly back and forward. Gradually her thoughts started to flow again too. Stark naked in a strange apartment with a man in the next room. All very intimate. If it goes on like this, everyone in D III will soon be calling me by my first name!

She reached for a square black plastic bottle. *Jil Sander Man Two*. He's still using it. Quite conservative our Roboldt.

His tastes are probably as simple as Oscar Wilde's. She took a squirt of shower gel and spread it over her hair and skin. You shouldn't have snapped at them like that. They really haven't deserved it. Using them to vent your frustrations. Schade in Fahlenkamp's travel agency – what did you expect! That they'd pull open a drawer and there would be the character who had delivered the karate chop to Herr-Second-in-Command's artery? And to those other gentlemen, Seifert and Neiss as well? And – for God's sake! – the other three too. Roboldt, he ... He just gets on the phone and immediately he's on the trail of a juicy scandal. Why didn't anybody tell us about those three corpses last year? We had briefings with them often enough ... Bisexual. If Roboldt ...

Shit, damn it! Why is this stuff stinging my eyes? Anyway, tomorrow the girls from COW will get a rocket. First thing tomorrow morning. Do you really want to tour the lesbian bars with Schade tonight? What else is in Krisztina Kędżierska's box? And if there's nothing in the notebook? Maybe she was just keeping a diary about her johns. I hope Kitty takes good care of it. Can it just be given to a translator, to a complete stranger to read? What if it's sensitive stuff about Solidarność? Maybe Krisztina Kędżierska wanted to blackmail them with it? That would at least be a motive for killing her and getting it off her. But they didn't get it off her. Zadko "found" it. He's more the blackmailing type. That's what Fritz thinks. And why does he pull a disappearing act? And where to? Fritz must go to that club where Zadko's playing tonight. If he is playing and hasn't already ... Well. Who'd want to kill him. He's so clumsy, it was child's play to get the notebook away from him. Wait a minute, wait a minute. You're turning Solidarność into a mafia gang. Murder Inc. They didn't kill her. Otherwise in Belziger Strasse my nose would have ... Well, we were going to forget about it. They aren't going to stamp a Nazi P on the forehead of a Polish woman! What on earth! For God's sake, now you're starting to talk like that Nazi block warden. On the other hand – it would be the perfect cover. But they couldn't have known anything about the guy's method. Method! At most about the first murder. That was in the media. Rubbish. Tomorrow ask Ewa Brzeżinska if she knows about the case, just to make sure. The black woman. At the end of April. Hopefully her husband will be at home then too.

Hharooash, hhroosh, hhrash, hrooash! Shit! Has Roboldt given you his germs? She turned off the water and picked up the towel, stepped out of the shower dripping wet and fished for the toilet paper roll. Now her nose was starting to itch! She dried herself and rubbed her short blonde hair in front of the mirror. Sure. You do look as if you've had a good break. She pulled the other shirt she had bought that afternoon out of the bag. Maybe they should keep an eye on Elvira Fahlenkamp. Or not? Maybe drop by there tomorrow, after seeing Henke. We have to take a closer look at him. And ask his wife some questions. A caretaker's wife always knows a little bit more. Like, where the son's hiding.

She groaned. No – let's not muddle everything up again! The JoAnne Little Brigade has to wait. She picked up a roll-on deodorant. First things – right. In dubio pro deo! First the old lady from the newspaper shop, whom Roboldt likes so much. If she goes home for lunch, she might have seen something. If she wasn't sleeping!

Roboldt wasn't sleeping when, fresh for five minutes anyway, she knocked on his bedroom door. He was stretched out under the covers, and only two feet and a face the colour of a fire engine were visible.

"I'm leaving now, Roboldt."

"Okay, boss!"

"That's all right. There is something I meant to ask you, Roboldt. What do you think of Herrmann's idea that some perverted pornographer is behind these murders?"

"Nothing at all." Roboldt, along with his blankets, shot

abruptly up from the horizontal and leaned against the wall. "Because I think nothing at all of Herrmann. He really . . ."

". . . pisses you off. You can say it. Me too. But even a blind man can sometimes . . ."

"Not him. He's worse than blind. Everything you've said about him would drive even the sickest man from his . . ."

"You'll stay in bed. Is that clear?"

There was a glint in Roboldt's eye as he said submissively, "Well, okay. But I'm allowed to make phone calls, aren't I? Where did you say Rambo was before?" He sounded a bit too submissive.

Deepest Wedding, Mimi Jacob sighed. For the last three-quarters of an hour she had been sitting in the passenger seat, pretending to wait for the driver. She was really proud of having thought up this camouflage. From time to time she looked demonstratively at the house opposite the one into which Herrmann had disappeared. It had been difficult to keep up with him on the city motorway. She had naively believed that speed limits would also apply to Roland "Rocky" Herrmann, and her Golf was no match for the Porsche.

It had been pure luck. A pile-up on the stretch between the exits for Tegel Airport and Wedding. She caught up with him there. If they're going to meet in Dahlem, she thought, and felt a quiet shiver again, then mazel tov! I want to know where he's going! I have to tell Karin. Everything. And the reason I was so bad-tempered before!

She jumped when the front door opened and Herrmann stepped into the street. She automatically reached for the key in the ignition. But – where's he going? He had parked his Porsche back there!

He came straight towards her. Smartly dressed in a shirt and tie, a jacket over his shoulders and his eyes hidden by sunglasses. Impossible to tell if he recognised her. But it wasn't very likely. The green Golf was on the other side of the street, she wasn't at the wheel and he didn't turn his head in her direction. But he could have looked without moving his head. Why is he wearing such dark glasses? Does he want to avoid being recognised?

She didn't dare turn around as he was level with her car. She sat there as if frozen to the seat and stared straight ahead. Until he had vanished from her line of vision. Then she waited another ten seconds. When she felt that feet, backside and head were gradually thawing, and still nothing happened, she turned her head very, very slowly. He was still swaggering down the street. So he hadn't seen her?

As soon as he had disappeared around the next corner, she got out and followed him. Pull yourself together, Mimi, she tried to encourage herself. This isn't the Six Day War. He's just a little Nazi – but still! That was exactly it. It was the word. That word. And everything that was indissolubly bound up with it. This annihilating . . . Go back. No. Keep on. Find out where he's going, look at the people. This is 1989!

"Did the old bag say she was leavin' right away?"

The small wiry one nodded.

"So how come she isn't here yet? Man, we're gonna be late. It's like almost seven, an' we've got to go all the way up north!"

"The car with the guy and his curry sausage. It's still gone?"

"Yeah yeah," growled the beefy one, who was now dressed all in black and standing behind the curtains. "C'mon, we'll get him downstairs. He's going to take twice as long as normal."

They grabbed Thorsten Vogel under the arms and pulled him up.

"We'll have to carry him," said the wiry one. "No way can he manage the stairs on his own."

"Shit! In this heat!"

It took seven minutes for the two of them to drag him upright down the stairs. As the wiry one leaned Thorsten against the wall just behind the front door and looked out at the street, the beige Mercedes cab was just pulling up to double park.

A man of about thirty, dressed in jeans and a t-shirt, who had for a short while been at a fast-food stand one house down, threw a beer can into the garbage bin, waved an exaggerated goodbye and swayed over to a blue Ford Capri.

"All clear. Let's get him away," said the wiry one.

Why in the evenings? She paced back and forward in front of the bar. But it wasn't nerves. It was the glass splinters. Still rubbing against each other. Sydney's was still empty. The editor sat on a bar stool and followed her movements like a game of ping-pong. She knew it. He can't take his eyes off me. A good surface offers a lot of starting points. He's been staring like that since he looked at my pictures. That did it. He didn't think I was capable of that. Wanker. You think I would be as one-dimensional as you! *I've penetrated the male attitude* . . . You stare at my ass and the way I walk. And that, and your surprise as you looked at my pictures, will give me the second thousand. So that I cross the border for you and bring back pictures for you. Pictures that are different. With which you can make your mark. You and your fucking paper.

"Eva-Ma . . ." he said, as she passed close to him again.

"Forget the name. She doesn't exist any more!" She laughed provocatively in his face. And get used to the new prices. Two grand. Your risk. Why I want to go is none of your business. None at all. *Penetrate the male attitude.* Is that why my skin is tinkling? Because of the chance to get right into it. Deep into those secrets of double crosses and state security. Good citizens dressed in chamois and grey, leading secret lives. Uniforms and military barracks down to the marrow. Over there. Where it's worth it. That's exactly where to find one. Why just one! One every day. An endless series of candidates. And in broad daylight. Not in the evening. I need the night to myself! Why is it tinkling? Damn it, why now? Why can't I stop pacing up and down and listening for the tak-tak and the scraaatch on this plastic floor. Nothing happens. It has to be stone.

The editor went on about her pictures. ". . . to put 'things, things' next to a portrait, that's daring. Although – photography of course has created a chronically voyeuristic relationship to the world, which levels the meaning of all events. To that extent, of course, you can label people 'things, things'. It's breaking a taboo, in a way."

Plong-plong-plong-plong-roosh. "I'm never really implicated. Maybe it's in the nature of being a photographer." She looked at him in amusement and tossed her head back. Close the deal. The show's about to start. Offer me the two grand! At least. My risk is frustration. A gigantic frustration. You don't know a thing about that! These glass splinters, these nerve endings on my ass, on my hip bones, inside my thighs – and these damn stretch pants which don't give. You don't know a thing about the power of these glass splinters. The pants stick. I should have kept on the jeans.

"A disavowal of empathy, a disdain for message-mongering, a claim to be invisible – these are strategies endorsed by most professional photographers."

"You've stolen that from Susan Sontag too." Plong-plong. Sarcastic.

"Well done!" he exclaimed enthusiastically. "And where

did you get the captions for your pictures? Richard
Avedon . . ."

Very good, you idiot. And Arbus and Sontag and Holder
and . . . come on out with it, you coward, take the risk!

"Well, to cut things short, I want you to go there. Tomorrow morning. I don't give a fuck about the expense. But I
want pictures like that!" His face was a perfect expression
of humility. He couldn't offer her his throat, because he had
to crane his neck to watch her. "Even if I have to put my
own head on the line!"

His glance suggested that he would find it a pleasure.

The first person she saw was Kim. And that was not because
of the abrupt shift from glaring sunlight into the dim light of
a relatively closed room. Her first reaction whenever she
entered a room with more than one or two people in it was
always blindness. But because Kim was standing right next
to the door.

"Hi, Mieze!"

There was immediate applause. Lietze opened her eyes
wide, even though the ten seconds she always needed until
people sorted themselves out in space and time weren't up
yet, and stared at Kim in disbelief. The clapping faded and
people started moving towards a staircase at the back of
Sydney's.

"What're you doin' here? Do I have to pull another pack
of protectors outa the machine for you?" There were a
lot of women and probably even more men who would have
responded to Kim's dreamy gaze with instant meltdown.
Lietze wasn't one of them. At least not right now. "How
come you're looking so mean? Oh yeah, this is Ginette –
don't worry, she's one of us."

Out of politeness, Lietze looked briefly at the woman with
the soft, blonde curls and the heavy but perfectly made-up

face, nodded and then fixed her eyes on Kim again. She wondered if she should give her hell right now or first of all attend to the purpose of the visit to this café.

"Like, Ginette's in some of the photos too. You're kinda late, so you missed th' introduction. Now you've got to wait till upstairs clears out again."

"I've got a meeting here," Lietze finally said coldly. "Work!"

Kim whistled softly through her teeth. "One guy, good family man type, the kind who'd have to go behind his own back before he went to a hooker, an' she looks like she works on a construction site? Sitting upstairs. In the gallery."

Lietze was startled. She would never have described Schade that way. But it was true. Sonja Schade was quite a power pack. She hardly ever hesitated if there was a chance to get stuck in. Not even with the coffee ma . . .

"I figured right away they looked like slime!" Kim bubbled on. "Your people? Are they okay?"

"Not words they'll appreciate," Lietze growled and pushed into the crowd. This was the place we picked, to have a quiet corner to ourselves!

"Nobody could've guessed there'd be some culture vulture thing going on here of all places," Schade apologised, after Lietze had finally forced her way through to the table in the furthest away bay on the right hand side of the gallery.

Fritz fanned himself with a menu and watched the almost two dozen people of both sexes, but dressed in one and the same style, filing past a row of frames, looking alternately at the pictures and a young woman dressed entirely in black with long, loose strawberry blonde curls. "That's the artist," he explained.

"Really," said Lietze tersely and squeezed into a tiny chair. Did her eyes deceive her, or was Fritz trying to hide his honest married life behind his own back.

*

A draught isn't exactly healthy either! Roboldt thought, switching off the electric razor. And it doesn't do any good anyway. The apartment is still too hot and my scalp is damp again. And I just blowdried my hair!

The phone rang. He ran into the bedroom, picked up the receiver and fell back exhausted on his bed. "Mimi?"

She never called him outside office hours. Her voice sounded strange too. Not soft and melodious at all. More as if Mimi was trying to pull herself together in order to sound impassive. Presenting information without interference.

". . . I only recognised two. The idiot who used to be with public transport and the pimply Hering guy who changed over from the Young CDU. They were in all the papers. Also a bunch of skinheads in black and with boots and lots of tattoos."

"Where are you now?"

"In a phone booth around the corner. Give me some advice on how to get in there. There are bouncers checking everybody. They let him through right away."

"Do you have your car? – Good. Then go home immediately!" Roboldt felt goose pimples spreading all over his body. He was still lying in the draught.

"Detlev, I have to find out. I have to know if he really meant what he said in the conversation I overheard. I have to . . ."

"Mimi, you are driving home. You're not going in there!"

"Do you think I look Jewish?"

Roboldt sighed. How could he discourage her? "Do you think I look gay? It's just nonsense. Herrmann is inside, no matter what you look like. And you're not going in. Mimi, please!"

Oddly enough, Mimi suddenly got her old voice back. "Okay, fine, Detlev," she sighed warmly. "Oh, one more thing, is it possible that three men were killed in bed with a karate chop last year and Lietze doesn't know anything about it?"

Roboldt jumped up. "Where did you find out about that?"

"Herrmann. He got it from this Charlie guy he was talking to on the phone."

"Lietze didn't know anything about it either. I found out about it earlier by accident," Roboldt said. But Herrmann had had the opportunity to tell her. He had been at Belziger Strasse with her. "I'm curious whether he's going to come out with it. If not, we've got him on disciplinary grounds!"

That boy's ripe for a fall, he thought. You can forget something once. But if he doesn't bring it up first thing tomorrow morning – "Are you still there, Mimi?"

"Hmm. A waste to get someone like him just on disciplinary grounds. He's not keeping quiet about the information by accident, he's got good reasons – political ones."

"But it's easier . . ."

"I don't know if one should take the easy way out with something like this," Mimi said, but more to herself.

". . . and more effective. If you don't proceed with care, you make martyrs of them, of all people. Then they'll accuse you of prosecuting their opinions."

"That's true," Mimi admitted after a short pause, "and yet at the same time it's wrong. Because it only works as long as everybody starts with the same assumptions. You have to take the risk over and over again. That's what I think!"

Roboldt pulled the damp blanket up to his chin and immediately stuck his feet out the other end again. He couldn't tell if he was sweating or shivering. "That's how I see it too, Mimi. But what do we have? The Republicans are a party with seats on the council, not a paragraph 129 association. What we think about it is beside the point, it's simply reality. So, if you want to fight Herrmann – as you say – politically, then you have to come up with watertight evidence that he is breaking laws in connection with his political activities or at least abusing his duties as a state employee. Because it's his right to be in that party, if in fact he really is. And we all know damn well that the riot police in their barracks . . ."

"Exactly. We have to stop fifth columns starting among the detectives as well."

"Yes! Of course, Mimi, that's what I've been saying for heaven's sake. But the question is how? Nobody is going to be kicked out of the civil service because of antisemitic remarks. Even less for racist ones. How are we going to prove that Herrmann is doing things which make him unacceptable as a state employee? Proof, Mimi! Watertight!"

"Yes, Detlev!" Mimi's voice was dangerously soft. "I've understood you perfectly well. We need proof. I'll take it to heart."

He got up and put on the rest of his clothes. A little too warm for the furnace he was about to step into. He decided to get back on the phone tomorrow morning and see what he could find out about Herrmann's past. The oily tone of Mimi's voice hadn't made the goose pimples go away. On the contrary. But he knew that he really wasn't strong enough yet to drive from Goltz Strasse all the way up to Wedding. He simply had to rely on Mimi's common sense.

"That's fine," Fritz said. "I'll go to the Blue Note Club afterwards and buttonhole Zadko."

After the gallery at Sydney's had emptied again and they had had time to discuss plans for the next day, Lietze had decided to put the JoAnne Little Brigade aside and save herself and Schade a tour of all the women's bars. At least for tonight. She was only surprised that Fritz hadn't even blinked at the prospect of getting to bed at an hour which seemed ill-suited to the perfect husband he was. Did an ideal couple like Beate and Lothar Fritz ever fight?

"Well, Lothar," Sonja Schade teased him as she got up. "My regards to Beate. Anita sends her greetings in solidarity."

"Uh huh," Fritz mumbled absent-mindedly. "Hope I won't forget by the weekend."

"Ah yes," Schade said sympathetically. "I understand."

Fritz didn't look at her while she said goodbye, but stared with deliberate casualness towards the stairs and the three women coming up them. In front a tall, gaunt, neon blonde, followed by another equally thin woman – but muscular rather than gaunt – with a huge blood-red pout and soft, strawberry-blonde curls, which she shook out of her face at every second step. Now she took a thick strand of hair in her hand and tossed it back. The third, a smaller and plumper woman with wavy blonde hair and thick, no longer quite so perfect, make-up was talking insistently to her. She seemed to be complaining.

Look at that, Lietze thought, and watched Fritz. Beate's away. What makes you think of Elvira Fahlenkamp, she wondered.

". . . I think it's really mean! You took so many pictures. And then you only use ones where I – where you – can't even see my hair! That's shitty! How will anyone ever recognise me!" Ginette seemed close to tears.

In the meantime, Kim had arrived at the table.

"Good evening, ladies an' gentlemen," she said in her best manners and blinked questioningly at Lietze. "May I, um – introduce the artist and one of her models?"

Fritz seemed to be under a spell. He sat there motionless, his eyes as big as saucers.

"Sit down," Lietze said and grinned. That Fritz!

"This is Violetta," Kim announced dramatically. "You can recognise her by the nail polish, huh? Hahaha."

Violetta threw her head back again, smoothed down a transparent black blouse over a black bustier with her hands and opened her lips for a smile which should have had a licence as a lethal weapon. She looked into Lietze's eyes for quite a while and gave Fritz only a quick side glance.

"And this is Ginette Champs-d'Hiver," Kim bubbled on. "In good German Winter-Feld, 'cause that's the area she works."

Ginette forgot her anger about the flop with the photographs and granted Fritz wide eyes, a penetrating look and a professional smile. "Winterfeldt Strasse, between Froben and Potse."

Fritz jumped up. He didn't know whom to offer a chair first. But his eyes were fixed on the strawberry-blonde, who, for Lietze's taste, was making far too much of not paying attention to him. Strange, she thought, is it possible to smell that a man is ready – to what? To be picked up? Did Elvira Fahlenkamp smell it? Why can't I?

She blinked at Kim, who, with great skill, took up the conversation. After a few minutes it was getting to be too much for Lietze. She didn't know what made her more impatient, this irritating femme fatale, who was constantly tossing and touching her head of hair, or poor Fritz, who was twitching like a fish on a sandbank and trying to catch her glance. She was tired. She wanted to go home. But she had to take care of one more thing. She made eye contact with Kim, got up and went to the other end of the gallery, and began to look at the pictures. They didn't mean much to her. Black and white photos partly tinted. Like the femme fatale's finger nails. In different shades of violet. So, that's where the name comes from. Or the other way round. How original, she thought, bored, and hoped Kim had understood her look and would finally come over, so she could tell her off and go home. It must be fashionable to enlarge the whole negative. Together with the numbers and the trade mark. Do they get money from the companies for that? It's advertising after all! ORWO. Ah yeah. Right, that must be the brand for professionals. And the captions. *When I did it for the first time, I felt very much like a pervert.* What did that have to do with the naked arm sticking out from the flowered sheets? And next to it, something in English. Ah, the lady prefers sexual contempt.

"These three here – that's Ginette!" Thank God Kim wasn't thick.

Mechanically she looked at the three pictures Kim had pointed out. She was just about to start her sermon, when she realised that she was staring at a black ski mask. Beneath it was a nude body with perfect round breasts and – a prick.

The black ski mask was more interesting. But according to Kim's long-winded explanation, the photographer Violetta would be the last person to join even a feminist art group, still less a group composed of militant avengers hunting rapists, and Ginette was, anyway, too much of a man for them to accept her.

That made sense, Lietze decided. Especially considering how tired she was. Which was why she was only capable of being half angry as she shuffled along the row of pictures without seeing anything, and told Kim never to dare interfere with her investigations again.

"We never did," Kim responded sulkily, "we just went to talk to Solli because of the funeral."

"And Kitty at Zadko's?"

"Yeah, well. It won't happen again. Promise!"

"And don't ever call me Mieze again either!"

They were back at the table. Kim sat down next to Ginette. Lietze picked up her bag, put in the cigarillos and lighter and looked at Fritz.

"You really shouldn't forget to look at the pictures, Fritz," she said almost like an order. And with a winning smile at the beautiful, secretive femme fatale, "there's really a lot in them."

*

Sonja Schade almost didn't recognise him. Alfred Henke was wearing proper trousers and an equally proper shirt, though open at the neck. Even he isn't so proper as to wear a tie in this heat!

She had just removed a thin white chit from under her windshield wipers, cursed, and put the key in the car door, when she saw him marching down the other side of Maassen Strasse towards Winterfeldt Platz. He had stopped briefly in front of the little newspaper shop and looked in. That must be the old lady's shop, the one Detlev meant. What does he want there? It's long past closing time, Schade thought, opened the car door, sat down, pulled it shut and continued to watch him.

Now Henke was coming diagonally across the street. What's wrong with his chin? He was walking straight towards Sydney's on the corner of Maassen and Winterfeldt Strasse. Funny bar. He doesn't fit in there. Why on earth did Detlev suggest it? From there it would have been completely impossible to see if something was happening in the entrance to the Ruin. The other place would have been better, Slumberland, on the corner of Winterfeldt and Goltz Strasse. And anyway, Sydney's is closed by five in the morning.

Henke didn't go into Sydney's, but turned into Winterfeldt Strasse. Sonja Schade put the crumpled piece of paper back under the windshield wiper, locked the car and followed him. Oh, Anita, she mused, though not for long. Maybe at bottom I'm a real cop, married to my job!

Now Henke turned left into Zieten Strasse. She followed him to the corner and looked round carefully. He was stand-ing in front of the door of Club Olàlà. That really looks as if it was a hook to the chin! He rang. The door didn't open. He knocked, several times. But nothing happened. Quarter past eight. He knows the place because his stepson works there. Worked there. Well, maybe they'll take him back. But evidently he doesn't know it well enough to know it doesn't open till nine. And what does he want there now anyway?

Henke gave up, crossed the street and disappeared into a bar. Seems to be urgent, whatever he wants, Schade concluded, strolled up Zieten Strasse, pretended to look intently at the window displays, of which there were none on Olàlà's side of the street and sat down on one of the benches at the Zieten and Nollendorf Strasse intersection, among pensioners and Turkish- and Slav-speaking mothers, who were watching their children play.

The blue Ford Capri drove slowly into the empty space. The man, about thirty, dressed in jeans and a t-shirt, put his feet on the pavement and swung the rest of his body out. Then he went to the phone booth next to the car. He had an athletic walk and didn't sway at all.

He put three ten-pfennig pieces in the slot and dialled.

"Lang."

He gave his boss a very short report containing all the necessary information. ". . . so then I had a problem. Should I follow her or stick to our objects? But I thought if our Erika turns up again, and there, of all places, then that's more important. With the lads, we can be sure they'll be in Wedding tonight."

"It was the right decision. Where are they now?"

The man gave the name of the street. "They're in number 14 now. She had keys for it. I assume the boy is Thorsten. It was impossible to identify him. Baseball cap over his face, sunglasses. He was on the back seat and looked as pissed as a newt."

"Nope. He's got concussion."

The man whistled. "Are they having trouble in their club?"

Lang explained who had helped get Thorsten into his current state and heard how Erika had tried in vain to get into her own apartment at 17 Nollendorf Strasse. "Either she didn't have a key, which is unlikely, or Henke has locked her out. I could hardly follow her into the building as well."

"It was risky enough as it was! Holding cover is the most important thing at the moment."

The man nodded into the phone. "What shall I do next?"

"Stick with it."

She simply jumped up after Kim and Ginette had finally gone. She still didn't seem to notice him. In fact, pictures were racing across her retina, engraving themselves there, tearing loose again. It burned like dry ice. Her whole skin was flickering now, but at the same time she was falling back into that unpleasant tiredness. Like yesterday – but that was in the middle of the day. It had never come in the evening before.

She moved along the row of twenty-one pictures. She stopped in front of one of them. But she couldn't stand still. She kept shifting her weight from one foot to the other. She wiggled her toes in the violet open-toed high heels and stared at the picture. The diagonal corner of a bed, a sheet, striped in darker and lighter grey, hanging over it, and at the upper end of the bed an arm with an exceptionally large, long-fingered hand. *The male attitude – penetrated* . . . The upper side of the arm was lit from some source outside the frame to the right, and it was tinted cardinal violet.

Finally he got up. "Well – now I can look at the pictures in peace." A chair tipped over and a spoon fell on the floor.

She crossed her arms and imperceptibly pressed the muscles of her upper arms against the sides of her breasts and turned round. But she didn't look at him, only at the chair on the floor, giving it a cruel smile. She observed him come towards her, still without looking directly at him. Then she moved on a little. To the next photo. What does it mean?

shot through her brain. Him? Is it him? In the evening. At
night. But the light is missing. The burning hot sunlight. It's
dark now. And it will get even darker. Ever darker. And the
glass splinters are getting sharp. They will cut open my
innards. Is he doing that? This pressure. Like mugginess and
storm at the same time.

He seemed to be looking carefully at the series of pictures.
She felt it in her back. Carefully she turned just enough so
that she could observe him out of the corner of her eye. He
was standing in front of the picture showing the corner of
the striped bed. He stared at it for a long time. He appeared
to be searching for something. Then he looked up, turned
his head towards her and shook it. He seemed to be smiling.

Or is it the prospect of the ghost army? The lion's den.
Tomorrow. Tomorrow at noon. Will it be just as hot in
Budapest? This sun? 10:35 on Malev. Schönefeld Airport.
He's checked it all out, that idiot with his assignment. The
next one is 11:05 Interflug. Be there two hours earlier. That
means taking the bus from Kongresszentrum at seven thirty.
Will he really put an envelope with an advance in her letter
box tonight?

She had reached the twenty-first picture. This is what
makes the skin flicker. The prospect of – no, this guy after
all? He came closer. He pretended to be looking at the
pictures, but he didn't see anything. She could tell he didn't
see anything. But things still weren't clear to her. What was
burning itself on to her retina? What was frozen into a still
and crying out for heat? Heat! To be expelled! Why was the
sun not there and yet screaming so brightly on her
skin.

She forced herself not to turn around. He was standing
right behind her now. He cleared his throat. "I don't know
what kind of plans someone like you has," he said, and a
certain innocent embarrassment which trickled from his

mouth through her transparent blouse on to her naked back, obliterated all the other shreds of images, "but I had planned to go to the Blue Note Club. Would you like to – join me?"

1 + 1 = 0

The slight dizziness had still not gone as he had walked up Goltz Strasse and turned left into Hohenstaufen Strasse. His feet didn't seem to be quite on the ground either. Yet Detlev Roboldt had listened to the voice of reason and left the fawn-coloured loafers lying in the hall although they would have made a better impression on an old lady, and put on a pair of solid rubber-soled trainers instead.

He made a detour to avoid Winterfeldt Platz. The thought of running into someone from D III leaving Sydney's and having to play the contrite invalid again, drove ice water through his veins and right out of his pores. By then, it was steaming again. The climatic conditions inside his body weren't normal at all.

Pulling up the collar of his brown silk jacket round his neck, he turned right into Habsburger Strasse. Shivering and sweating he strolled past grand renovated old tenements and turned left again into Winterfeldt Strasse. A gentle wind from the west blew across his face. The dizziness began to disappear. You've just about made it, he thought. Now, right into Eisenacher, and the next right is already Nollendorf Strasse. Oh God – did she really say four flights on the phone?

After half an hour on Fräulein von Thurau's flowered settee and two orange liqueurs served in crystal glasses on little bast mats, the pressure behind his ears had eased. Roboldt trumpeted into his handkerchief one more time, but his nose remained stopped up. Nevertheless, he could have listened to Fräulein von Thurau all night.

"She couldn't really speak English, the Schröder woman!" she explained apologetically. "She mumbled the name, and that's how he got stuck with Herr Issyvoo . . . the Schröder woman – she's dead a long time ago too, I used to know her well. And certainly I met him at least two or three times on the street, because my brother was already living in this house and when I visited him . . ."

Roboldt had a soft spot for old ladies and their little whims. She seemed to like him for her part. Perhaps she was only happy that someone from the police was at last interested in what she knew.

"To think that you still remember Isherwood – he's my favourite writer," Roboldt interrupted a brief silence while Fräulein von Thurau sipped her liqueur until it was finished.

"It's nice that they at least put a plaque on the house," she began again and looked enquiringly into his swollen red eyes. "But they could easily have written on it that he was bent, couldn't they?"

Roboldt was silent and returned the gaze.

"That's why they put my brother in a concentration camp. And he never really recovered. Another kwangtroh, inspector?"

Her brother Johannes had died thirty years before and had left the apartment and shop to his sister. Roboldt promised himself he would just sip at the third glass of Cointreau, and discreetly change the subject. But Fräulein von Thurau didn't miss a thing.

"Oh my God, I'm just chatting away here," she chattered, "and you've got a stuffy head and a job to do. Well, if you ask me, I think Henke is a nasty piece of work. He's a completely lazy so and so. But he'll take your money, he'll do that. His wife has left him now, inspector!"

Roboldt interrupted his notetaking to whisper that she could just call him Roboldt, after all he wasn't from the tax office. She giggled and knocked back her third glass.

"He really bashed her about! And the boy as well. I've seen it with my own eyes – black and blue. Both of them!"

Roboldt listened to her description of the pair and asked about Frau Henke's new address.

"Oh God, I don't know that one, Herr Romold. But I doubt that she's going to move back here, because he's got a new one already. I assume that's what they were fighting about. Just imagine it! For years you're married to a man and you go through thick and thin with him, and all of a sudden he shows up with a new one!'

Fräulein von Thurau admitted that she was a real beauty. Blonde and slim. "But at least twenty years younger than him." She had met her in the courtyard once, just before five thirty in the morning, one day when she had to be at the shop very early.

"I can't even remember what the reason was. Well, anyway, she always only came late at night. You could tell, because he always turned on music, very loud, everyone could hear it. All his windows face on to the courtyard . . ."

Roboldt scribbled in his notepad and thought about a lover from years ago, whose apartment had also overlooked a small courtyard. And who had expressed his degree of pleasure in bed by the sonic level of his groans. It had been a beautiful summer and the scent of lime trees had wafted intoxicatingly through the open window. But every time some neighbour had shouted "Shut up!", and every time Tobias had stepped to the window like a Prussian sergeant-major and yelled: "It isn't my fault you can't open your mouth when you fuck!" And had crawled back into bed.

". . . the Bolero, I think, by Ravel. Over and over again, imagine that! Last Sunday again, at four in the morning, Herr Rohgold!"

Roboldt nodded sympathetically.

"Herr Fahlenkamp was the only one who gave him a piece

of his mind, and now he's dead too. But you're not drinking, Herr – " She poured more into her own glass. "Do you know already who did it? But I'm sure you're not allowed to tell me, Herr – Gromoll, are you?"

"As long as you don't call me Kobold, it's all right by me, Fräulein von Thurau." Roboldt improvised the most charming, queeny smile that he could manage, given his fevered head, and told her about the investigation.

"By yesterday at noon? Well, I was here at a quarter to two, because Herr Henke was supposed to come at two to fix my tap. And he was gone again in fifteen minutes and took forty marks! Then I quickly ate my cold cherry soup, it's the only thing in this heat isn't it? And I always go back to the shop around a quarter to three, because it has to be open from three."

"And you didn't notice anything unusual?"

"Of course I did, young man! Herr Henke himself was sweeping the pavement. He's never done that before."

A disappointed Roboldt sat back on the couch. "I see. Nothing else? In the courtyard? Did someone leave the house? Did . . ."

"Well, that redhead, but I'm sure Henke has already told you about her. No? He must have got a good look at her! I only saw her from behind."

His temperature suddenly seemed to rise, his nostrils were tickling, and Roboldt was waiting for a sneezing attack. But nothing happened. He merely had some difficulty taking down Fräulein von Thurau's description of a red-haired beauty, before his eyes swelled shut again.

"That Herr Henke didn't tell you about her! Well, perhaps she distracted him, I mean, Frau Henke. She was just arriving in her cab. They didn't see me. At any rate, they didn't say hello. Neither of them!"

*

Sonja Schade stared out the window of the bar across from the Olàlà, and wondered how long someone like Henke would need. He had disappeared into the Olàlà about ten minutes ago, and she had taken over his observation post. Could she risk calling Anita?

She finished the mineral water and was signalling the waiter for another one and to ask about the phone, when the door of the club opened and Alfred Henke came out. He looked pitiful. His face should have been dark red. Instead it looked, except for the bruise on the left side of his chin, like a mildewed shroud. He crept along the walls of the houses as if he needed to hold on to them. She paid.

She crossed the street up to the corner of Winterfeldt Strasse and watched him. He staggered towards the square. Then she ran back to the Olàlà and held her finger on the bell.

"You're fast movers, eh?" Minou threw open the door and looked out into the street behind Schade. "All by yourself tonight? No man with you?"

Schade entered the red plush semi-darkness and the clouds of hair spray and deodorant and went to the bar. Ramona was sitting behind Natalie on a bar stool and giving her a neck massage.

"Why am I fast?" Schade asked.

"Well, because that was one of Martha's regulars just now," Minou answered and held out her empty champagne glass enquiringly.

"Ah, because of that!" Schade shook her head. "He was pale as a sheet. I thought maybe he had done something here . . ."

"The police, your friend and helper! Isn't that sweet," Minou mocked. "Nope, he just broke down completely when I told him what happened to Martha."

"He was shattered," Ramona joined in. And Natalie added, without the accent, that she had never seen anything like it.

"Maybe what Martha told us was really true." Minou went

on polishing the glasses. "That he wanted to marry her. Not just to get her out of here, that's what they all want. Still, I didn't believe it."

Schade lit a cigarette and tried to imagine Alfred Henke as the husband of a beautiful Polish woman in her late twenties. It didn't quite fit, and not just because of outward appearance. She must have been at least an inch taller than him.

". . . on the other hand, then she would have had a secure situation here, not just been on a tourist . . ." Minou clapped her hand over her mouth. "Oh fuck!"

"It's okay," Schade said. "We knew she was here as a tourist. We're not interested . . ."

"But that joe who was with you yesterday, I bet he's interested!" Ramona released Natalie's neck.

"Don't worry, he's just a trainee."

"We even found out the client's name!" Ramona was whispering conspiratorially, even though, apart from the four women, there was no one else in the place. "Alfred!"

"Thanks!" said Schade in a friendly tone. "And the others – regulars? Do you know them yet?"

"Nope, none of them has been back," Minou said. "Can I ask you something for a change? How long are – ah – I mean, dead bodies kept?"

Sonja Schade looked at her in astonishment. "It depends. Why? Did you want to see her?"

"No no, not at all," Minou said quickly. "Just wanted to know."

"Well, then I'll wish you – well, what should one wish you?" Schade looked from one to the other.

"Loadsa money!" Ramona yelled.

"Well then: loadsa money! You don't happen to know if this Alfred is the man Martha left with early on Saturday night, do you?"

They didn't know.

*

Visibility inside the Blue Note Club was poor and the air was stickier than Lothar Fritz would have thought humanly endurable. Nevertheless, a few people were dancing. The music seemed to be taped. There were no musicians in sight and the little stage, like everything else apart from the bar, was in darkness. This wasn't his kind of place, he concluded, and wondered if it showed. He wondered if she noticed it too. She moved between the tables and the people as if she belonged.

"Do you know who this is?" he asked, just as she turned towards him to point to a free table in front of the stage. Again, without looking him in the eyes.

"If you mean the music – Madonna," she said.

"I thought it was familiar, it makes me think of our – " he swallowed the word "daughters" just in time, but felt her watching him out of the corner of her eye, as he squeezed clumsily into a chair.

She turned to the neighbouring table and asked when the Marek Zadko Group would be on. Interested, he leaned over the table and only at the last moment saved the ashtray from falling. Had he bumped it? He felt like an idiot. The matter of fact way in which she talked to people and excluded him was irritating. Her disinterest worked on him like a magnet. For the first time in his life, Lothar Fritz knew how a hooked carp might feel. "Supposed to be on at ten," he heard from the next table. "But my guess is not before ten-thirty."

Violetta waved at a black woman in short red satin shorts and black and gold boxing boots, who couldn't have been more than seventeen. Light-footed as a gazelle, he thought, and wondered why he was constantly thinking about animals. All of a sudden Violetta looked straight into his eyes. But only to allow him to order. Perhaps he was already goggling like a carp?

She mumbled an irritated, "Campari Orange," and threw a glance at the waitress.

What was he doing here? He knew what he was supposed to do. But if he had something else in mind – nonsense! I'm simply on duty, Beate. And there's something about this photographer which might give us a lead. I feel it. You're always saying one has to rely much more on one's instincts.

"The same for you?" The annoyed gazelle shifted her weight from one foot to the other and tossed back her thick, curly black mane

"What? Ah. No, do you have – beer?"

If Violetta had at least looked at him reproachfully! He leaned back, pulled a handkerchief out of his pocket and wiped his face. But she was sitting bolt upright on her chair, her long, shiny black legs crossed, and contemplating one of her feet, which was just barely covered by her violet high heel, turning the shoe, playing with her ankles and tendons and muscles, before finally allowing her gaze to wander in all directions again. Except his. But he couldn't shake off the suspicion that she was keeping a close eye on him nevertheless. More than that, he noticed, disturbed: it was as if she even controlled where he looked. Now she was fanning her transparent blouse, looking at her cleavage.

"Tell me," he said, "how long does it take to train as a professional photographer?" He held out his pack of cigarettes.

She ignored it and grabbed her strawberry blonde curls with both hands, pulling them together behind her head. The full breasts – he noticed guiltily – were barely protected by the black bustier. "No idea. I never trained."

She shook her head, her breasts swayed and she loosened her hair with both hands. "When I knew I wanted to be a photographer, I picked up a guy who was a photographer. And I fucked him for as long as it took to know what it means to be a photographer."

Fritz tore his gaze from her cleavage and looked into her eyes, which, surprisingly, she turned towards him for a second. Once again with the smile that seemed cruel.

"Have you ever heard anything about shamans?" she asked.

He nodded, lit a cigarette and frantically tried to remember what he'd heard.

"Appropriation of knowledge through the senses," she instructed him. "They wear the clothes of people whose energy they want to acquire. Or fetishes of gods. During initiation. Cannibals are the same . . ."

Was she winding him up?

". . . they don't just eat anyone. They consume their adversaries in order to gain their power."

"And you're trying to do it with – " before he could decide whether to say "fucking", the gazelle placed two glasses on to the table.

"Sure," Violetta said, took the orange slice from the edge of her glass and sucked on it. "Sex is the most sensual way of gaining access to the world. And the most dangerous."

"And you like – danger," he heard himself say from a great distance. The only thing within reach was this sight, which he couldn't take his eyes off. Her lips and teeth around a slice of orange above a glass of kitschy, blood-red liquid.

He looked round the room one more time, but the tables on both the ground floor and the gallery were empty apart from two couples, and nobody he was looking for was sitting at the tables outside on the pavement either. They've all gone home long ago, he thought and noticed a small poster on Sydney's open front door. "Violetta – Twenty-one new pictures. Exhibition until August 31. Opening August 1 at 8 p.m."

He decided to phone from home rather than from Sydney's and strolled diagonally across Winterfeldt Platz. His nose was still almost completely stuffed up. That was why he couldn't smell the air. He only noticed that the earlier gentle breeze had turned into small, sharp gusts of wind. He looked at the sky. It was as stuffed up as his nose, sealed off by thick yellowish-black layers of cloud. Was the storm finally coming? Tonight? Brimstone and pitch?

He walked towards the brick-red church and looked left towards the Ruin. She had been lying right there, next to the entrance, in a roofless and windowless rectangle surrounded by sand and dirt and crumbling pieces of wall. The green-blue-brown strangulation marks on her neck, the eyes bulging out of the scratched, blood-encrusted face, blue and terribly dead. Like steel. He tried to stop his inner eye from moving down her body. Not to look at her torn, pulled-up skirt, nor at the red-brown carnage between her legs. He forced himself to stare straight ahead at St Matthias Church and to remember how incense smelt, and how full the church had been the time he went there for the Christmas Eve service with his mother, and how he could no longer imagine that he too, a skinny little boy in a white batiste shirt, had stood very close to the red wine, and he felt sick. For a moment he was sure he was going to throw up on the reddish-grey synthetic stone squares. He took a deep breath, turned his head slowly to the right and tried to fix his eyes on the new buildings on the west side of Winterfeldt Platz. But there was too much of that ugly red there also. Someone with a mania for wine red must have had a hand in the renovation decisions. Repulsive colour. Like violet.

The nausea was gone by the time he pushed open the front door of his building on Goltz Strasse and ran smack into someone who was coming leaping down the stairs and seemed to be in a hurry. It was Larry.

"Man, Detlev! *Where the fuck have you been*! I called, nada. I came over, nada. So, I left you a note. *Come on*!"

"Stop. What is it? Wait a minute, I've got to phone." Was this a delirious dream?

"You can call from *TAZ*. Later. Come with me now." Larry pulled him along, put him in a car and put the seat belt in his hands.

"Where to? What's the matter? Am I or am I not sick?"

"You're after the Ku-Klux-Klan, aren't you? You told me you want them! They've raided *TAZ*, and I'm going to smuggle you in. Before the other cops, *oh fuck*, what do you call it, destroy the evidence. *Get the picture*? I'll explain it to you on the way.'

It took two left turns and one and a half minutes of strong headwind before Detlev Roboldt finally understood that Larry was talking about the JoAnne Little Brigade.

There was nothing special about the thirtyish man dressed in sports clothes who turned away from the big window with the "Physical Therapy" sign, walked slowly across Nollendorf Strasse, opened the door of a Blue Ford Capri and got in, leaned over to the glove compartment and finally studied a street map for a while. If someone had been observing him, which was unlikely, they would by now have been distracted by another, really conspicuous scene. Coming up the other side of the street was a heavy-set man in his mid-forties, his face mottled red and shiny with sweat, and a bruise under his left cheek. He was gesticulating wildly and from time to time shouting something into a cab driving along at walking pace next to him. In front of number 17 he waved his arms, as if he were trying to chase something away. But the taxi stopped and a woman about the same age wearing big dark glasses lurched out and ran towards him.

The man in the Capri kept the street map in front of his face, but went on watching the quarrel over the top. She yelled louder than he did. It was about a mortice lock and how it was an outrage, but that didn't surprise the man in the Capri.

The man with the military haircut got even more flushed, cradled the left side of his chin and seemed to be on the verge of exploding. But he tried to talk quietly, and looked around all the time, and up at the windows of the surrounding houses. It was obvious he wanted to get rid of her; at any rate, the last thing he wanted was for her to follow him.

The man in the Capri waited until the scuffle was over and they had disappeared into the building, the woman first. Then he counted to twenty, got out, went over to the cab parked at an angle across the pavement, the windows open, and looked in. He decided to get a little closer to the action. Because they hadn't locked the door to the courtyard. For a caretaker couple like the Henkes, this was unheard of. And possibly a reason to request reinforcements.

The glass of the phone booth in front of the kiosk on Winterfeldt Platz was so fogged up Sonja Schade couldn't even make out her car, which was still not parked in accordance with the by-laws. She had both a guilty conscience and urgent news. The guilty conscience was stronger. Not a cop after all, she thought with relief, as she dialled her own, and Anita's, number. Just a detective who does her job and believes a crisis-free home is important.

The phone had already rung six times. And that was bad news. Schade felt panic in her limbs and images shot through her head. She saw Anita lying on the floor somewhere in the apartment, after a fall, unable to get up because not one of her muscles would obey her any more. Helpless. The tenth ring. Eleventh.

"Yes," the voice panted feebly at last.

"Anita! What's happened? Are you okay?" What could she do but try to shout louder than her feeling of guilt. She already knew what had happened, and she knew above all that she hadn't been there. Again. Anita had been alone during an attack. Again she was too late, and all she could do was call the emergency ambulance and race with her to hospital, blue light, the metallic rattling of the swaying first aid equipment, the noise of the siren, which sounded even more shrill inside than outside, usually some excitable doctor who didn't know the ropes yet, and Anita, pale, thin as a wraith and both ancient and childlike at the same time, smiling soothingly at her with those green eyes, which seemed to be telling her: "You know, it's not my fault, it was your idea to be a cop . . ."

It was happening again. Schade pushed down the hook, but kept the receiver in her hand, put three more ten-pfennig pieces in the slot and dialled.

"Lietze!"

"Schade. I have a –, well I was –, I mean I've seen Henke. He was one of the regulars. I went to the Olàlà and there . . ." She was more upset than Lietze had ever known her. And more than could be explained by whatever she had to report about Krisztina Kędzierska's murder, Lietze thought.

"First of all, just slow down, Schade. There's bound to be a storm tonight at last. Drive home carefully. The man isn't going to run away from us, we'll squeeze him out tomorrow."

Schade was grateful that Lietze obviously had no desire to be up all night. But it didn't calm her down. She knew that she'd be up all night and that tomorrow morning she would report for work punctually, without having slept a wink. But that was nothing compared to the reproaches, the fear and the nagging sensation of having done something wrong. Of doing something wrong all the time.

She ran back to her car, pulled the ticket off the windshield, crumpled it up and stamped on it.

Was the first of August another one of them? A special day? This guy was boring. Probably happily married. That makes him immune. The last one was married too, but at least he was used to playing around. Playing around! Tsk-tsk. *Strange brew.* How did it go? *Girl what's inside you ...*

She uncrossed her legs and slid both hands along her thighs to straighten out the sticky, yielding material of her stretch-pants. Fucking pants. Hydroplaning on her skin. Flushing away the splinters. What is it? What does it mean? The daylight's gone. The smell of sun on skin is missing. No pulsating aroma.

She raised her arms above her head, stretched, shook her strawberry blonde hair and sniffed unobtrusively at her armpits. Sweat. Common sweat. What was his name? They had called him Fritz, his – were they his colleagues or what? Probably a nickname. Or are guys his age still called Fritz? He was old-fashioned enough. Obedient too. Had followed her every move and didn't seem to want anything as desperately as that she look at him.

She let her hands with their nails in shades of violet fall to her lap and realised that people must have been moving around on the stage for a while. Nevertheless, Fritz wasn't a candidate. The shrill burning between her thighs must be coming from somewhere else. His gaze wasn't grateful. More like – curious. Searching. Distanced.

If she was honest, she didn't find him boring. On the contrary. And she didn't know whether she rejected him as a candidate because something about him disgusted her, or because she was frustrated that he didn't relinquish his immunity. But she didn't want to be honest. She tried to imagine his marriage. Home and hearth.

"You're a journalist. Am I right?" she said suddenly and nailed his surprised look with her cool, sarcastic gaze. Now he'll drop his beer glass, she calculated, no, she really hoped he would. But he simply looked her in the eyes. Did they signal approval or was this merely optical arm-wrestling?

She quickly looked away and at her empty glass. Threads of orange were sticking to the inside. She felt the tinkling of glass splinters grow more violent and noted with a touch of panic that she had never before felt hopeful in such a situation. Hope kills all magic. Hope is the opposite of the erotic. The erotic only exists if one knows one will win. No. Wrong. More than that. There is no possibility of not winning. She picked up the glass, looked at her long, violet nails, and put it to her mouth. When she remembered that it was empty and he was still looking at her, she closed her eyes and leant her head back as if to indicate that she needed more to drink. When she opened her eyes again and looked at him, he was leaning back in his chair with his arms crossed. This isn't a candidate! She tried to drum it into her brain. A candidate is always a promise. This one promises trouble at most. Let the storm come and put an end to this tinkling.

"Why do you want to know that?" she heard. She shrugged contemptuously and turned back to the stage. Spotlights came on. *I am a camera*. Why is he here? To talk to one of the musicians, he said. *With its shutter open, quite passive*. So he's a journalist. What does he want from me? Does he want . . . *Recording not thinking*. What kind of fucking sentence is that. Where's that fucking book? This isn't a candidate! This isn't a special day. Otherwise I'd have to go home immediately, put on the right pants, get the camera and – she focused on the musicians who were picking up their instruments. He did the same. Each watched the other out of the corner of an eye.

*

Of course the cops arrived before them. They weren't actually destroying possible evidence, as Larry had feared, but their mere presence prevented Roboldt from even looking for it. At least, thanks to Larry, he could pass as one of the staff and keep his ears open. Some ten staff members were there. He recognised a couple of them because he had seen them yesterday in the library. Nobody had the time to doubt that Detlev Roboldt was either a free-lancer or one of Larry's lovers.

He fitted in effortlessly. He glanced into a big room on the ground floor, whose grey partitions had been completely covered with spray-painted threats and abuse. There was nothing original or new. Not even sentences which commented on the reasons for the action. Only the old slogans like "Cut off their pricks!", "Men piss off – women won't miss you!" and "Porn is the theory – rape the practice", which the big letters didn't make any more convincing.

The room, which also served as a cafeteria, was a mess. Tables and chairs had been thrown around and partly smashed. A door on one wall had been torn off and food and dishes tossed about. The drinks dispenser in the hallway had been smashed with a hammer, the windows to a little porter's lodge were broken, and in the room itself there was a charred pile. The caretaker, a gaunt young man with long hair, shorts and sandals, was sitting in front of it, with his hands pressed to his stomach, his face bleeding, and a group of editors around him.

"I was just about to lock up and leave," he said as fluently as the shock and pain allowed. "There were at least a dozen. I thought, now you've had it. I could only see their eyes, but that was enough. Nothing but hate, really, nothing but hate!'

The world didn't make sense any more.

"*Of all people,*" Larry whispered to Roboldt. "He's the

biggest softy here. He's in a men's group discussing violence . . ."

"So now at least he knows what it feels like," Roboldt heard a woman's voice behind him. And a second woman next to her said, "Right." He felt a wave of heat go through his body and whirled round. "What do you mean by that!" he heard his own voice say.

"It's what I said. This is what women are confronted with every day. With pure hate from men. Powerless!" He realised that in his mind he was trying to pull a black ski mask over this woman's face and stopped himself. "But this won't make things any better either."

"Do you think I like it? Unfortunately it's reality. It's about time you realised it."

"And felt it," the other one added. "Being gay is no excuse."

He turned away. They were right, there was no denying it. Probably everyone instinctively has more empathy for the victims among their own people, he brooded as he stumbled behind Larry. And as a professional who was confronted with the sight of victims of violence every day, he knew there was only one way to stop himself becoming completely unfeeling. Somehow one had to retain the ability to have sympathy for everyone. Equally. And that didn't make things any easier.

"Look here," Larry said proudly and pulled him over to a door leading to the stairs. "They managed to open this one, but that was as far as they got."

Roboldt looked at the spray-painted walls, while Larry explained the advantages of the system of fireproof doors.

"You can't beat this technology. Except with a key. And the same with the editorial rooms and the library too. What do you want to do?"

"Listen, and hope that none of my colleagues recognises me."

*

Just check one more time that all the windows are properly closed. But she was following him. Didn't let him out of her sight for a second. Didn't stop talking at him. And the further they got from the living room where the tv was turned up full, the more clearly he could understand her words. Only something inside him tried to argue against it. It'll all be over soon. Once and for all. Won't be long now.

He went into the workshop. His glance fell on the big flat wooden box. He pulled off the dish towel. That's good, Blondie my angel. You didn't disturb it when you jumped down. Left it as it should be. Discipline and order in small matters.

"Yes, you – " he heard the voice again, and it sounded unusually high, "take a good look at it!"

Slowly, very slowly he wiped his face and neck with the towel. Was what was running down his skin hot or cold? "Why don't you ever shut up," he heard another voice say, and it sounded very high-pitched and quiet. Was it his voice?

The air hung in the narrow room as if it was stuffed with glass wool. He went to the window. Open it, he thought. Open everything. But later. Later. Not yet. First . . . The moon was full in the sky. But only a few clear, dark blue patches remained. Yellowish-black clouds coming from the south-west were slowly gathering beneath it and cutting off the air.

He checked the window. It was securely closed. He looked into the courtyard. Blondie was nowhere to be seen. There was too much fighting for you my queen same for me same for me I can tell you no comparison no comparison at all my queen so refined and so tender and so but now she is she is now it's over with once and for all it doesn't make any yesyesyes you'll get something my angel just stay outside for a while you must hunt that's your nature –

Erika's voice and the chatter inside Henke's head broke

off as he threw open the window. "What are you doing here!" he yelled into the courtyard.

The young man in sports clothes closed the door to the courtyard with particular care, and strolled towards the rear house. He stayed a good distance from Henke's well-lit window, so that Henke couldn't recognise his face.

"Where are you going?" he barked again. What on earth! He isn't even turning round. He's not stopping . . .

"I don't know that it's any of your business if other people have visitors," the man said. And then he had already reached the door, pushed down the handle and disappeared into the hallway of the back house.

Henke closed the window and waited until the light in the stairwell had gone off.

"There you go again! You're interested in every little piece of shit, but your wife doesn't exist for you," she shrilled in his ear.

"Shut up! I'm telling you for the last time!" he heard himself with this clear, high voice again, which he recognised now. All the blood in his body seemed to shoot to his head. The bruise on his chin started throbbing again. All I did was clean up like you always told me to and as soon as I've done it I forget it I forget everything, but not her not Mata my Mata –

". . . Polack whore, yes, haha, so that's what you thought, you thought I'd put up with that! Nope. You. That's over. I'm telling you. For the last time. What are you doing?"

Very, very slowly, Henke opened the wooden box. Erika grabbed his arm. He pulled it away, took out one of the trays and put it down.

"When – did you notice?" The voice was small, very small, and something in his head registered it. Notice what? He took out the next tray.

Paralysed, Erika stared at the letters all lined up in formation, in alphabetical order and according to size. Old German letters from N to S. She lowered her arms but the trembling didn't stop.

He put a third tray on top of the other two without paying any attention to her.

Erika heaved a sigh of relief as the second tray disappeared. In slow motion she took her eyes off it and looked at his face. Even more slowly, with almost tender calm, Henke took the biggest G from the bottom of the printer's case.

But for Erika's eyes it was still too fast. As was Henke's sudden lunge for the light switch. And after that it was too late. She couldn't have seen his fist coming.

After midnight, the moon had disappeared, and with it any light. The air was too thick to cut with a machete and saturated with exhaust fumes, foul smells from the sewers, and all the exhalations which accumulate in the asphalt pores of the streets, the walls of the houses and the living creatures in the course of a seemingly endless heat wave, and try to escape with the first breeze. If one looked carefully, it was possible to see a few sulphurous yellow patches in the pitch black sky. The cloud layer was not quite uniformly thick yet. But nobody was looking carefully, not on Belziger Strasse. A big storm was in the air. The gusts grew stronger and more frequent. Sudden whiplashes which sliced through the air for a few seconds. They swept cigarette ends from the ashtrays and menus from the tables in front of the Pizzeria Due Emigranti. Soon, tables and chairs, customers and their glasses, plates and bags, had all disappeared inside. Only one of the owners stood, legs apart, in the open doorway, looked at the sky and mumbled something that, with his expression, was like a brief prayer against an inescapable catastrophe. A *terremoto* at least.

There was nothing remarkable about the two cars, one

close behind the other, coming down Belziger from the direction of Schöneberg City Hall. At the time a few people were fleeing home, or had decided to transfer a picnic in some park to some apartment after all.

The two cars stopped close behind one another too in front of the head office of Julius Grieneisen & Co. Funerals and Cremations. Two men got out of the first, a sports car, unusual in this neighbourhood, four men got out of the second, a big jeep with tractor-like tyres. Three of these four were dressed entirely in black, from boots to bomber jackets with bulging pockets, zipped only at the waist. One of the men from the first car went up to number 29. He was small, stout and muscular and behaved like a Boy Scout leader. His companion, bigger, heavy, but almost without muscles, followed close behind him, unobtrusively looking in every direction. But nobody in the surrounding houses or among the passers-by seemed to take any notice.

The bomber-jacketed four shuffled behind, short, or almost no, hair, hands in their pockets, weighed down by the effort of looking tough.

Nobody followed them when they disappeared into the passageway leading to the courtyards in the back. Nor did they encounter anyone coming from the back houses. Nobody wanted to leave home at this time of night, and nobody needed to check the boxes in the passageway any more for their mail.

At least ten minutes passed before Fritz got suspicious again, jumped up and looked round for the waitress. He cursed the vodka he had drunk because Zadko had insisted and paid, he cursed his naivety which had made him assume Zadko was hot for the photographer and would come back to the table, and he cursed his own interest in Violetta. It made him uncertain, and he cursed Beate for that. But only as an experiment. The experiment didn't work.

Violetta had been charming Zadko and that had annoyed him more than he liked to admit. She seemed really talkative suddenly, wanted to know all kinds of things about the most absurd subjects, like men in Eastern Europe. Fritz had let them talk and had listened half frustrated, half fascinated. Sex maniacs together, he had thought. Or artists. He didn't understand anything about music, especially that kind, or about photography. And for some reason, which he wouldn't have liked if he had really thought about it, he didn't want to ask Zadko about the notebook, while she was listening. Who likes to catch himself thinking he's ashamed to be recognised as a cop?

The suspicion that Zadko might have left instead of getting another round of vodka came to him first. But he had kept an eye on the instruments which were still on stage, and told himself Zadko couldn't give him the slip. They had him on file. But with Violetta, he didn't even know her surname. When had she left? Five minutes ago? Not right after Zadko anyway. Had she said she was going to the toilet or had he just imagined it? Are the two of them together...? You really are too dumb even to be a cop.

He ran to the entrance. If he remembered right, that's where the toilets were. The waitress burst into his wildest fantasies. "Twenty-three marks, if you please!"

Had he really thought of a gazelle? The woman who blocked his way no longer looked either light-footed or graceful. Fritz mumbled an excuse, paid and asked where the toilets were. She counted the money and nodded towards the exit.

The gents was empty except for a young guy in one of the cubicles who seemed to be puking up his guts. Fritz stood near the door to the ladies, waiting for someone to come out so that he could glance in, at the same time wondering if he dared to go in himself. The door finally opened. The women's toilet also seemed to be empty.

He went back to the bar and asked the waitress.

"The instruments are gone," she said, glancing at the stage. "That means the group is gone too."

"And the woman?" Fritz asked.

"Which woman?"

"The one – who was with me, with us – "

"No idea." The look she gave him was a mixture of scorn and pity.

Then he was out on the street and the next thing to hit him was a strong gust of wind. He stood there dazed for a moment. Then his head seemed to clear a little.

What did she say? What on earth! What did she say? How could she still say anything at all? I got her. She couldn't any more. I saw it. I never looked at the others so carefully. Not one.

He stumbled against the frame of the living room door. The hallway seemed to stretch for miles. He pulled open the workshop door, found the light switch, pressed it, and immediately pressed it again. He ran to the window and pulled the dark curtains closed. The curtain rod came away in his hand. He threw it aside. Ran back to the light switch. The three trays from the printer's case were still in the same place as before. He looked for the right one. His hands refused to obey his love of order. Letters flew about, some of them to the floor. Then he found it. Yes, it really was. What on earth! Used. That animal. I got her. The same way. Why doesn't she just die? She has to go. I have to clear up. Clean up. It won't do. It won't do at all. What on earth!

He hardly felt his dizziness. He almost fell against the cupboard door when he tried to yank it open. But it didn't open. Finally he remembered he had locked it, since she

had . . . All a mess. The smallest gimlet. Order is the most . . .
Under the cupboard! Under the cupboard! What on earth
she can't do it it won't do that's that the end if not with the
small things it starts with the small things her too yesyes
even the way she looked the little rat the cheeky just fresh
taking my stamp what on earth her that's the end end end
yes my end that's my here it is my Mata my queen you of
all people but you are honest and upright you're not one
of those Polacks you love me you aren't dead you it isn't
possible where's that damn key here here they all are hanging neatly as they should be but I don't need a screwdriver
now no no not any more where did I stick it it it must be
it's been a while I did put some of that stuff aside down
there here yes here it is steady hands have to be steady
down that will take a bit until I how did it work how much
of it here's the piece of paper is the curtain drawn yes
properly so that nobody sees so that nobody interferes the
Thurau woman that nosy old bag her too everyone of them
here and especially her especially her her too. Once and
for all!

Was he really unable to see the wood for the trees or what?
Detective Inspector Lothar Fritz's pace grew quicker to the
rhythm of the gusts. Not that they made anything cooler. On
the contrary. But if walking faster increased the force of the
wind on his face, maybe it would clear his brains out, or so
he hoped. Maybe he was only walking faster down Bülow
Strasse towards Nollendorf Platz because he was growing
more and more angry with himself. Instincts! Instincts! What
instincts did he have? Just the usual one.

At Nollendorf Platz he turned into Maassen Strasse. He
would pick up his car, which he hoped was still in front of
Detlev's door. Should he ring his bell? At this time? Nonsense. He wouldn't cry on Detlev's shoulder, but drive home,

get some sleep and tomorrow morning do everything properly! If only he had hinted to Zadko that they had the notebook! He would have had to react! And wouldn't have been able to drag off that woman as if nothing had happened.

When he stopped at the corner of Winterfeldt Strasse and looked left to let a motor bike pass, he found himself looking at Sydney's again. He hesitated. Reflected. He hadn't really looked at the pictures. Maybe that would tie up the loose ends?

He crossed over. Sydney's was still pretty full. Hardly anyone was sitting at the tables outside. Presumably they didn't like a gale force 12 wind in their cocktails. What does someone look like who is head over heels in love and wants to reach the object of his desire? He tried a face and went over to a young woman cleaning glasses behind the bar. "Em, excuse me, is em – Violetta still around?"

He felt he really was going red.

"We don't have a Violetta here," the woman at the bar said, and glanced briefly at him.

"I mean the photographer, who had . . ."

"Oh, yeah. No idea. You've got to ask the boss. I've got nothing to do with openings."

The boss was in the cellar, and Fritz allowed himself to be drawn upstairs to the gallery. Reluctantly following an instinct once again. And then he saw the wood. Behind one of the twenty-one trees, as it were. And suddenly he got the whole picture. It wasn't the three pictures with the black ski masks. But the one with the striped sheets from which the long-fingered hand protruded. In his mind he made the frame disappear and enlarged the detail. Yes. That was him! No doubt about it. He had seen just that picture once before. Live. That is – no longer live at all!

He closed his eyes in order to concentrate on the hurricanes inside his head. When he opened them wide again, his glance fell on the frame. FILLMORE HP5. He hurried past all the other pictures. Every one of them ORWO. Another arm among flowered sheets caught his eye. He didn't know that one. But two others. The same motif six times over. Three he didn't know.

He ran down the stairs trying to decide if he should now say he was the police. He decided against it. He had a better chance as an idiot in love.

The owner smiled at him pityingly. "I'm sorry, but I can't help you there."

"Do you maybe know her second name?"

"No." He seemed to hesitate and looked Fritz up and down. Fritz tried to look as if he was about to come. If there's any point to male bonding, then it has to be now!

"Well, I think her first name is Eva-Maria. I picked up that much."

Oh, how nice, Fritz thought. That's as rare as the man five foot ten, about forty with dark blond hair and the beginnings of a paunch whom witnesses describe at every crime.

"But it won't get you anywhere," he heard the owner continue. Was he wrong or was there a sadistic undertone to his voice? "As far as I know she's just sorted out a commission in the east. And that might take a while."

East? Zadko! Oh my God. He had to drive over to Zadko's before he turned into number seven! He could assume that Violetta had decided to become a saxophonist.

Fucking shit! There was no time for play-acting. He grabbed the phone from behind the bar and dialled. Detlev seemed to have taken his phone off the hook. Sonja wasn't answering either. And he preferred not to call Lietze. He ran out of Sydney's and reached his car in two minutes. While he was still figuring out the fastest way to the heart of Wedding, he remembered the transi. With that damned ski mask which had misled him for so long. What was her name? Yvette? Ninette? Didn't matter. She'd said Winterfeldt Strasse.

Ginette didn't take his bullshit about being in love. "You can just be straight with me. You're in Lietze's squad, and that's in your favour. What do you want to know, Mr Police President? Or may I call you Police Senator? Hahaha."

"Do you know the photographer's name and where I can find her?"

"Not exactly. I don't really know her either. She gave me a phone number once. What do you want from her?"

"Just – I need her to make a statement – as a witness," Fritz lied.

"Well – why don't you call me tomorrow afternoon, I'll have had a sleep by then and I can look for the number."

And if I put her in the car now and drive her home and she looks for the number right away? No. Violetta wouldn't drag Zadko to her apartment. She would go with him. She had always gone to the men's apartments.

He scribbled Ginette's phone number in his notepad.

At about half past one the lights in the caretaker's apartment also went out in every room but one. The whole side wing of the house had been dark and remained so. Must all be on vacation, concluded the athletic thirty-something man.

There were lights on in a few windows of the front house. Someone nervous seemed to live on the third floor. Bright lights in every room. He pulled open the door of the back house and went out into the courtyard. The two professional Teutons have probably made up. Interesting that she left her son all by himself in the other place! Even though he urgently needs medical care. Could it be his flat? Anyway, he could smoke once again! Hours of surveillance are usually a trial of biblical dimensions. At least for nicotine addicts like him.

He left the same way he had come in. Casually, as if he lived here. In the passageway he stopped briefly and looked up at the back house. All the windows were dark there too now. Before, there had been lights on the second and fourth floors.

He unlocked the blue Ford Capri, groped for the cigarette pack on the dashboard and lit one. He looked at the sky. Not long now, he thought. Before it blows up. If the storm doesn't come tonight, then – he let the gusts waft through his clothes and hair. And then he saw the flash of lightning. A yellow-blue zigzag due west. And immediately afterwards he heard the bang. It was an odd bang. Unusually short and muffled. And a little too soon after the lightning. But the man only realised that when the real thunder rolled.

He looks so different! What's happened to his hair? And why is he making me an accomplice to his infidelities, damn it! Beate is standing at the back there, and here he's telling me not to say anything to his wife. I don't want to know anything about my subordinates' private lives. Basta! Why does Beate have dark hair? Isn't she blonde? That evening dress doesn't suit her either! And I don't care if he's governing mayor a hundred times over, we're not on first name terms! I hate all this casualness! Bang, that's it!

But the banging didn't stop at all. It came again. And again. How had Fritz turned into Governing Mayor? Why doesn't anybody tell me? Bang?

Karin Lietze ran through all the female and male senators in D III until it dawned on her that it was the window that was banging at regular intervals. She shot up in bed and tried to open her eyes. No, I don't want any fireworks! I don't want to be at this party at all! And I don't want to have a department for same sex forms of investigation. We're all the same – that was, that wasn't fireworks at all? That was lightning! And now there really was a bang.

She switched on the light, got herself out of bed, staggered over to the window and secured it properly. There was a bang in the kitchen, which was directly opposite. She secured that window properly too, and remained standing in front of it to enjoy the wind on her skin. She shook her head and grinned. Had she really dreamt that the current governing mayor had confessed an infidelity to her? To Karin Lietze, detective chief inspector. And had begged her not to tell his wife? Had that damn Fritz and his interest in that crazy photographer made such an impression on her? My God, Lietze! It must be a joke. Some sneaky red herring. Hope it didn't make him forget Zadko.

She sighed and went back to the bedroom to light a Lucky Luciano. She inhaled deeply. But it didn't taste good. She ran into the bathroom and let water run over her hands, arms and cigarillo, threw away the cigarillo and went back to bed. Why wasn't there another flash of lightning? And, more important, why was there no rain! There should be tons of water falling from the heavens. It's not enough, there won't be a real storm. Tomorrow our skin and our brains will be as sticky as ever, and we'll go on fumbling with our inquiries. We'll get on to that block warden and then we'll look at Krisztina what's her name's notebook, look for witnesses from Fahlenkamp's circle and – oh yes! That comes first of all! Give that Rambo wannabe a rap on the knuckles. And at some point, at some point all the knots will come undone. At some point, all the scraps of evidence will fall into place and the puzzle will be solved. And then you'll see, Lietze Karin, that the only connection between all these cases which have been wearing out your last ounce of grey matter all these months is this city, this city, these times and this weather! The Zeitgeist – the spirit of the age – pure shit! These times don't have spirit. This city is a pressure cooker in the middle of a sea, in which a few waves ripple and spill over. It's time for the lid to come off. This is the – the spirit – of things, of the times – bloody noise! What does that idiot neighbour think he's doing! Letting his stupid phone ring in the middle of the night – oh well! At least he seems to have an answering machine. Congratulations. But turn it down next time, please – and – and – don't leave your phone in my hallway! Wait a minute. Isn't that – the voice sounds like – Lang?!

After she had hung up, she wasn't quite sure whether everything she had experienced since returning from Amrum might not simply have been the result of a large ozone hole in her brain. Lang was in Nollendorf Strasse, and number 17 was on fire. Why was it burning? And what was Lang doing there?

She staggered into the bathroom and let water run over her head. Then she dialled Schade and then Fritz and let the phone ring for minutes each time. She cursed, tried Roboldt's number and let it ring too until her scruples at waking the poor man from his fever bed had turned into pure rage. Why is nobody ever there when you need them! Then she pulled on the nearest clothes, grabbed her bag, hoped her car keys were in it, and slammed the door behind her.

It didn't look like anyone was at home. It didn't sound like it either. The soft squeaking of old floor boards came from the opposite direction. Fritz took his ear off Zadko's door and looked straight into the neighbour's peephole. The light in the stairwell went out. Not a sound. No light behind any of the closed doors. He switched on the light again, and held his police badge up to the peephole. Still no sound. He pulled out his I.D. and held it closer to the little round hole. After a while, he heard what sounded like the click of a metal flap, the floor boards squeaked again, a chain rattled, a key was turned. A short fifty-year-old man with thick black hair and a moustache appeared in the doorway, wearing striped flannel pyjamas. He looked distrustfully at the I.D. picture, then at Fritz's face.

"I really am a detective. My name is Fritz, excuse me, Herr – Şaniş?"

"Schanisch," the man with the blue-beige-silver pyjamas corrected him politely, and opened the door wide.

Fritz entered. "You weren't perhaps standing behind the door last night by any chance?"

"Me no. No. Ella! You can come here too."

Şaniş switched on the light in the hall and closed the front door. A small, chubby woman, also around fifty, with a flattened ash-blonde perm, emerged from one of the rooms.

"My wife saw."

She came closer and blinked at Fritz. "You were there too, weren't you? Later, with the police."

"Frau Şaniş – "

"Hartmann. My name is Hartmann. We aren't married."

"Yes, yes," Fritz said impatiently. "I'm not concerned about yesterday. Have you seen Herr Zadko tonight?"

Frau Hartmann and Herr Şaniş looked at each other and shook their heads in unison. "No, not at all since – yesterday afternoon, right, Ella?"

Frau Hartmann nodded. "Young Marek" had left around three thirty with "the young girl" and "a lady" with beautiful red hair. "We've been worried because of the break-in," she added as an excuse for their curiosity.

"Offer something to this gentleman, Ella," Herr Şaniş suggested.

"Red hair? What did she look like?"

"How should I describe her? Very – attractive, Mister, er. Do you want mocha coffee or Turkish tea?"

"My name is Fritz. No, no. Thank you very much. What was she wearing?"

Had Zadko and this Violetta – Eva-Maria been winding him up? Did they know each other?

"What was she wearing? Well, frightfully high heels. I said to Adi, how can they possibly walk in them! It's amazing. And at her age! I saw her hands, Herr Fritz, because she was playing with her car keys. She looked like thirty, but her hands – at least ten years older, I would say."

Fritz was relieved. Violetta wasn't forty yet for sure, and she didn't drive either. He heard the two whispering and looked at them.

"My wife had seen that lady before," Herr Şaniş said.

"Yes, with Christina. Oh my God, what is she going to say about the break-in when she comes back!" Frau Hartmann suddenly clapped her hand over her mouth and gave Fritz a scared look.

Fritz slowly put his I.D. into his back pocket in order to gain time. They didn't know anything about Krisztina Kędzierska's death yet. And Frau Hartmann was worried that he could cause problems for her when she entered the country again. Or with her residence permit. He thought about what to tell them first: the good news or the bad news. He opted for the bad news and forgot to mention that he wasn't from any immigration office. He urgently needed to phone for reinforcements. Herr Şaniş showed him into the living room and took the weeping Frau Hartmann into the kitchen. When he returned to the living room with a bottle of brandy and two glasses, a grim-faced Fritz was holding the receiver to his ear. Şaniş put a glass and the bottle down in front of him and disappeared. Fritz gave the machine a telegram style message. Then he dialled another number and waited. He dialled a third number and let it ring a dozen times too before angrily hanging up and rubbing his damp forehead. He tried to remember who was on duty tonight and dismissed the idea. He didn't think much of his colleagues in D III. And he had good reason to assume that the idiot who had made sure that no connection was made between the six murdered men was among them.

He would take care of it on his own! He would get this female murderer on his own. Well, suspected murderer. Maybe he had really blown a fuse and was seeing ghosts. A woman, killing men, just like that. To take pictures of them. After she had been fuck...! God, there's never been anything like it. Men yes, but a woman? She's a bit cracked, somehow, all that stuff about shamans. Everything about her really. But a psychopath? Or did she have something to do with the JoAnne Little Brigade after all? Maybe she was a perfectly disguised avenger? An undercover feminist? He would have liked to ask Beate.

He decided to accept the offer of mocha coffee. He went to the kitchen to ask the upset amateur voyeurs if he could use their apartment as a temporary headquarters, ask a few more questions about Krisztina Kędzierska, Marek Zadko and the break-in, and wait for Zadko's return. With Violetta in tow. Or the other way round.

The bomb damage wasn't extensive, but it had ripped a hole in the ceiling and a room in the apartment on the first floor of the side wing had been set on fire. The Henkes' living room had also been wrecked and gutted, apart from the outside wall with the windows.

The young man in sports clothes, whom Lang introduced as "Borgel, one of our people", advised her to take off her sandals and roll up her trousers. But Lietze's foot was already in a puddle in the hallway. "What's worse is that the water washes all the evidence away," she growled and defiantly put her other foot into the lukewarm, sooty, dirty water.

The living room, or what was left of it, was crowded with people clambering over lumps of masonry and bits of furniture. Two firemen were tapping the walls and the caved-in ceiling, three men from the police lab tried to pick out what might be evidence that should be kept, a colleague from D I fumbled around the charred remains of a man who must have been Alfred Henke. A young woman in a white coat, whom Lietze didn't know, was busy with a woman who lay in front of the window and appeared to be dead.

"Erika Henke," Borgel said. "She's almost intact."

"You think that's funny?" Lietze snapped at him, and worked her way across to her. "Good morning, are you from forensic?"

"Yes. Weber."

"Lietze. You look like you're new – but I don't imagine you'll be sick, will you?"

"Not any more. I was responsible for abused children for three years. If anyone broke down, then it was the really tough crime squad guys," the doctor responded coolly without taking her eyes off Erika Henke's corpse.

"That's not how I meant it." Lietze crouched down. The back of Erika Henke's head had been smashed by pieces of falling ceiling. But otherwise, apart from a soaking, the body was apparently undamaged.

"She was raped," the forensic doctor said. "With this beer bottle. Can I turn her over?"

Lietze stared at the blood-smeared bottle neck the doctor held up, and then looked away to the brown-green marks on Erika Henke's left arm which was now lying on top of the body. And then she saw it and almost lost her balance. On the corpse's forehead, only partly obscured by blood, was a G, about an inch and a half high, in old German script. The left eye was bloodshot. There was a gag in the mouth. "Signs of strangulation?"

The doctor bent over the neck. "Yes."

Slowly Lietze got up and waved over the photographer from the police lab. "Take a few of her head and forehead, please." Then she went over to the duty crime squad man, who was still crouching over Henke's presumed corpse, and asked him to come outside with her.

"This is a most peculiar mix-up of departments," he complained, when she had steered him into the workshop. "What are you doing here Lietze?"

"Lang called me because . . ."

"Ah. And what is Internal Security doing here, if I may ask?"

"You may," Lietze said. She was friendly, but a little sharp. "Do you have anything to smoke on you? I forgot my cigarillos."

He didn't smoke.

She explained what she thought necessary. ". . . I didn't, however, expect to find the fifth victim of the stamper here. Until a few hours ago, this apartment block figured as the scene of the most recent male murder, the other series we're working on – but you know about that."

Even the few details Lietze restricted herself to were obviously too much for her colleague. He seemed to be grateful that he could go back to just being on stand-by. "We have to question quite a number of people," he added, for the sake of appearances.

"I think I can take care of this with the two from state security until my crew arrives."

If only, she growled to herself, once the man from D I had left and she was alone in the workshop. They don't even answer the phone. She considered asking one of the uniformed men to drive to the three addresses and drag Fritz and Schade out of bed and yes, damn it, Roboldt too! Her glance fell on the big, flat wooden box. It had been left open. In front of it there were three trays of letters with old German script, one on top of the other. A few of the letters had fallen on the floor. Lietze stared at them. Then everything happened very fast. She ran into the hallway and ordered one of the photographers over. "And bring me a pair of gloves!"

The largest letters were about an inch and a half high. The G was missing. It was probably under Erika's corpse or had been swept away by the jets of the water. The other four letters were there. The P, the C, the N and the T. Two were remarkably clean. The N and the C, on the other hand, had slight traces of smeared ink, as if someone had tried to clean them very quickly.

Henke is much too tidy, he would never have left them like that, she thought. Krisztina Kędzierska was the only victim of two killers. But the P was clean. It was the cleanest of them all. Had Henke abandoned his mania for cleanliness? Was Thorsten a cleanliness freak too?

"So, this is where you've got to!" Lang's voice broke into her ruminations.

"Take pictures of those boxes there, please," she said to the photographer. She stuck each of the four letters under Lang's nose, before putting them back in their places.

"Found something?"

"And how. Death is a caretaker from Germany," said Lietze.

"How original, my dear. The explosives Henke used are not known exclusively to the German police."

The previous night's break-in had paid off – for Detective Inspector Lothar Fritz. Ella Hartmann and Adi Şaniş needed no convincing that Marek was in some kind of danger, without Fritz having to reveal what. In his opinion. As for Krisztina Kędzierska's murder, he only had to hint that it was probably one of a series whose victims were all foreign women. Whereupon Şaniş had taken his brandy glass, now filled for the third time, posted himself at the front door and put his eye to the peephole from time to time.

Ella Hartmann had stopped crying a while ago. "You see, Marek is, God, what shall I call him, a rogue. An eternal child. You know what I mean, don't you? But they do say he's very talented. Christina, she is – was – ," she fell silent and once again blew her nose into a huge paper towel, " – quite a different calibre. Down to earth and practical. Goodness, she was always organising something! Once she took our old Mercedes to Poland to have it freshly painted. I don't know, she must have known someone there who does that kind of work. First class, I tell you. Immaculate. The car was like new. And we had to talk ourselves blue before she'd take any money. No matter what you need done Christina always knows someone who can do it. Knew. Yes."

"Shh," the voice came from the hall and then the peephole flap clicked again. Şaniş returned to the kitchen and put his empty glass on the table in front of Ella Hartmann. "Just someone from upstairs."

She poured in a drop. "That's all, Adi. Look at our Herr Fritz. He hasn't drunk anything at all yet. And he's much younger!"

Şaniş shuffled "back to work", as he said giggling.

"The other day she asked me why we aren't married, Adi and I. But why, I say. Then I'd lose my little pension. But then Adi can stay here, she said. I say, he can stay anyway, he has German citizenship. But I knew what it was all about, Herr Fritz. She wanted to stay here, and I assume she had someone she could marry, on paper at least. But she didn't want to come out with it."

"But you know who it was anyway," Fritz hinted in a friendly way.

Ella Hartmann looked at him in surprise. "Nooo. Whatever made you think that! Christina could be very discreet. I only told her to make sure that it's a decent man. Because you can really fall flat on your face with that kind of thing." Unexpectedly, she burst into tears again and sobbed for several minutes. Fritz looked at her in consternation. But she seemed oblivious to him and immersed in her pain. He looked at his watch. Three thirty. He asked himself if it hadn't been the last big mistake of the night to come here instead of chasing after Violetta's address.

"Excuse me, Herr Fritz. I feel so sorry for these poor people. You can't understand, or do you have a wife who isn't German? No? I had to fall in love with Adi first to get a feeling for it. One is so afraid here as a foreigner ... cold-shouldered is far too mild a word. And when your own son looks down on you, just because you have a Turkish companion ... yet Adi isn't even a Muslim! He's a Christian like you and me. Well, like me. I don't know if you are ... it doesn't matter. Everyone knows whether they believe in something or not. Do you have a son, Herr Fritz?"

Şaniş was whispering excitedly again and waving his arm by the kitchen door. Fritz jumped up and went into the hall. Şaniş nodded, and Fritz put an eye to the peephole and recognised Marek Zadko. Alone.

He pulled the door open. Zadko, who had been fumbling at the lock, spun round. The sudden move seemed to make him lose his balance. He looked a little worse for wear, almost fell into Fritz's arms, and stank of alcohol.

"He looked so poorly! Do you have such a small staff he should be in bed such a nice young man ..." Fräulein von Thurau's adrenalin level had evidently been pushed sky high by hours of waiting. She seemed to want to tell the two police officers everything she knew at record speed and in condensed form. She must mean Roboldt, Lietze thought. Poorly? Who could have – How on earth did he ...

"... tell me, just between ourselves, I'm sure he was born on May 17, wasn't he?"

Fräulein von Thurau really did stop talking for a second and looked at Lietze. She, however, was totally baffled. The old lady grabbed her arm and continued in a whisper: "Well, 17th of the 5th! One seven five! You know, paragraph 175 . . ."

Lietze knew that she mustn't laugh now and looked pleadingly at Lang, who was discreetly examining a little gallery of pictures in old-fashioned frames above a flowered bed settee. "When did he leave here?"

"Two minutes before quarter to ten, because then I watched current affairs upset as I was it all upsets me so very much with that Henke man! The poor woman how he knocked her black and blue and that rascal too and then all the noise at night when he had a visitor . . ."

At the word "visitor" Lang started listening officially again. Lietze noted down Fräulein von Thurau's description of the visitor. "Krisztina Kędzierska," she muttered to Lang. "I'll tell you later."

". . . and always that Bolero again and again imagine that poor young woman living above him what she had to put up with well she wasn't around the last time thank God she's on holiday because imagine if she'd been there when he blew up the apartment! There are a lot on holiday right now luckily otherwise it's unimaginable Elvira Fahlenkamp is back again do you think he did Fahlenkamp too – ?" Fräulein von Thurau paused again. Startled, she looked from Lietze to Lang, as if only just realising that her life had been in constant danger in this house.

"What makes you think that?" Lietze asked.

"Well because Fahlenkamp gave him a piece of his mind. About the late-night Bolero and other things as well."

The idea that good citizen Fahlenkamp had crossed good citizen and arsonist Henke because of the latter's little infidelities, made Lietze smile. "No, no, for a change he didn't kill him, Fräulein von Thurau. He was after women – foreign women."

Before the old lady had time to turn this thread into a

tangled knot, Lietze signalled Lang with her eyes and said goodbye.

"Shit, damn it!" She grumbled at him on the stairs. "Why didn't any of us talk to her this afternoon! It would have prevented Henke's fifth murder."

Sweating and cursing, she briefly informed him about the stamper case and the pointless, aimless circles that the whole of D III had been going round in for months.

Just before the last set of stairs, Lang grabbed her from behind by the shoulders. She spun round, confused, looked into his eyes, then at his inviting, wide-open arms and then back into his eyes. But now she was no longer confused but angry. She shoved both hands deep into her trouser pockets.

"Karin, you could have worked out when we talked on the phone earlier that Henke is your stamper." Lang's voice was unbearably friendly. "I told you that story about the student . . ." No, it was patronising!

"It's very helpful of you to remind me of that now!" Lietze said cuttingly and jumped down the last few stairs. "Are you coming along to arrest Thorsten? Because at least I've worked out that he must have been Henke's accomplice in the murder of Krisztina Kędzierska."

Was he laughing behind her back?

"Of course I'll come along. I have to show you where to find him, little one. I also want to find out for myself . . ."

Lietze stopped in front of the house door, turned round, and gave him an angry look. "Don't ever dare call me 'little one' again."

What made her more angry, his choice of words or the fact that she really did need him to find out where Thorsten Vogel was hiding? Perhaps simply that he went on smiling and talking.

". . . what I can't understand is why someone like Henke invited a Polish whore in."

"Still a prostitute to you," she said in a businesslike way. She

had the unpleasant sensation of running up against a rubber
wall. And the suspicion that even what was supposed to be a
look of anger, was nothing more than the ludicrous attempt
to look down on somebody from the perspective of an insect.

"Thank you nurse. But I really can't eat anything right now."
Sonja Schade tried not even to glance at the tray of sand-
wiches, which the delicate looking woman with blue-black
bobbed hair and the orange-red overall was offering her.
She was afraid that even the sight of food would make
her throw up.

"But you haf to be reasonable. It doesn't help your priend,
ip you don't keep up your strength!"

Schade closed her eyes because they were starting to
sting again. Somehow she would have liked to fall into the
arms of this Florence Nightingale from the Philippines, as
she had said, and cried her eyes out. But somehow that was
impossible. Somehow nothing was possible. And who knew
how much longer things could somehow work out with
Anita. Somehow! But how? That she would no longer be
able to stand on her own feet or walk, in the foreseeable
future, was sad, but not a catastrophe. She would have a
wheelchair and her easel, paints and brushes could be
attached to it. It was the problems with her eyesight which
were the catastrophe. Nobody knew when Anita would go
blind. And it was only too probable that she would go blind,
even though she insisted sarcastically that the nice thing
about MS was precisely its chaotic lack of logic, so Sonja
should be prepared, suddenly and unexpectedly, to be
attacked and thrown to the floor by her one day.

She forced her eyes open again and looked at Anita's pale,
sunken face, at the skinny arm with the IV and the tube
leading to a bottle on a stand, and she tried not to think
about the pain Anita was now spared only because morphine

was stronger. But the pain would be back. At some point. Unpredictably. More and more often, probably. How long would she be able to stand it, these nights in intensive care units, keeping her panic at bay? How long would she be able to hide it from the others at her home away from home, D III? Did she want to hide it? Yes, of course, they had to be able to rely on her! Maybe she would have to quit the job soon. Or – leave Anita to a nurse? Who would be with her all day . . .

"I know, nurse. It's very good of you really," she said finally and jumped down from the window-sill where she had been sitting. "I think I'm going to go home now and get ready for duty." Not a woman, no way. A male nurse.

The air into which she stepped from the air-conditioned hospital rooms almost took her breath away. She looked at her watch. Just before five thirty. What had happened to the storm? Or had she just not seen or heard it? Once, when she had been in the ward nurse's room smoking a cigarette with the nurse, there had been a flash of lightning and thunder. She shook her head, unlocked the car and fell on to the seat. Take a shower, she thought. Wash away the hospital smell. Far away. Not have to smell it any more. The memory stayed anyway. Of this damn night. Far worse than the most exhausting tour of all the women's bars with Lietze could have been. Angrily she pushed aside thoughts about the other chaos that was waiting for her in about an hour and a half. And it was the much more important one, wasn't it?

Thorsten Vogel didn't just look terrible. He was in no condition at all to be interrogated, and according to the emergency doctor who had immediately taken him to hospital, he would stay that way until at least the following afternoon.

There was no reason to try to convince the doctor otherwise, Lietze decided. This time "Rosso" would be guarded and in three days time he'd still be able to say why his stepfather had induced him to take part in murder, and whether he had been involved in the other three stamper murders, and what he knew about the JoAnne Little Brigade.

"And anything that would be of interest to you as well," she concluded in a voice that didn't allow for any contradiction, and then asked Lang for another cigarette.

"We'll see," Lang responded grinning. "But I promise you, if he tells us something which could be of interest to you, you'll be the first to know. Do you want to come for a drink?"

Lietze couldn't think of a good excuse not to. She just wanted to make a call first. The woman in whose apartment Erika Henke had taken up temporary residence was still in shock. Or maybe the tranquilliser the emergency doctor had given her hadn't taken effect yet. Lietze left Lang with her, grabbed the phone and took it into the hall.

"So Roboldt, in the mean time I've found out that you've known since last night that Krisztina Kędzierska was at Henke's just before she was killed. But what I would like to know is why you went to sleep and unplugged the phone instead of reporting it immediately!"

"What? Who? That was her?" Roboldt stuttered on the other end. "Oh shit! I was only paying attention to the other one. I did want to call immediately, but when I got back home, Larry was there and . . ."

"So you went out for a good time, rather than taking care of your damn flu!"

"No, I went to the *TAZ* office!" Roboldt yelled, half offended, half angry. What he reported grew more hoarse from sentence to sentence. "I just got back home, but with zero results. No clue, nothing that would lead us closer to the Brigade," he concluded, his voice barely audible now.

"Don't be offended, Roboldt," Lietze grinned. "You can't have everything. I spent the night on the demise of the stamper – that is, he took his demise into his own hands."

Her report seemed to breathe some life back into Roboldt. "Congratulations, boss!" he croaked.

Tired, Lietze said, "Now tell me about this other woman you were paying attention to while you were enjoying Fräulein von Thurau's flowered couch."

"Oh yeah. It's just one of those silly ideas, but I suddenly thought your theory that the men were killed by a woman might be right after all. Because the old lady did see a woman leaving the house on Monday afternoon shortly after Fahlenkamp must have died. Henke must have got a much better look at her, but he can't tell us any more, to that extent . . ."

"True, true. Just tell me anyway to complete the picture," Lietze looked at her watch and decided that there was no point in going back to sleep; she would go for a drink with Lang and maybe have breakfast and hopefully find an open tobacco shop which sold her cigarillos. "What did the lady look like?"

"Approximately the same age and size as Krisztina Kędzierska, long red hair, dangerously high heels, violet jeans, something about 'aggression' on her t-shirt – "

"What?" Lietze yelled at him. "Violet? Did you say red hair? Long curls? Did she have a camera?"

"Oh my God," Roboldt gasped. "That photographer, with the show at Sydney's . . ."

"Roboldt, damn it, why didn't you call me, you idiot! Get dressed, I'll pick you up!"

"Why, what's the matter, I am dressed. What is it?"

"She's dug her nails into Fritz!" She slammed down the receiver and took a deep breath.

He rolled his eyes and looked angrily into the glaring sun which was straight ahead of him as he turned from Froben into Winterfeldt Strasse for the third time. He was just in time to see Ginette Champs-d'Hiver's ass disappear into a car. "She seems to be making a lot of money today!" he grumbled and decided not to drive around the block once again but to give his acidic and rumbling stomach a chance. He parked the car in front of a kebab place and went in.

Lamb kebab and UHT milk at five in the morning was certainly one way to add something exotic to his life, he thought and hoped that calming down his stomach would make him more relaxed. There was no reason to hurry. He didn't need to save a Zadko from being murdered. He just had to find Violetta's address in time to keep her from escaping to the East. If what the owner of Sydney's had overheard was true. If it was true it would be rather difficult to lay hands on her in the foreseeable future. And precisely because there were suddenly holes in the Iron Curtain. But they led in the opposite direction, from East to West. A paradox, he thought, and couldn't help but be impressed by himself for having such philosophical thoughts at an hour which, despite the glaring sun, was still between night and day. It must have been his talk with Zadko. Despite twenty-five years on the force, Detective Inspector Lothar Fritz was still astonished whenever he saw what happened when the system flipped out of balance. Nor was he so naive as to believe that people were basically good. But he was firmly convinced that it was humanly possible to balance good and evil instincts. After all, he had learned to do it! Hadn't he? What had all that been about tonight – with that vamp, who had him – yeah, yeah! There you go again. You're getting sidetracked. Not that she wanted you, and if she did, so what. But you – you wanted her. Right. And you were the one who lost control when you smashed that guy's teeth who raped his little daughter! It's not like somebody else couldn't hold his horses, that would be understandable, blah, blah, blah. So stop getting all worked up about the fact that a talented saxophone player wanted to be a lousy little blackmailer as well. To turn a profit from something that from close up isn't even all that dirty, though it could be made to look that way by some Mr Clean. With a silly notebook, though he didn't even know what use it was. And which was stolen from him anyway. That's the way of the world. One big paradox.

As he stuffed the last of the bread with the meat and salad into his mouth he saw Ginette stalk down Potsdamer Strasse and take up position opposite the kebab snack bar. He paid quickly and ran across the street.

"The next car you get into is mine. I'll bring you back right away. It'll take quarter of an hour at most," he started shouting even before he was close to her.

Ginette gave him a surprised coquettish look.

"You've arrived at just the right moment, Herr Police Senator, haha. I was beginning to feel like calling it a day. I just hadn't decided whether to allow myself a cab or enrich the public transport system for the last time today."

The phone number which Ginette found after some searching must belong to a Schöneberg address. Possibly around Winterfeldt Platz. "Where were the photos taken, Ginette?"

"In some old factory building in Kreuzberg, but it didn't belong to Violetta. It was something cultural funded by the government. Those are the things they fund, rather than us! It's really a scandal, because I really don't see how a little theatre or a painter or whatever can contribute more to culture than we do. I think that sex is part of culture too, and that's why we've organised and . . ."

Fritz stared at Ginette in disbelief. Was this happening? A transsexual prostitute wanted to talk politics just before six in the morning? Yes. Evidently. As strange as it sounded. But if he wanted to find his sex murderess, whom he still didn't quite believe in, then he'd better get on the phone immediately.

*

"And now?" A tired Roboldt asked and looked at Lietze with red, wet eyes.

"Now I'm taking you back to your little bed, Roboldt. You remind me of the dog my mother used to have. He had the same look!"

Roboldt looked away from her and focused once again on the heavy wooden door with the sign: "Fritz Lothar Beate Nicole & Jennifer," in a child's handwriting. He pressed the bell once again and once again the Swedish gong typical of terraced houses in respectable Lichtenrade, vibrated in his impaired ear drum.

"Fritz is a grown man – "

"So were the others!"

" – and a detective. We can only assume that he knows how to take care of himself. Or perhaps you want to embarrass him with a big manhunt?"

That was the last thing Roboldt wanted. The second last thing was to go to bed. "Well, take me to Keith Strasse. At least, I can – if Mimi – " He almost let out a scream. "Heaven's sake, I'd completely forgotten about her!"

"I'm not worried about Mimi," Lietze said, after Roboldt had told her about Mimi's urge to go out on night-time surveillance. "Mimi's never been thoughtless, and besides, she found out what she wanted to know. Herrmann's a problem, Roboldt. I want to get rid of him. Even though it goes completely against the grain. Just because I can't stand him . . ."

"Just because he's probably on the far right, is that what you wanted to say?" Roboldt croaked hoarsely.

"I'll think about it for the next hour or so," Lietze said and stopped in front of the Norman castle. "Why don't you put coffee on, but be careful with the mach . . ."

In the time it took Roboldt to answer, Lietze had already got as far as the Cornelius Bridge, and was waiting to make a right turn into Stüler Strasse.

*

"That's her! Just a moment – Adam, Eva-Maria. Yeah. Goltz Strasse . . ."

It had to be very close to Roboldt's place. He promised Ginette a longer discussion about culture in West Berlin some evening in the near future and said goodbye.

Roboldt's car was parked right in front of the house he was about to enter to arrest the serial killer of three, no – six men. Hold on! Without his weapon. Alone? That wasn't just against the rules. But nothing was going according to the rules now anyway. On second thoughts – he decided to wake Roboldt, who he hoped had taken his gun home. There was no time to drive to Keith Strasse. Every minute counted.

No one stirred. By now having lost so much time, Fritz had had enough and he mobilised his inner hero. The left hand wing of the house, second floor. Sometimes it works. He pushed open the door to the courtyard, ran across to the house in the back and up the stairs, rang the bell, shut his eyes and tried to prepare himself for anything that might happen. He was only a part-time hero, but nevertheless. He opened his eyes again, stared at the door, rang again and listened. Nothing.

He bent down and looked through the letter box. A hallway with several doors. In semi-darkness as if curtains had been drawn. If she hadn't come back since last evening, the curtains ought still to be open.

He ran down the stairs. So she must have been home and left again. Look at the list of names in the hallway. Find the caretaker. Maybe he has – in the courtyard he ran into a round, older woman in a flowered smock, her grey-black hair tied up in a knot. She looked him over suspiciously. He waved his I.D. under her nose and asked for the caretaker.

"I, I," she said, very slowly and still suspiciously. "What want!?"

"Frau Adam – " Fritz panted.

"Meier. Vionoulla Meier."

"No, I mean Frau Adam up there!" He pointed to the windows. She had gone away. Holding a big bag and with a square one on her shoulder. The camera bag! Maybe an hour ago or half an hour. "Do you know where she was going?"

"Me? Nothing. Frau Adam not talking to me."

"Then she didn't give you the key to her apartment?"

"Me? Key? No, never!"

He cursed, apologised to the caretaker, who looked at him disapprovingly and asked to use her phone. It was next to a snoring, beer-bellied, straw-blond man. She picked it up and brought it to him in the kitchen. "My husband night-shift," she explained and concentrated on doing the dishes.

Prague, the café owner had said. And Warsaw and Budapest. Damn it, that was where the West German embassies had been taken over. Was that the assignment the café owner had overheard, because they had talked about it at the bar? That's how she could be found! With a bit of luck. And if whoever had hired her could be found.

He opted for the alphabet. Budapest first. That was the most overcrowded of the three embassies. More precious minutes were lost because the 100 per cent official wanted to know his I.D. number first. Rules. Nothing from West Berlin. From Schönefeld seven to ten daily. "It's not a question of what I'd like Mister – " Fritz snapped. "I have to know all the times, damn it! I don't care what airline."

"Sixthirtytenthirtyfivetwelvetenfour – " "Stop!" he yelled into the phone. "Only two flights in the morning? At six thirty and at ten thirty-five?"

"That's Malev," was the icy response. "Interflug leaves at eight-o-five and eleven-o-five."

Fritz slammed down the receiver and looked at his watch. Six thirty. The six thirty flight and the one at five past eight were out. You had to be at Schönefeld two hours before departure. The bus ride took almost an hour. All the buses left twenty past the hour. And she had to get to the bus station. With a cab from here – a quarter of an hour at least. The rush hour traffic was already starting. She could make the ten thirty-five or the one at eleven-o-five. If she was flying. And if she was going to Budapest first!

There was no sense going to the bus station. The bus she must have taken was already gone. But he could try to catch it at Rudow, the last stop before it crossed the border.

He was too late. According to the timetable, a bus had left about seven minutes before and was probably just crossing the border, which for the moment remained insurmountable for Fritz. He waited for the next bus. But there was no strikingly beautiful woman with strawberry blonde hair and violet finger nails on it.

All of a sudden his inner hero was tired. She had given him the slip. Definitely. She must have. She had taken advantage of the damned, fucking, shitty border, which kept him out. There was only one other possibility – the embassies. A procedure he didn't know anything about. And there were only two things he still wanted to know – whether his suspicion that he'd given himself away somehow was correct and she'd shaken him off on purpose, or if she'd slipped through his fingers quite by chance. He drove the family car back towards the city motorway and all the way back to the bus station across from the radio tower and the International Congress Centre. After running back and forward and talking to a number of people, he knew at least that she had been there. One of the somewhat dusty, worn-out men who seem to belong to the inventory of West Berlin's fast-food stalls had seen the woman Fritz described. Fritz also listened to half the story of the man's life. He had come here as a GI and stayed because he had no desire at all to be sent to Vietnam. Fritz hoped that at some point he would be able to pick up something useful about Violetta from the whole lecture. But all he got was an alcohol-soaked description of the student movement in West Berlin in the late sixties and early seventies and a handwritten note of the slogan on Violetta's t-shirt. He didn't know enough English to write it down himself. *USE WHAT IS DOMINANT IN A CULTURE TO CHANGE IT QUICKLY.* JENNY HOLZER

Lietze didn't believe her eyes. Since when were there four? Or was she already seeing double because of nicotine deprivation and hunger?

The really existing fourth was Anna. "Zadko's girl," Kitty explained. "I've, like, adopted her for now. I couldn't leave her with him 'cause she got us the notebook. No way of knowing what he woulda done to her, Karin!"

Lietze shook her head and didn't tell them off, even though she had intended to. She was too tired, it was too hot again, and she didn't think it desirable for Anna to find out even more about Lietze's unofficial relationship with the trio from Tiergarten Strasse. That they were all on first name terms – that was already more than enough.

Anna thought everything was great, especially the fact that Berlin's cops weren't getting on "the whores" nerves. She thought that was just wicked.

Lietze gave Helga a conspiratorial look, shrugged, nodded at Kim and went with Kitty to the navy-blue Mercedes, to take possession of the box labelled "family medicine cabinet" and the black notebook with red corners.

"I don't know if this isn't almost procuring, my dear," she said with a glance at Anna.

"Naw, why should it be. She'll fuck anybody for a concert ticket or for a backstage pass. What's the difference if she does it for good money as well! What's up, Karin?"

Lietze shook her head and didn't know what to say. She had the unpleasant feeling that she needed to think damned hard about too many damned things. The best thing she could do was leave all the rest of the stuff about stampers, Violettas and women from Brigades to the others at D III and go back to Amrum. "Would you see it that way, if Anna were one of your daughters?"

"Sure! Why do you think I'm working my ass off with all this fuckin' politics? Our daughters oughta have it easier. Or do you think anybody's gonna give me a pension? I don't know what's up with you, Karin! You still mad 'cause we stuck our oar in?"

"Probably," Lietze said and pulled the door of her old rattlebox Renault shut. And because I still have to deal with Rambo.

It was seven thirty-three on Wednesday morning and still the hottest summer in living memory when, head and limbs already sticky, Detective Chief Inspector Lietze entered the secretary's office, exuding a sour cloud of sweat and carrying a box under her arm.

"God, I was right," she sighed with relief.

"You can still call me Mimi," Mimi said, and a bright melodiousness which even drowned out the wheezing of the brown plastic machine was back in her voice again. "What were you right about?"

"That you were the only one who spent the night where you belonged."

"True," Mimi laughed. "Because I only had one mark seventy left in my purse and . . ."

". . . that doesn't even buy a beer. Yes, indeed. We'll talk about it later my dear Miss Jacob! Has Fritz turned up too?"

Mimi nodded, opened the door to Lietze's office and looked enquiringly at the box.

"Evidence. Maybe. Where's that lout?"

"Making more calls to find victims of the Brigade."

"Very good. Did you get hold of a Polish interpreter?"

Ignoring the three figures hanging around at the conference table, Lietze walked straight to her desk, put down the box, opened the drawer, rummaged around in it and found a pack of Lucky Lucianos. It's always good to have something stashed away, she thought, as she at last inhaled the taste she had been longing for.

"Good morning seems to have gone out of fashion around here!" Fritz said loudly to Roboldt and Schade.

"Good morning!" Lietze said and came over to the table, her head wreathed in a blue cloud. "Nice to see you here fully dressed and without a dented carotid artery, Fritz!" she said sharply. "As a reward you'll get study leave. A crash course in how to use a telephone."

"How nice!" Fritz growled. "I'll do it right away. But only if everybody else learns how to answer one when it's ringing!"

Lietze sank down on a chair and looked round with a grin. "If someone could see us they would think we were holding a vampire convention. How come you smell like the perfume department at KaDeWe, Schade? Did you tour the women's bars after all?"

Sonja Schade looked down, stared at her notepad and doodled on it. "No," she said briefly and very softly. And only after a pause did she go on to explain briefly and just as softly where she had spent the night. "I just didn't want to have to smell it any more." She looked first at Lietze and then at the others. It was a look Lietze had never seen from her before.

"I'm sorry," Lietze said and took another draw. Then she put her hand on Schade's arm and squeezed it. Only for a moment. Embarrassed, she cleared her throat. "Can we get started on wrapping this up?"

It took forty-five minutes, three Lucky Lucianos, seven filter cigarettes of various brands, two pots of coffee and four tissues before, thanks to creative improvisation, they had coordinated the results of their investigations.

"Conclusion," Lietze said, throwing her pen on the table and her cigarillo stub to one side of the ashtray in frustration, "the women's murders are cleared up, the men's murders are cleared up, the JoAnne Little Brigade had nothing to do with either of them, unless Thorsten Vogel tells us otherwise, when he can be questioned again. And the flattering result of all this is: now that we've managed to put one and one together, everything has dissolved into thin air! Nice work! So now we'll take our right hand and pat ourselves on the left shoulder."

Silence. Roboldt hid behind his tissue, Schade stubbed out her fifth cigarette and slumped down sullenly in her chair. Only Fritz didn't seem to have fallen victim to the general mental paralysis.

"Nothing's dissolved into thin air! Violetta hasn't disappeared from the face of the earth, only from the Western half!" he growled. "And it isn't certain that she knows or even suspects that we know about her. We've still got a chance there."

"Why were you so sure she took a plane?"

"Instinct." Fritz gave Lietze a challenging grin. "Sometimes it still works. It also tells me that there's something about the rubber stamp case that doesn't quite fit, something doesn't add up . . ."

The phone on Lietze's desk rang.

"Frau Brzeżinska? Have you found out some – what's the matter?" Lietze pointed at her notepad. Roboldt brought it over and stood next to her while she scribbled. "Herr B. beaten up around six p.m. Women. Foreigners out Polacks-Pimps mailbox at night . . .

"Are you sure? Does it really say pimps together with Poles?" Lietze asked agitatedly. "Thanks. Yes. You've really been a great help. I'll take care of it. Right away."

She slammed down the receiver and jumped up, almost knocking Roboldt over. The last thing the three others heard before the door banged shut was: "Now I've got you!"

Epilogue and prelude
I AM NOT A CAMERA

It happened right in the middle of it and without warning. Nobody behind the three dozen pairs of sunglasses had noticed that the sky had grown darker. Suddenly a gust of wind swept through the fancy hairstyles, wigs and hats, ripped the sheets of paper from the hands of the elegant lady in a black suit, and twisted the sentence she was about to utter into a surprised "merde alors!"

It was still hanging suspended in the air when three or four flashes of lightning lit up the whole southwestern sky in blue-green-yellow for a fraction of a second. Immediately there came a crash, ringing and loud, like a roof truss cracking directly overhead. Then the bursting noise turned into a dark roar that seemed to bounce back and forth between two loudspeakers and re-ignite itself again and again. A heavenly match point which only went out of play minutes later, mingling with high-pitched yells and suppressed whines. Poodles and pitbulls were snatched up and hugged tightly to chests, sunglasses were pulled off or pushed up into dishevelled hair. The masses of water coming out of the clouds now made what came out of the water cannon when the cops broke up demonstrations seem like a gentle shower, and lashed eye make-up into a terminal state that no flood of tears could ever have accomplished. Somewhere some young men hiding behind a couple of bushes took to their heels, although their hairstyles were not at risk. They didn't have any, just a short one-day stubble on the scalp.

No one who belonged there made any attempt to run

away. Right in front of their eyes, which they could only keep open with difficulty, the pieces of paper with notes on them fluttered into the grave and stuck fast to the coffin. Those without dogs to console hugged bouquets of flowers to their drenched blouses and dresses.

Lietze clutched the chain with the small silver fist. It had taken some manoeuvring to get it out of the impounded evidence locker legally so that she could throw it into Krisztina Kędżierska's grave. Lietze had never liked cut flowers much. She looked up, in so far as the rain pouring down would allow, and watched the fireworks in the sky. Every flash was still closely followed by thunder. The storm was directly above the Matthäus Cemetery between Grossgörschen Strasse and Monumenten Strasse, just where the sun at its zenith had been beating down only a little while before. It was a few minutes past one on a Friday in August. Summer time.

She wiped her eyes and looked round. Kim, Kitty and Helga stood bunched together holding a wreath of all white flowers, on which a white ribbon with green letters proclaimed on one side in English: HER NAME WAS MCGILL, SHE CALLED HERSELF JILL, BUT EVERYONE KNEW HER AS NANCY. The other side said: FOR SHISHI, MARTHA AND KRISZTINA FROM HER COW. A short distance from Kim a petite blonde woman stood crying. The long hair which had originally been tied loosely at the neck was now dripping down her back. She held a bouquet tied with red and white striped ribbons and a pennant with the red Solidarność insignia. Lietze smiled. How on earth had Ewa Brzeżinska managed to get hold of that? Having found her version of German again, Nadine improvised a few closing words and reached into a wooden box. When she pulled out her hand, it wasn't holding the anticipated loose earth but a mudpack. Nadine stared at it, then at the girls next to her, and put her free hand over her mouth to hold back the laughter. Too late, Banana Mae and Dominique had already burst into smoky laughter, Rosi-Gülay joined in. Ginette's first giggles earned a few sharp nudges from the very Catholic Maria, but when even Manu began to laugh heartily, Minou, Natalie and Ramona fell swaying and cackling into each other's arms, which Ramona's dog seemed to find even more threatening than thunder and lightning, and it bounded from her embrace into the ankle-deep mud and ran around the three of them barking loudly, and when Kitty finally let go of Kim and Helga, who grabbed the wreath at the last moment, and sat down on a nearby half sunken post and burst into giggles, then at that point even Maria let matters take their course. "Sacramento!" she squealed at Nadine. "Take shovel, cretina! Is there for that!"

Lietze smiled at Ewa Brzeżinska who, after the briefest moment of hesitation, smiled back. She had talked her into coming when she'd gone to see her with Roboldt to check out the spray-painted mailboxes and to look for evidence to harden the case against Roland "Rocky" Herrmann. That he was the only one who could have known about Krisztina Kędzierska's financial ties to Solidarność wasn't enough. But Ewa Brzeżinska had asked around and found out that during the night from Tuesday to Wednesday morning a white Porsche had been parked right in front of her building. Just when the storm was threatening to break. After talking to her boss, Detective Chief Superintendent Dettmann, Lietze had decided to confront Herrmann with it, but nevertheless have him officially dismissed from the police force for disciplinary reasons. Herrmann hadn't mentioned the six male corpses on Wednesday morning either. Finally Dettmann had faced him with it, claiming that he had by accident overheard the phone conversation with "Charlie". Lietze had talked him into the lie in order to protect Mimi.

In theory, Herrmann could go back to being a beat cop. But he's too vain to do that, she thought. It's a kind of dishonourable discharge,. He doesn't know the meaning of the word honour, Schade had protested. He'll make a career with the Reps, and now he's got one more reason for revenge. Yes, I know, we've provided him with that, Lietze had said. But do you have a better suggestion?

Who were the guys who had run off at the first drops of rain? Bomber jackets, combat boots. Acquaintances of Herrmann's? Sent by him? Is he going to send them after the avengers of the JoAnne Little Brigade next? Or will he himself take a hand if he doesn't need to worry that I'll recognise him? But what should I have done? Talk with him? Take him by the hand and educate him? The man is thirty years old! I must have a word with Lang.

She noticed that everyone, even the two elderly men, the only males at this strange funeral – two of Krisztina Kędzierska's regulars, Minou had whispered to her – had already thrown one flower from their bouquets on to the coffin followed by a shovelful of wet sand and were moving towards the gate. She went to the grave and dropped in the chain with the fist. An amulet which couldn't save Krisztina's neck from the stranglehold of a boy who took every opportunity to give vent to his hatred of everything. Probably she hadn't even been suspicious when he got out of the cab and approached her on Nollendorf Strasse very early that Sunday morning. She knew him. And once she was sitting in the cab, she didn't have a chance. Because for the first time in his life, he was doing something useful. In his mother's eyes. She needed him. She couldn't have done it alone. And she could have left him to his stepfather's mercy because she had caught him with the printer's case, Alfred Henke's tabernacle. So he had put his hands around Martha's neck and squeezed, squeezed until at last she stopped hitting out and scratching him. And for the first time he heard his mother spurring him on and praising him. Him, the unwanted product of an affair that had allowed Erika Henke to rise to the position of publican at a neo-Nazi inn on Lüneburg Heath. Provided that she didn't name the father. She hadn't admitted who it was, just as she had probably not admitted, even to herself, that she wanted to abort the child. A German woman doesn't have an abortion. "Na!"

Lietze closed her eyes and shook her head, but the images stuck, and, deep under the retina they blended with the rain still pouring down and the thunder fading into the distance. A beautiful, successful woman with a goal which made life worth living, murdered by a betrayed child of seventeen, who had never been allowed to develop any feelings and who seemed to have only two instincts: bottomless fear and boundless hatred. Unmoved, exhausted only by his own injuries, Thorsten had told how afterwards his mother had attacked Krisztina's sexual organs – and nobody from D III had any reason to doubt it. She had also stamped Krisztina's forehead and her passport. Thorsten hadn't understood why and told her to hurry because he had to take the printer's case to an address in Steglitz. "I promised them I'd get hold of it. They need it for a leaflet!" And so, after unloading Krisztina's corpse at the Ruin, she had driven him there and then back home and had helped return the printer's case to the workshop, unnoticed.

Lietze turned and walked down the waterlogged path to the gate. The two regulars had disappeared, and about half of Krisztina's colleagues as well. Kim talked Ewa Brzeżinska into joining them. "Get a skinful! You know 'bout that? 'S a custom here, we go for a drink after a funeral. C'mon Ewa, you've earned it too."

Kitty organised the cars. "You're joinin' us, aren't you?" she whispered to Lietze.

"Not for a drink, I'm on duty. But I have something in my car I'd like to give to you and Helga and Kim."

"So come to the office, we can take care of it there. Can you take Ginette?"

Ginette's appearance had suffered most in the rain; she looked pitiful. But she didn't seem to mind. She beamed at Lietze when she had sat down next to her in the old Renault, proud of the honour and, above all, curious to hear details about Violetta's case. "And she's really gone? And you've no way of getting at her? Can't you do anything through the Foreign Ministry?"

Lietze wondered why Ginette was so well informed. Had Fritz done more than "interrogate" her again?

"Yeah, a spectre is haunting Eastern Europe . . ." Ginette thought out loud, when she realised that Lietze wasn't interested in passing on too much information. "The old guy would never have dreamt . . ."

"What old guy?"

"Marx, of course."

Lietze looked at her and forgot to take her foot off the accelerator. The car lurched around the corner.

"Now you're trying to figure out how someone like me knows something about Marx, right?" Ginette giggled with satisfaction. "I'll explain. I used to be an economics student."

"You used to be what?"

"A student of economics. In Frankfurt. I was supposed to take over the family drug store. But even as a boy I had the feeling I was in the wrong movie, and a drug-store owner was the last thing I wanted to be. It took a few years until I had worked things out about gender, I mean, that I want to be a woman, and so then I changed from economic theory to practical economics. Applied market economy, you see? That's what whores know all about. Do you know what horizontal financial adjustment is? No?" Ginette grinned provocatively at Lietze. "Poor federal states are supported by the richer ones. Now if you think of us women as the Saarland or an impoverished border region and men are Baden-Württemberg . . ."

Lietze had to laugh. She couldn't think of a counter-argument. And why try. She was in too much of a hurry to come up with a socio-economic gloss on her previously entirely sentimental feelings for three particular whores from Tiergarten Strasse and their activities.

"And – " Ginette paused theatrically in her lecture, "our trade is even socialism-compatible!"

"I beg your pardon?" This time Lietze almost hit the car in front.

"Well, we trade with our own property, right? We don't trade with other people's goods. From that point of view, we're squaring the circle. Compatible with socialism and with the market economy. That surprises you, doesn't it?"

Lietze was too busy to be surprised. After she had manoeuvred her Renault out of danger, she sighed. "Tell me about something totally different: this studio where Violetta took pictures of you, who does it belong to? How do I get in there?"

"It's not a studio. Just a huge space without a thing in it."

"No cupboards? Darkrooms?"

"Oh, no. Not even a toilet. Are you looking for the negatives of the men who were murdered? I'm sure she took them with her. She can turn them into cash. Who knows, she might come back in a couple of years with a new name, perhaps as a cult figure from the Leningrad underground, or something like it. Maybe she'll talk then! No, but don't count on it. Violetta is the anarchy of the free market personified. She could have been a good whore, if she – stop! That's the house. 37 Bülow."

Executing a final foolhardy manoeuvre, Lietze turned the car sharply to the left on the right hand lane in the middle of Bülowbogen and pulled into the parking lot in front of the church. She would wait here for Kim, Kitty and Helga, and show them what she had written up earlier. Krisztina Kędzierska's diary and her family medicine cabinet would be presented to the COW Archive on condition that they were not misused. All three would have to put their signatures to that, and then she would hand over the bag with the two items.

"Come up to the office. You have to take a look at the room. We even have a fax!"

Lietze promised to catch up on the visit soon. In her rear view mirror she saw a navy-blue Mercedes drive up Bülow Strasse.

"By the way, do you know what used to be in this house?"

Lietze shook her head.

"Club Violetta!"

"Oh God," Lietze burst out. "What's that?"

Kitty's car turned into the parking lot and stopped right behind Lietze's Renault.

"Don't worry, it wasn't a killer's office. Just a civil rights organisation for lesbians." The twinkle in Ginette's eyes as she offered this piece of information was not entirely unambiguous.

THANKS

SPECIAL THANKS TO MY (IN/VOLUNTARY) ACCOMPLICES:
Baronowski, Birnbach, Dietze, Döll, Dordel, Drews, Eichstädt,
Erhardt, Haag, Heine, Hermans, Hober & Cotton, Karau, Knobloch,
Lang, Langrock, Laufer, Maerker, Malzahn, Marwedel, Moor, Myers,
Poplawski, Poscich, & Skai, Radusch, de Ridder, Schnell, Slevogt,
Treut, Westhoff, Yilmaz

VERY SPECIAL THANKS TO:
Reingard Jäkl for her determined research in the Schöneberg
entertainment mecca!

ONE FROM THE HEART TO:
Gabriele Dietze, Michael de Ridder and whores of all countries for
the patience and guile with which they endured the side effects of
the occasional absence of sociability on my part

AND FINALLY:
It was once again a pleasure to plunder the highs and lows of world
literature. I hope that many of the plundered will find true pleasure
in my recycling of the loot. For my part, I found much pleasure in
plundering many a corpse.

Founded in 1986, Serpent's Tail publishes the innovative and the challenging.

If you would like to receive a catalogue of our current publications please write to:

FREEPOST
Serpent's Tail
4 Blackstock Mews
LONDON N4 2BR

(No stamp necessary if your letter is posted in the United Kingdom.)